STEALING DEATH

STEALING DEATH

JANET LEE CAREY

EGMONT
USA

New York

In memory of my mother, Margaret Saxby, and my stepfather, Doug Saxby, who touched so many with their generosity and love.

EGMONT
We bring stories to life

First published by Egmont USA, 2009
443 Park Avenue South, Suite 806
New York, NY 10016

Copyright © Janet Lee Carey, 2009
All rights reserved

1 3 5 7 9 8 6 4 2

www.egmontusa.com
www.janetleecarey.com

Library of Congress Cataloging-in-Publication Data
Carey, Janet Lee.
Stealing death / Janet Lee Carey.
p. cm.
Summary: After losing his family, except for his younger sister Jilly, and their home in a tragic fire, seventeen-year-old Kipp Corwin, a poor farmer, must wrestle with death itself in order to save Jilly and the woman he loves.
ISBN 978-1-60684-009-2 (trade) — ISBN 978-1-60684-045-0 (lib. binding)
[1. Death—Fiction. 2. Brothers and sisters—Fiction.] I. Title.
PZ7.C2125St 2009
[Fic]—dc22
2009016240

Map illustration by Heather Saunders

Printed in the United States of America

The land is dry and death not far;
Ride home, boy; ride home.
He will cut and leave a scar;
Ride home, boy; now ride home.

—ESCUYAN SONG

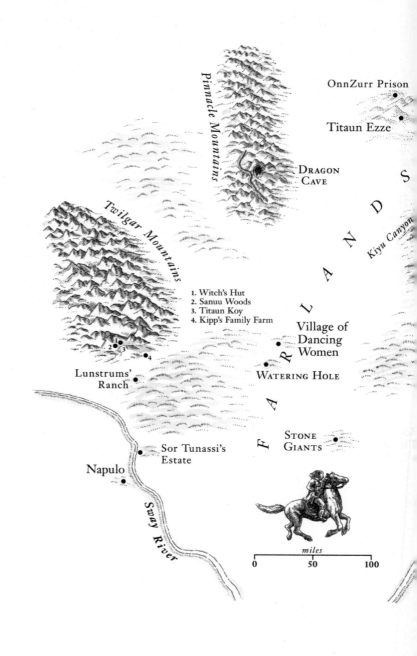

OnnZurr Prison

Titaun Ezze

DRAGON
CAVE

Pinnacle Mountains

Twilgar Mountains

Kiyu Canyon

F A R L A N D S

1. Witch's Hut
2. Sanuu Woods
3. Titaun Koy
4. Kipp's Family Farm

Village of
Dancing
Women

WATERING HOLE

Lunstrums'
Ranch

Sor Tunassi's
Estate

STONE
GIANTS

Napulo

Sway River

miles

0   50   100

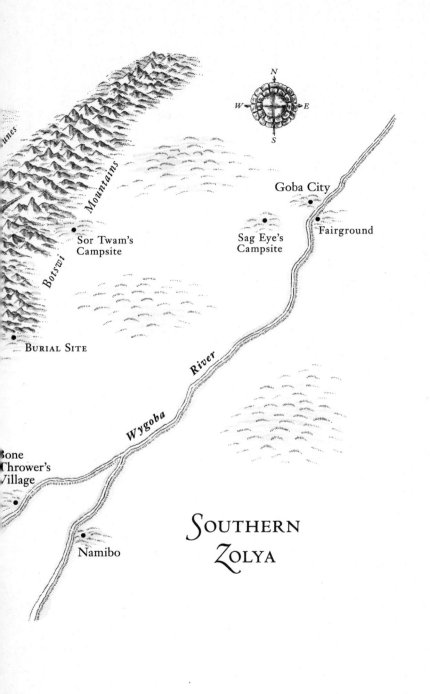

SOUTHERN
ZOLYA

CHAPTER ONE

I N HIS SLEEP, Kipp heard hounds baying in the
foothills. He dreamed of sweeping human bones into
a sack. His mouth was dry when he awoke, and the
thornbush scratching the window whispered the same *kush-
kush* sound the broom made in his dream. But there was no
howling now and no scattered bones to be swept off the
floor.

Under the frayed covers, Royan sighed and turned on his
back. Kipp scooted away from his little brother and dropped
his feet onto the dusty floorboards. He looked out the window at the high mountain shelf called Titaun Koy—a name
that meant "dragon's jaw" in the old Escuyan tongue—and
blinked at a sudden flash of white.

The wild horse he'd seen two weeks ago was back,
galloping across the plateau in the moonlight.

"Lightning." The horse vanished the moment Kipp whispered the name he'd given him. Still Kipp jumped up, threw on his clothes, and slipped his hunting knife into his boot. The drought was killing the crops, their animals, his family; but he was a Corwin, and Corwins didn't give up easily. Capturing this wild horse could turn things around.

The day's stark heat was long gone, and the cold night air shaped his hurried breath into misty ghosts. Two gray shapes floated over Royan and flattened themselves against the window. Kipp's teacher, the Escuyan elder Sor Joay, would have called that a death warning, a sign that the Gwali would ride out tonight to steal the souls of the dying. Kipp told himself it was only his breath slipping out between his teeth.

"Where you off to?" groaned Royan sleepily.

"Nowhere, little sprik mite."

"You going after that wild horse?"

It had been hard to keep his secret from Royan, who'd seen him practicing his roping these past few days. "Quiet. You'll wake Jilly."

"Take me with you." Royan sat up, yawning.

Kipp crept over to the bed. "How would you like to do my chore and light the iron stove for Mother this morning?"

"I might do it if you promise to take me fishing."

"I'll take you to a place Sor Joay showed me in the Pinnacle Mountains."

Royan's eyebrows shot up. "In the Farlands? Are there lions there?"

"Could be."

"And titauns?"

"Only people with Naqui powers can see the dragons, Royan."

"Dragons?" Jilly said. She, too, was sitting up on her bed across the room. Kipp swore under his breath. Was there no way to escape this *detching* house without everyone in the world knowing about it?

"Go back to sleep, Jilly."

"I'm hungry." She looked up at him in the dark. Her face was too lean for a seven-year-old. Kipp was sick of the tight feeling in his gut, the hungry looks on his brother's and sister's faces. He would change that if he caught Lightning and sold him in the market. He pressed the worn blanket in around his little sister and hurried back to Royan. "You will light the fire like you promised."

"I didn't promise."

"Shh! Here." Kipp pulled his tinderbox down from the shelf.

"Mine?" Royan thrust out his grubby hands for the soap-stone box. It was green as new grass, with a tree carved on the lid.

Kipp held on a little longer. Sor Joay had given him this box three years ago before he left the farm. His old friend was dead now, and this was all Kipp had left to remember him by. "Yours to use this once, but if you so much as scratch the tree Sor Joay carved on the lid—"

Royan snatched the box. The flints and twigs rattled inside. "I'll take care of it."

Royan's only nine. Too young for my tinderbox, Kipp thought, *and mother's stove is difficult to light. You must watch the fire spirit Techee,* Sor Joay had warned. *She is always hungry.* Still, he left his brother cradling the prize and snuck outside. In the barn he saddled Cassia. The old red roan was thin, but she didn't complain as he led her out the barn door. They rode past the orchard where the drought-parched kora bushes stooped row on row, wrinkled as old men. Every day Mother prayed, "Ahyuu, God of all, give us rain." Papa just squared his shoulders and worked harder, as if his sweat could water the land.

The Corwins, like many immigrants, had sailed the six-thousand-mile journey south after war swept across the northern continent. The people of Zolya hadn't been too welcoming, calling the refugees "pales," for their light skin and hair. Kipp's father had hoped to start a new life here, but the drought had withered his father's dreams along with their orchards. With no roasted kora beans to sell at the market this year, no money to pay the landlord, they would be kicked off the land.

Kipp fingered the red bead woven into his shoulder-length braid. His father had awarded him his first manhood bead for helping Sor Joay capture and break a wild horse three years ago. At the time, they'd made just enough money from the horse sale to save their farm from ruin.

Alone now without Sor Joay's expert horsemanship, he'd have to rope the wild horse on his own. *I'm seventeen now and* no longer a short-haired boy, Kipp thought. *I will do what a man does to help his family.*

Vultures circled in the sky, their moon shadows whirling black on the ground below. Looking up, Kipp counted them once, and then again. Seven. The number was a death sign. He shivered and strained his ears for the shadow hounds whose howls forewarned the coming of the Gwali, collector of souls.

Crickets sang; vultures gave their stark scratchy cry, cheewii lizards winged through the sky in search of insects, their scales shining like fireflies. But the hills beyond were silent. Kipp rode bravely under the seven, letting Cassia's hooves trample their winged shadows.

Two miles into the hills, Kipp scanned the terrain. No sign of the horse now. Maybe Lightning had galloped higher up the mountain into Sanuu Wood?

Kipp flicked the reins and urged Cassia to a gallop. He'd have a better chance of capturing the wild horse if he had Naqui powers. The heightened senses gave you an advantage. Sor Joay had said Kipp might come to have the gift as he got older, even though Kipp wasn't Zolyan and had no Farland soil in his blood. But if he had Naqui powers, wouldn't he have noticed keener eyesight? Wouldn't he have been able to see titauns by now?

Cassia headed up the steep incline. Tonight he'd rely on what he had—his horse, his hands, his lasso—to help his family. Half an hour later, they reached the great flat terrace of Titaun Koy, the place so high up in the world, he'd once seen Sor Joay pluck a star and eat it. Kipp was seven then, but that was still his strongest memory of the night the old man visited the witch of Sanuu Wood and made a wish.

Riding between the giant granite teeth, he followed hoofprints to the trees on the slope above the bare shelf. Under the boughs he watched and waited. Horses who lived east of the Twilgar Mountains roamed in herds and rarely came so close to farmlands. This horse was alone.

Sound. Movement. The white horse emerged from a stand of oaks. Kipp hadn't known until this moment he was tracking a mare, not a stallion. Well, Lightning would be a good name for either one. What mattered was her power, her speed. He guessed she was a three-year-old, a good age to corral and train. He kicked Cassia to a gallop. Instantly, Lightning took off. Clumps of dirt flew out behind her as she ran.

Spinning the lasso, Kipp caught up with her and swung past. Aiming for her bobbing head, he threw out the loop with a grunt and missed. She slowed her pace, huffed, and nodded at him. She was close enough now for him to see her muscular shoulders, her strong back and proud tail. *She shines against the dark as brightly as a cheewii lizard*, he thought. Kipp fumbled with his rope. She shook her head, snuffing. Or was she laughing? Then she broke into a run.

"Come on, Cassia!"

The wild horse veered left, making for the sanuu trees. Rope in hand, Kipp kept her in his sight, riding Cassia along the edge.

6

The mare could race down the mountainside and escape him easily enough, but she was playing with him.

"So you like a good game."

Kipp laughed. She teased him the way the landlord's daughter Zalika had, the time they'd met in secret down by the Sway River.

Lightning had a muscular beauty, a perfect swift stride. Kipp liked the way her white mane lashed against her neck as she ran. But most of all, he liked the way she lured him closer before she galloped off again.

Swift. Bright. She'd earn him plenty of money. He could see the coppers raining down from the sky and piling up around his feet. He and Royan and Jilly could stuff themselves with sweets. They could buy a better farm: a fertile piece of land by the Sway River. If he became a rich landholder living next to the landlord's estate—Kipp held his breath, felt his heart beat as he let it out slowly—Zalika would look at him differently then.

Not far ahead, he spied Lightning through the trees. "You'd better not climb farther up the slope," he said. "The Sanuu Witch lives up there." He was talking under his breath to the horse, giving her a warning she couldn't hear or understand.

Suddenly, Lightning darted from the woods, racing between Titaun Koy's teeth.

"Run, Cass!" They chased Lightning down the steep, moonlit hillside fast, faster. Cassia galloped close enough for Kipp to swing his lasso. Flinging the rope high, he whipped it in a broad circle overhead, tossed, and missed.

"Detch! Hurry, Cass! She's getting away!"

At the base of Titaun Koy the land grew flat again. Riding hard in the moonlight, Cassia half-stumbled over a dry, stony riverbed.

Kipp whipped her flank with his rope, a thing he'd never done.

Swaying unsteadily, Cassia freed herself from the riverbed, snorting as she sped on. But even now Kipp could see Lightning vanishing in the tawny grass. She was no more than a white speck flitting, mothlike, through a pale yellow landscape.

They chased her through the valley another hour until he was sure she was gone. The coppers he'd imagined at his feet vanished with her.

Throwing himself from the saddle, he whipped the grass until his arm ached. Something was caught in a bush. Kipp bent down. Three white horsetail strands fluttered in the breeze. He took the hairs Lightning had left there for him like a calling card or a challenge of more night games.

"Tomorrow night," he said as he carefully wove the strands into his braid. Still he had a bitter taste on his tongue. She might not return. This might have been his only chance.

Leaping on Cassia, he gave her rump one hard, disgusted slap before bringing his face down on her neck and kissing her over and over.

"Sorry, Cass. I know you're too old to run so fast so long. I only wanted . . ." He choked on his want, hating himself for whipping her.

His eyes were still blurry when he lifted his head and turned for home. Four miles away, or was it five? A gray plume rose in the predawn sky.

"Cass?" he whispered.

A howl echoed from the distant hills and then another. The sound the Gwali's shadow hounds had made in his dream. He followed the smoke trail with his eyes. Fire, too far off for Kipp to see what was burning. He kicked Cassia to a gallop, remembering Royan clutching Sor Joay's tinderbox.

CHAPTER TWO

THE SMOKE PLUME was broader now. *Maybe it's the Lunstrums' ranch.* Kipp hoped, prayed it was. They had grown sons to fight a fire and, after four generations of struggle, a large herd of cattle they could release and capture unharmed later. The Lunstrums could afford to take the loss. His family couldn't.

Kipp drove Cassia to a hard gallop. She was too slow! If he were riding Lightning, not this lame, half-dead mare . . . ! No, he didn't mean it. He only had to get there now. Now.

They crested the last hill. The fire was on his farm, not the Lunstrums'. His house and barn both were burning. Kipp leaped to the ground and raced downhill past the flaming orchards toward the house.

"Jilly! Royan!" He shouted their names as he burst through the door.

Papa, his clothes blackened, staggered through the smoke, carrying Jilly rolled up in a green rug. He pressed her into Kit's arms. "Take her outside!"

"But Royan! Where's Royan?"

"Get her out!" Papa covered his mouth with his shirt and ran half-stooped back through the room. A roof timber crashed down behind him. Kipp flew outside and carried Jilly all the way to the well. No fire near here. He put her down and lowered the bucket.

The Lunstrum boys were always up before dawn. Couldn't they see smoke from their ranch? No time to run and get them.

Kipp hauled the full bucket from the well. "You'll be safe here, Jilly."

She grabbed his leg. "Don't go, Kipp."

"I have to help Papa find Mother and Royan."

Jilly sobbed, wouldn't let go. He pushed her away. "Stay there, Jilly!" The bucket knocked hard against his leg as he ran, sloshing precious water on the ground. One small bucket. Not enough.

"Papa!" *Ahyuu, why hasn't he come out!*

The front door was engulfed in orange fire. He raced around the side, where the burning roof tilted down into the kitchen like a seesaw. The other side then. The sound of horses from behind. The Lunstrums? No time to look. He found part of the wall outside his parents' bedroom, kicked the window in with his boot, passed the bucket through, and jumped in after.

Smoke coiled around him. He gasped, choking. Eyes stinging, he pressed forward in the overpowering heat. *Ahyuu, help me find them.* "Royan! Mother!"

Someone gripped his shoulder. Relief flooded through his body. Papa was here. They'd rescue Royan and Mother together. But it was Carl Lunstrum clutching him, dragging him back toward the broken window.

"Let me go! My family!"

"Too late! The roof's about to cave in!"

"I don't care!" Kipp struggled savagely, elbowing Carl's ribs and kicking his shin. Carl strong-armed him back through the window and dragged him across the fallen fence.

Kipp hunched over coughing, sucking in ragged breaths.

The blazing farmhouse roared. Twelve feet away the bedroom wall collapsed. A few seconds more, and he and Carl would have been crushed.

Techee's high-pitched wail sounded like a sea storm as she drank all the air from the hollow wooden shell. But now the roof tumbled in with hardly a sound. *Poof,* like a nest falling from a tree.

What had Carl done? Mother, Father, and Royan were all still in there! Flames flashed out as the roof beam fell. Fire leaped from the falling house, setting Kipp's pant leg alight. He rolled in the dust, frantically trying to smother the flames.

Wiping his eyes, squinting, coughing, he rose to his knees. He had to get back inside. "Papa! Royan! Mother!" His arms were shaking. He tried not to be sick. There was a woman at the well, too square set to be his mother. Mrs. Lunstrum was holding Jilly. Kipp started to crawl back toward the house. *Get up, you detcher! Run! You might still be able to save them!*

Tall figures raced past with buckets from the well. All three Lunstrum brothers were here to help put out the fire. Now Kipp was up, running for the well.

"A bucket!" he screamed. "I need a bucket!"

Mrs. Lunstrum shouted back above the sound of the roaring fire. "There are no more buckets here!"

Get back to the house. Kipp raced past Carl, who was freeing the chickens. Confused hens tumbled out of the henhouse and scattered across the yard. Lars flung open the barn door. The terrified cow stampeded through, bellowing as she clattered up the hillside.

Choking, Kipp stumbled around the burning timber pile. No roof. No walls or doors, only a raging spire of flames where the house used to be. *Too late.* Still he shouted their names over and over, screaming through the fire, summoning his family from the smoke.

"Kipp's gone mad!" shouted Lars as he and Jon ran toward the barn with buckets. They did not run to the kora orchards, already burning up, already dead.

Kipp sped up, circled the fallen house again. Above the roaring fire he heard howling—not the sound of flame but of animals. Rounding the inferno, he saw shadows, first flat, then growing upward in the air.

13

Hounds.

The Gwali's shadow pack had come, sniffing death. The seven hounds became flesh before his eyes. All black. All growling.

Behind them the black-caped Gwali descended from the night on his ghost mare.

"Get back!" Kipp screamed, standing sentry before what had been his front door; he spread his arms out wide against the Death Catcher.

It was the Gwali and no other. Yet he could *see* him. Only people with Naqui powers could see the Gwali unless the Death Catcher chose to show himself. He remembered the seven vultures, the dream he'd had of sweeping human bones into a sack; Sor Joay had taught him to pay attention to such signs. He should have heeded the warnings.

The Death Catcher rode closer in on his mare. She was white as Lightning had been, but leaner, and the hot wind blowing back her mane exposed a hand-sized reddish-brown spot on her neck.

"I said get back!"

Lars tossed a bucketful of water at the barn. "Who's he shouting at?"

His brother stopped dousing the barn wall to stare at Kipp.

"Come on!" Jon called from the well. They turned and went for more water.

"They can't see you, but I can." Kipp felt a flood of power as he stood his ground before the towering mare, the looming figure on her back. Techee washed heat up his backside. His leg smarted, his neck throbbed, and the backs of his arms stung. He didn't move. "You can't come in!"

There was no house and no door, only a pile of blazing timbers, but Kipp wasn't going to let the Gwali get past. He was the wall. He was the door. And he was locked.

The Gwali did not speak. He sat long and lean atop his mare, darkness under his hood. Kipp couldn't make out his face, wasn't sure he wanted to. Did he even have a face? The mare stepped closer and shook her mane, pale as summer grass. The shadow pack gathered in a blackened clot, lowered their heads, and hunched their shoulders. Still Kipp didn't move.

Just left of the burning house, the Lunstrum brothers struggled to save the barn, but Kipp could no longer hear them shouting, nor could he hear the roar that must be coming from the inferno at his back. He was alone with the Gwali and his pack, surrounded by thin swirls of smoke.

The Gwali slowly drew a sack from his saddlebag. Kipp trembled and pulled out his knife. Sor Joay had told him about the soul sack called Kwaja—*the taker*. The bag the Gwali used to steal the souls of the dead.

The sack was blacker than night sky torn from empty space. It was but a foot wide and a yard long; it still looked immense. Kipp could almost feel himself falling into it. He averted his eyes.

"Stay back!" Kipp ordered. The words sent misty breaths across the night air. Or were they trails of smoke from the fallen house at his back? One gray puff glowed softly as a pearl as it lengthened into the shape of his mother's spirit. Her sleeping gown ruffled silently in the hot wind as she flew toward the Gwali.

Kipp screamed and flung himself forward. The mare reared up, her legs swimming in the air above Kipp's head. He dodged her hooves, leaped at her side for the Gwali, who held the sack open like a gaping mouth. Two more spirits floated past, following his mother's spirit into Kwaja.

"Royan! Papa!"

Kipp dropped his knife, caught the bottom corner of Kwaja, and pulled with all his might. Two shadow hounds sank their teeth into his right pant leg, growling and tugging him back. Another bit into his flesh where the cloth had burned away. Pain shot up his leg; Kipp held on to the sack, his fingers clamping down tight as the hounds' teeth. He would let his mother's spirit out, free Papa, free Royan.

The mare strutted forward, dragging Kipp and the dogs along. The horse took off as the Gwali yanked Kwaja upward. Kipp dangled from her side, banging hard against her ribs as she galloped. He tried desperately to keep hold but he was losing his grip. The dogs raced beside him barking. His head knocked against the saddle.

The Gwali tore Kipp's fingers from Kwaja. Kipp hit the ground and tumbled head over heels. Dust. Moon. Stars. Pain. Blood. Sweat. Rage. Smoke. He crashed to a stop, sucked in a breath, and jumped to his feet. The Gwali and his shadow pack were already up the hill.

Kipp stumbled off in search of Cassia. Where had he left his mare? He couldn't remember. "Cassia? Cass?"

He had to catch up, to steal the sack and free the souls of his family before the Gwali could get away.

CHAPTER THREE

KIPP'S LUNGS WERE RAW with smoke as he fled past the barn and back to the well. Jilly ran to him. He drew her to himself and hugged her hard. "You're alive." He sobbed into her hair, then quickly put her down.

Jilly cried, lifting her arms up to him.

"Get back," he warned. Not because he didn't love her, or want her, but because he was going after the Gwali and he couldn't do that with her along. He was already running up the hill.

"Wait, Kipp." She raced after him, jumped on his back, and clung to him, her arms about his neck like a catch rope. *Don't stop. Find Cass.*

"Put her down," screamed Mrs. Lunstrum. "Carl! Go after him! The boy's lost his mind!"

Kipp spotted Cassia by a lone oak on the hill. Jilly still clung to him. How could he leave her? He peeled her from his back and hugged her hard. "Stay here with Mrs. Lunstrum."

"No—K-Kipp." The words came in gulps between her sobs.

Kipp leaped into the saddle. Jilly cried, running after him, but he couldn't stop to explain. He'd come into his Naqui powers at last. Sor Joay had seen the possibility in him long ago, though it was unheard of in an immigrant, but he wouldn't take time to wonder at that now. He had to use his new powers to catch the Gwali, free his family.

Cassia dashed up the steep hill above the burning orchard. The rising smoke pierced the sky with the rich scent of kora as the bushes served their last hot brew.

Rope in hand, Kipp chased the Death Catcher, his pack fleeing like molten moon shadows. Blink and they'd vanish. But with his eyes wide and staring hard, he could clearly see the hounds racing alongside the Gwali's ghost mare.

The noose was tied just right to catch a horse. He'd knotted it for Lightning, not the Gwali's mare, but he'd rope her. Here was the horse he was after now, this horse, this rider, and his wretched black sack.

Cassia bounded toward Titaun Koy, the flat terrace where he'd tried to rope Lightning, where Sor Joay had seen his wife's spirit sprinkle down from the stars the night Kipp turned seven. If anyplace was magic, it was there. He'd run down death, shake him, make him give it back.

The sun rose tongue-red across the land. Thick clouds blew across the crimson sky, ringing the blue-black Twilgar peaks in white. The Gwali's mare sped into Sanuu Wood. Kipp drove Cassia into the trees. Thunderous sounds of flapping wings filled the air as the dawn sky blackened with thousands of bats returning to their mountain caves.

Kipp urged Cassia on. He couldn't see the Gwali and his hounds in this overgrown forest. Couldn't hear them with all the *detching* bats!

The last wave of bats flew overhead. Silence. Kipp listened. There it was. Crackling underbrush just up ahead. He peered through the branches. Low black shapes wove between the tree trunks. Dogs.

Kipp's muscles tightened. They couldn't run here in these thick woods, not fast anyway. In the swirling mist beyond the shadow pack, the Gwali's shape suddenly appeared, his black cloak hanging listless as a wind-free sail. He was riding his ghost mare at an easy trot.

It's like as if he doesn't know I'm after him or . . . or he doesn't care. Kipp's gut twisted. Was the Gwali ignoring him? He'd attacked the Death Catcher, grabbed his wretched sack, and nearly wrenched it from him! He would have it still if it weren't for the detching dogs! Anyway, he was on horseback now, and his rope was ready.

Cassia whinnied. The Gwali turned his head. The hope of a surprise attack fled with that single glance. Kipp had to act now.

Racing for the Gwali, he spun his lasso overhead. His foe sped up, dodging left and right between the oaks and sanuu trees. Kipp swung the rope higher, twirling it out in a wide arc. All his years of roping practice would pay off now.

Thundering hooves ahead. He had them on the run, and he was closing in! Swing it out. Control the spin. Now.

The loop snagged on a branch.

Two startled birds took flight, and Kipp drew back angrily. He flicked the lasso to loosen it from the tree, but his movements only cinched the rope in tighter.

"Bloody detch!"

Kipp abandoned his rope and sped on. Dawn shot spears of orange light through the trees. Higher up the trail he saw the ghost mare take a great leap. Her pounding hooves left the ground, and she rose up in the air.

Spirits could ride wind, he knew. Still he tugged the reins and drew up in the saddle, shocked at what he saw.

The hounds were next. They threw themselves upward in a mass as if flinging themselves against a wall, but there was no wall, only sunlit air. Their paws paddled as they rose, gathering speed over the thorny sanuu boughs.

Kipp tried to follow them along the forest floor, but it was as elusive as chasing a flock of birds. They appeared, disappeared, appeared again above the canopy.

His breath came hot and fast as Cassia hoofed up the steep path. There was a clearing ahead. Breaking free of the trees, Kipp suddenly reined Cassia in.

The Gwali and his shadow pack were flying straight for the witch's hut.

The white mare soared over the thatched roof, her ghostly form wavering in the chimney smoke. There was a last pearly glow before the Gwali and his pack vanished.

Kipp raced around the edge of the clearing to the other side of the shack. Squinting up, he was met with empty sky, now golden yellow with sun. Birds sang sweetly in trees. A fresh morning scent filled the mountain air. The Death Catcher and his hounds were gone.

CHAPTER FOUR

KIPP WIPED THE SOOT from his knuckles and knocked, his breath still coming hard from the chase. He was afraid, but he had to stay and find out what the Sanuu Witch knew about the Gwali. He knocked again and steeled himself. Sor Joay had brought him here once. The old man had not been afraid to go inside and ask for what he wanted.

Footsteps came from within, and the door opened a slit. A brown index finger poked out, wormlike, and beckoned. Kipp edged closer. The finger touched his chest and he jumped back, startled.

The door opened wider. The hearth fire on the far wall burned green. Saddlebags hung from hooks, as if this were a rich man's stable. *Stolen*, he thought. And if that were true, what had happened to all the riders?

He felt for his knife, then realized he'd dropped it when he'd tried to take the Gwali's sack. *Deysoukus!* As the door clicked behind him, the witch smiled. Her teeth gleamed white as sea pearls. Sor Joay had said the Sanuu Witch was very old. He saw she had smooth dark skin, full cheeks, bright eyes. Old. Young. Both. Neither. The witch had long braids, man fashion, only hers were not a single, dignified braid worn down the right side. There were dozens of them, some black, some brown, some gray, one wheat-colored like his own. They sprawled every which way like roots.

Kipp's eyes adjusted to the pale grass-colored light coming from the strange green flames. What wood burned green? The room was swept clean. On the high shelf to his left he saw a row of sparkling glass jars. Each of the smaller ones had a single perfect wildflower floating inside. All the wildflowers up here had died in the drought. Where had she found these? What kind of magic suspended them and kept them turning slowly in the jars? He eyed the contents of the larger jars—a floating scorpion, a tarantula. In the last jar, a wingless cheewii lizard glowed.

"Aum, Kipp," said the Sanuu Witch.

"Aum." She had a name but he could not remember it.

"You've been fighting Techee."

It did not take magic powers to see that he'd been battling fire. His clothes reeked of smoke, and he was covered in ash, his face likely as black as his hands.

"How many died?" she asked.

Her question spurred him into sudden ferocious speech. "They didn't die. They didn't have to. That's why I'm here. I saw the Gwali and I had the soul sack in my hands." He lifted them, shaking. "I had Kwaja. I almost freed my family. I swear I can still free them. I saw him disappear in the smoke from your fire. Tell me where the Gwali's gone!"

She took in his tirade as if he'd said no more than "good morning." Sitting by the fire, she stirred the pot hanging from the hook. "You think you can pull souls from the Gwali's sack once they've gone in?"

"I can. I will. He has my mother and Papa and my brother, Royan. He stole them."

"He took their souls." She turned and waved the spoon. "What bodies would you put them in if you retrieve them?"

What bodies? The question sent him reeling back against the door. He pictured what Techee had done to the house, the solid beams, the roof and walls. Under the smoldering rubble there must be charred bodies, blackened bones under the ashes. Nothing there to put a soul into.

He sucked in a sob. His knees were going under him. *Stand. Fight.*

"I had the power to see the spirit and grab his sack," he said. "With that kind of power, couldn't I—?"

"Raise the dead?" she finished. "That is beyond human reach."

"But one with Naqui powers—"

"Have you ever heard of such?"

He gripped the door behind so tight his nails scratched the wood. "But . . . I had the sack!"

He slumped to the floor. His skin felt hot, then cold. He'd grabbed Kwaja, chased the Gwali all the way up Titaun Koy through Sanuu Wood, but it wasn't enough. His family was gone. There was no way he could ever get them back.

An angry animal cry ripped through his chest.

He stayed crouched against the door, too weak to leave. The witch had given him water, but he'd refused the broth and the goat meat offered on a skewer. He would leave as soon as he could stand.

The yellow-white lily in a jar overhead made him think of his sister. Mother and Papa used to call her Lily Jilly, which later turned to Illy Jilly. The second nickname stuck. He thought of Jilly chasing him when he rode off, crying for him to take her along. Of Mrs. Lunstrum calling for Jilly to come back to her. His sister paid no mind to the woman but ran after him in her blackened sleeping gown. He felt a sudden fierce need to protect her. Jilly was just seven. She was all he had left.

"I want that soul sack," he said suddenly.

"What?" the witch asked around the scrap of meat she was chewing.

"I want it so no one I love will ever, ever, ever have to go inside again."

"It's not for mortal hands to have." The witch spat out a bit of bone.

"You know magic. I saw the Gwali disappear in your chimney smoke."

"The Gwali comes and goes as he pleases."

"Give me the power to steal his sack."

He was feeling stronger, just saying these impossible words. He'd seen the blue powder the witch once sold Sor Joay years ago. The powder had given him the magic to bring his wife, Safra, out of the spirit world. When he was seven, he'd watched Sor Joay burn the powder on Titaun Koy and seen the spirit light come down from the sky, but the flash had only lasted a moment.

Kipp wanted more than stardust or spirit light. He wanted Mother and Papa back. He wanted Royan real, in the flesh, his brother's cold feet bothering his sleep. What he'd pay to have Royan next to him again, hogging the bed at night, or talking all day about fishing in the Sway as they worked in Papa's sweltering orchard. What he'd give for that. Anything. Everything. But if their bodies were too burned, too far gone to hold life inside them ever again, if he couldn't save them, he'd keep Jilly safe, never let the Gwali draw her into his hideous sack.

"Mix up the potion or whatever it is you do."

The witch peered at him thoughtfully. "There will be a cost."

"Tell me how many coppers you want."

"Coppers do not pay for such strong magic. This kind requires a sacrifice."

"Anything." Jilly wouldn't ever have to die. He would make sure.

The witch scratched her ear. "Your braid," she said suddenly. "Cut it off."

"What?" Kipp leaped up as if he'd been bitten. "If I cut it off, I will be called a little boy, or treated as an outcast." He gripped his hair, his fury rising at her outrageous request. He'd grown his braid, earned his first bead of manhood. "Something else," he hissed. "Ask something else."

"That is the cost," she said flatly.

He looked at the clean-swept floor, saw the prints his ash-covered boots had made. The witch gnawed her bone, waiting. He'd once seen two thieves paraded through Napulo. In the town's central square, drummers played as the thieves' braids were publicly shorn. Townspeople spat in their faces as they were led, shackled, through the crowd and loaded into a cart. His father said the men would be imprisoned in OnnZurr. Kipp had heard of the place deep in the desert, which had served as Zolya's prison for the last three hundred years.

He'd also heard that men were shorn for lesser offenses. In the outer townships, where people were poor and a man's word was as valuable as his property, a liar or a cheat would lose his braid in a public ceremony before he was exiled.

"Why?" Kipp asked. He was swaying. His shadow moved across the green-lit wall, darkening the saddlebags.

"How much do you value this power you ask for?" she asked back.

If he returned to Jilly shorn, how could she look up to him? And worse than that, how could Zalika ever respect him? He would have to hide while his hair grew back. How could he take care of Jilly if he were in hiding?

"Impossible," he whispered.

"Then go."

He felt for the door handle at his back. Did not turn around. Sweat dripped from his brows. The room swam. The witch opened a window, put out her hand, and caught a sparrow. Drawing the bird back inside, she held it lightly, the small dark head poking above her encircled index finger. "Everything that lives will die," she said.

He suddenly felt afraid for the sparrow. "Don't kill it."

"Is this the hand of fate?" She held the fisted bird over her head. "Was it this sparrow's destiny to be caught today?"

"Let her go."

"Why?"

"Because you can." He'd hunted for food. But this was different. The witch was killing out of cruelty, just to feel the pleasure of her power over the little bird.

He went for her, grabbed her wrist. She let the sparrow go. It flew about the room frantically before finding the open window and darting back into the daylight.

He was the same height as the witch, though she carried the weight of a well-fed person, and he was thin with hunger. He let go and stood back as she pulled out her knife and ran the blade through the green flames in the hearth.

Kipp didn't move, though he could have. Both knew he would stay and let her take what she meant to take.

"I could have bled the sparrow. Now I'll need your blood to mix the potion."

The knife blade reflected the fire.

Kipp felt suddenly sick. Would she kill him and bury him out back, add his saddlebag to all the others on her wall? He listened for the Gwali's hounds. If he heard their warning howls, he would run.

She held the knifepoint to his neck, then cut his braid at ear level. The shock of what she'd done made his blood pound. The braid slit with the soft sound of a scythe through grass. In Napulo, guards pounded drums when the thieves lost their braids, and there was the wail of the desert skree pipes. Here, nothing. The swiftness and near silence of his loss hurt him deeply.

She put the braid on the table between the meat bone and a spoon. The single hunting bead he'd earned this year and the three white strands he'd woven in from Lightning's tail gleamed green in the firelight. Kipp looked away. It was done.

The witch chose a small jar from the high shelf, spun open the lid, and touched the tender iris floating within. The bright purple flower turned to dust.

Clouds passed in the sky outside the window. Kipp tried to control his breathing as the witch turned with the knife a second time.

"Easy now," she said in the kind of voice one used to calm a jittery horse.

She made a swift, stinging slit on his neck, pressed the jar against his skin, and began to fill it with his blood. Kipp felt dizzy. The walls wavered, the floor heaved. The witch steadied him with a firm grip. The fire was a single eye, the room a hollow face. Panting. Low and steady. Shadows. Dogs circling.

Suddenly, she took the jar away, pulled a rag from one of the hanging saddlebags, and handed it to him. "Press this against the wound."

Only then did he let himself tumble onto his knees, panting. The shadows fled.

"You must tread close to the edge to battle death," said the witch.

Still holding the cloth to his neck, Kipp fumbled for the chair, got himself up, and shifted on the seat so he could watch her without looking at his braid. She could, at least, have placed it on a clean shelf. Not directly on the table by her leftover meal.

The witch stirred the blood and powder together in the jar, speaking half in the familiar Zolyan tongue and half in Old Escuyan so he could not make out the full meaning.

"Eepi ynn kor tuta yoy.

"Akki tan yom ipak noy."

Steal death and do not turn back

Become the master of the sack.

The potion thickened. Leaning over the table, she hummed as she worked, the way Kipp's mother had hummed when she prepared the morning meal. He blinked back tears.

The witch touched the bone on the table. It, too, turned to powder. She had not crushed it any more than she'd crushed the flower, only touched each thing lightly with her fingertip. Kipp trembled. Could she do the same to him if she willed it?

He watched her add the bone powder to the potion, the white powder turning the mixture a lighter purple-black. She placed the lid on the jar and held it out to him.

"What do I . . . How is it to be done?"

"When the Gwali comes riding, you will take out the jar. Rub the potion on your hand. One hand, not both. Then grab Kwaja. The potion will hold fast. And in the moments of that holding, no one, not even the Gwali, can wrest the sack away from you. But run quickly once you have what you desire, for the sticking spell will not last long."

Kipp saw a flash of white outside the window. It was followed by a deep rolling sound and the crack of thunder.

"And now the storm," said the witch.

CHAPTER FIVE

KIPP RODE THROUGH THE sanuu forest in the rain—the first shower in more than eleven months. Under the forest canopy he lifted his palm, felt the drops prick his hand.

On the edge of Titaun Koy, Kipp dismounted between two granite teeth and watched the rain sweep across the grassland below in broad sheets. He could see his farm two miles away; the rain was putting out the last of the flames. A yellow flash still burned upward from the distant orchard. The storm had come in time to save nothing but a single barn wall, which even now was tilting hard to the left.

Kipp heard a sob, spun around startled, and realized it had come from his own throat. He let out another, this time forming the word like a curse, *"Rain!"* The storm had come too late.

A pool formed in the low, flat boulder by his knees. He stooped, drank the rain, and let the sky come into him, though he did not forgive its treachery. Cassia's soft muzzle pressed against his cheek, waiting her turn. "Go on," he whispered. "Drink."

Later, riding downhill and through the gully, he spotted the Lunstrum brothers far below, leading his family's one remaining cow toward their neighboring ranch. They passed the charred kora orchard, where puffs of smoke rose and bloomed outward in the rain.

Mrs. Lunstrum and Jilly followed behind. He had no thought of what he'd say when he reached Jilly. Only that he'd pick up his little sister. Hold her.

The Lunstrums were likely halfway to their ranch by the time Kipp rode through the lingering smoke at the farm. He dismounted and let Cassia's reins hang where they were. On the ground he found his knife. He'd had the Gwali for a moment: gripped the sack just here. Drying the blade on his pant leg, he sheathed it in his boot. By the well, he found his hat. The rim was blackened with ash, but he put it on against the rain and headed for the remains of the house.

In the charred and broken woodpiles, he ran his hand along his mother's cast-iron stove. It was the only thing still standing. The stovepipe had fallen over. Nothing else, not even a doorframe, had escaped Techee's hunger.

He found Sor Joay's stone tinderbox in the rubble by the stovepipe. Royan must have used it carelessly when he started the fire. *Stupid!* Kipp kicked it hard across the ash piles, sent the flints flying in all directions. They fell soundless in the mud. *Stupid little boy!* He kicked the box again and again until the pieces had flown beyond the fallen walls and lay on the ground by the burnt henhouse.

Cassia paced anxiously, sniffing the smoky air. Kipp mounted her, rode halfway up the hill, then jumped down, and ran to the scattered pieces of the tinderbox. He wiped the stone box hard against his shirt until the tree carving on the lid was clean. Wept.

"Where have you been?" asked Mrs. Lunstrum. Kipp closed the back door and stood in the mudroom, a small entry adjoining the kitchen. Water dripped from his hat brim, adding to the growing puddle at his feet. He'd ridden round and round for hours, unable to come inside this farmhouse so like his own, unable to face a warm kitchen where Mrs. Lunstrum and her daughter, Kinna, prepared the family meal.

Kinna Lunstrum blushed when she saw him, then busied herself sweeping onion skins from the counter into her open palm. She was fifteen, blonde, and big-boned, with blue eyes and pretty peach-colored cheeks. He watched her toss the skins into the trash.

"I am sorry," he blurted out. He knew how filthy he was, a stinking smoky smudge on the edge of this clean kitchen.

Both families had hoped Kinna and Kipp would someday have an understanding. But he did not have feelings for her as he had for the landlord's daughter, Zalika, who was beautiful and daring and nothing like any girl he'd ever met. There was no real hope of a pale immigrant marrying a wealthy, dark-skinned Zolyan girl like Zalika, but he could not change his heart. Anyway, Kinna was like a sister, though he sensed she wanted to be more to him than that.

Avoiding his eyes, Mrs. Lunstrum pulled the steaming bread from the oven. The last words he'd heard her call out as he rode after the Gwali were, "Carl! Go after him! The boy's lost his mind!"

He should say something to let her know why he'd ridden off that way. But if he told her where he'd been, what he'd done, it would only prove to her that he *was* mad. Who but a madman would chase after spirits, sell his hair to a witch for a potion?

"Where is Jilly?" he asked as politely as he could.

"I put her to bed," she said. "Hat, coat, and boots off, Kipp Corwin."

Kipp struggled with his boots, then hung his coat on the hook, turning the pocket with the potion jar in it toward the wall. It worried him to leave the jar there, but it was not small enough to slip into his pants or shirt pockets unnoticed. Kipp fingered the damp brim of his hat. Many men tucked their braid into their hat while working or riding, so Kinna and her mother hadn't guessed that he was shorn. He knew he should remove it, get it over with. "Is Jilly all right?"

His family had visited this farm many a time, more so lately, hoping he would think to court Kinna. But Kipp felt like a stranger here. Mrs. Lunstrum stood warily by the open stove where Techee burned in the black iron belly.

"Your sister is resting. She took in too much smoke and has been coughing all day so I . . . Wait!" she shouted as he blew past her and Kinna and hurried down the hall, opening doors until he found her in her bed.

"Jilly?" He knelt down and stroked her curly blonde head. Her skin was warm. Was she feverish? His heart ached.

"She needs her rest." Mrs. Lunstrum's tone was stronger now, a mother lioness protecting her cub, but her reprimand awakened Jilly. She sat up, rubbed her eyes, and coughed. Kipp patted her back.

"I saw the fire," said Jilly. "It ate our house."

"It did." He wanted to ask if she saw Royan start it, but he couldn't get the words out. He'd ask later or maybe never at all.

"Are you hungry, Jilly?" Kinna asked from the doorway.

Jilly didn't answer. She wrapped her arms about Kipp's neck. He lifted her and carried her down the hall to the kitchen. Mrs. Lunstrum had bathed her and given her one of Kinna's old dresses, but she still smelled like smoke. They both did. He was pushing in Jilly's chair when the Lunstrum boys clambered inside, jostling each other as they hung up their wet coats. They all spoke at once.

"Big storm. Mud everywhere."

"I'm starving."

"Thank Ahyuu it's raining at last."

"I smell stew."

"Watch where you put those boots!"

"Kipp's here."

Suddenly, all three blond-haired Lunstrum boys stood at the table in their stocking feet. Like his family, the Lunstrums were immigrants, though their homeland of Svenlund was hundreds of miles north of Kipp's homeland Gare, a land of dark winters and heavy snow. Kipp's family was new to Zolya compared to the Lunstrums, who had ranched for four generations. They owned their land and kept a good herd of cattle here in the highlands.

"Manners, Kipp," said Lars. He reached over and knocked off Kipp's hat. Carl's jaw fell open. Kinna bit her lip. Lars let out a guffaw. "Look at you!"

"Now don't be rude," said Mrs. Lunstrum.

Carl, Jon, and Lars took their seats. The chairs creaked under their weight.

"The fire," said Kipp. "My braid caught fire. I had to . . . cut it off." It was a lie but he could not tell them what the Sanuu Witch had done.

"It's a terrible thing," Mrs. Lunstrum said as she sliced the bread, "to lose your family and your farm in a fire." She was speaking to her sons, rebuking them for their obvious scorn over his short hair. But her attempt only made him feel worse. A boy might need a woman to defend him. A seventeen-year-old did not.

As Kinna buttered the bread, Lars wiggled his braid at Kipp. Most immigrant men adopted the Zolyan custom of earning braid beads to show their strength and prowess. The Lunstrum boys were likely just as proud of their braids as Kipp had been of his. Lars already wore two hunting beads. Kipp jabbed his meat. The beef stew tasted like the dinners his mother used to make before their larder was bare. The thought made his stomach go hard. This was not his kitchen. Not his home.

They would take this meal; stay tonight and no more. He still owned some hens and the milk cow, Tish. If he sold them for a few coppers, that would be enough to get them on their way.

CHAPTER SIX

AN HOUR LATER, he was tucking Jilly into bed when Kinna came in with a shining glass jar.

"Cheewiis," said Jilly. "Where did you find them?"

"I know a rock where they like to soak in the sun."

"Kipp never got me any."

"I have tried many times and never succeeded," he said.

"My brothers could not find them, either. You have to know where to look." Kinna put the glass jar by the bed. The two wingless male cheewii lizards inside flicked their tails. The glow would dim when they slept, but they were awake now, their scales glowing a bright yellow-green.

"Say thank you, Jilly," Kipp reminded.

"Taka, Sa Kinna."

His sister didn't have to address her as *Sa*, the polite Zolyan word for *Miss* or *Ma'am*, but Kinna must seem very grown up to Jilly. Kinna circled to the other side of the bed to kiss Jilly's cheek before she left the room.

Jilly touched the jar. "They are baby dragons."

"Not dragons. But some say they are a distant relation."

"They can fly like dragons."

"They'll grow wings in a few months. Then we'll have to let them go."

Jilly said, "I don't want to."

He remembered wanting to keep his cheewiis, too, when he was a young boy. "They can't live in the jar once they know how to fly," he said, running his hand through her tangled hair.

She coughed. "You said cheewiis swallowed fire and that's why they glow."

Kipp nodded. "That's what the story says."

She was silent a long while before she said, "The fire doesn't hurt them."

Kipp couldn't speak or move. He knew what she meant. If fire did not hurt the cheewiis, why did it hurt people?

Jilly's eyes welled up. "Sa Lunstrum said Mama, Papa, and Royan went to Ahyuu's paradise."

He put his arms around her. Held her.

"They t-took Royan. They didn't take me," she cried into his shirt.

He let her cry.

Mrs. Lunstrum hurried in with a handkerchief for Jilly and stood at the foot of the bed. "Let me help her," she said at last.

He rocked his sobbing sister. "I'm here with her. Please, would . . . leave us alone."

"What did you say to the child?" She seemed offended that Kipp didn't want her help.

"Nothing, Sa. Please go now."

Mrs. Lunstrum left the room.

"Do you want me to sing to you now, Jilly?"

She wasn't ready for a song. "I want to go with them."

"Not now, Jilly. Stay here with me." He was holding her too tight. She pushed against his chest, looked up at him. "But you left and rode away on Cassia, and you wouldn't let me come with you!"

"I'm sorry, Jilly. I had to go, but I won't leave you again. I promise."

She sniffed and tugged the button on his soggy shirt. "Sa Lunstrum said Ahyuu's paradise is a beautiful place and people are never hungry or thirsty and there's lots of happiness."

"Yes," he whispered. "That's right." His parents had taken him to temple, where he'd heard the priests speak of Ahyuu's paradise. People all over the world worshipped the Great Being. Sor Joay had prayed to Ahyuu, too. But he'd also told Kipp about the Gwali. Would Ahyuu send a Death Catcher to gather souls? It didn't seem right.

Jilly lay down again. He wiped her face with the hand-kerchief.

"Sing to me," she said.

• • •

When Jilly slept at last, Kipp walked out through the rain to the barn and laid his head against Cassia's neck.

"I don't understand," he whispered. "Help me understand." His mind went back before the fire, before Sor Joay had left him with the tinderbox, all the way back to the night they'd spoken of the Gwali in the mountain cave.

They'd been on one of their many hunting trips and were riding through a rough rainstorm when Sor Joay sickened with a fever. Deep in the Pinnacle Mountains, Kipp found them shelter in a cave. He'd nearly missed the dark entrance hidden behind a jagged rock. In the cave he'd rolled out Sor Joay's blanket and guided him onto it before lighting a fire.

Kipp remembered that night so clearly; Sor Joay's head had been wet with rain, and his dark eyes were glassy with fever. "I am thinking of Safra," he said.

They had talked of his wife many times. Sor Joay still wore the white bead of marriage in his braid, though Safra had died a long time ago.

Kipp said, "She used to cook such fat griddle cakes."

"They were very tasty." Sor Joay closed his eyes and folded his dark hands across his chest. Kipp saw his hands were shaking.

There was a waterskin in the knapsack. "Drink this, Sor."

Sor Joay took a sip. "I have lived a good life, Kipp. If the

Gwali comes for me tonight, I do not want you to be afraid."

Kipp wiped Sor Joay's feverish head. They had rarely talked of the Gwali, though Kipp knew there were many stories. In Gare, people also told Death Catcher tales. In Gare they called the Death Catcher the Shonheen. It was the Shonheen who rode with a wolf pack to take the souls of the dead. His papa had stopped telling those stories when they gave Kipp nightmares. He had also cautioned Sor Joay not to speak to Kipp about the Gwali.

"The Gwali won't come, Sor," Kipp said. "You will get well."

"My spirit is ready to leave the old hut of my body. I will go to paradise and see my wife again."

"This is your fever talking, Sor," Kipp answered nervously. Sor Joay had always been a strong man. He did not like to hear him talking this way.

"Open your eyes," Sor Joay said. "Tell me what you see."

It was an old game they used to play. Kipp had been so busy trying to make his teacher comfortable; he had not looked around the cave. In the soft firelight he turned and saw the wall paintings of bright creatures with enormous silver wings.

"Titauns," he'd whispered. "Dragons." He saw the people running below. "So many people. I thought only those with Naqui powers could see the titauns."

"In the beginning days, all people could see them. Before

the titauns left our world to fly in and out of time, they left us a gift."

"Fire."

"Yes, fire. You have brought me to the sacred cave, Kipp. These titaun paintings are ancient. Only Zolyans who follow the old ways come here to pray."

Kipp could not tell if he was pleased or upset with him. "Sor, I only wanted to take you out of the storm."

Sor Joay touched his arm. "You are not Zolyan but you understand the land. You might have a gift." He let his eyes wander across the titaun paintings. "I think the cave would not have opened its mouth to you if you were not meant to come inside," he whispered.

Kipp had trembled with delight. He was fourteen that year, the age a Zolyan boy took his Lostwalk, the age when the first signs of Naqui powers appeared if you were lucky enough to have them. He boiled the tea leaves for his teacher. "This will help you to get well, Sor."

"You can fight this fever, but you cannot change the hour of a man's death," Sor Joay said. The firelight dancing across the dragon paintings made it seem as if the titauns' wings were moving.

"Tell me a story," Sor Joay said. "I have taught you what I know."

"Drink this tea and I will." He put the cup by Sor Joay's side.

Kipp's family could not go to the temple very often. But

Sor Joay said you did not have to go to a temple to learn the sacred tales. Kipp scooted in closer to the fire and looked up at the titauns. The painting showed them flying in a great circle under the moon. He thought of the tale called "Tiatuu's Egg," a good story that featured dragons and the birth of Omaja, the Daughter of Time. Kipp cleared his throat.

"The First Beings who dwelled in the One World did not know day or night, only Ahyuu's primordial light, for time had not yet begun. There was no death and no end to the glory that was the now of Ahyuu's world. . . ."

In the chilly stable, Cassia's neck was warm against his cheek. The night in the dragon cave was long ago. "I did not ask Sor Joay anything more about death that night," he whispered, "or about the Gwali."

Rain pattered on the barn roof. He looked into Cassia's large brown eye. "Sor Joay wanted to talk to me about the Gwali. He would have told me whatever I wanted to know that night. I was too afraid to listen."

CHAPTER SEVEN

TWO NIGHTS LATER, they were seated around the Lunstrums' dinner table when the door swung open. A tall man stepped into the entryway. Kipp and the Lunstrum boys leaped up, hands on their hunting knives.

"Is Kipp Corwin here?" The man stood in shadow, the Lunstrums' work coats on the walls hanging limp as boneless bodies on either side of him.

Kipp's thoughts raced. *This man's not . . . the Gwali. The Lunstrum boys can see him, too.*

"What do you want with him?" asked Carl.

Kipp could see him better now. The prominent scar on the left side of his face scored him from eye to lip. It drew the base of his left eye down, exposing the red underneath, and puckered his upper lip. His skin was a little too fair for a Zolyan. There were likely a few northern immigrant branches in his family tree.

"The landlord sent me here to collect the late land fee. Seems the Corwins have destroyed his house and orchards. The boy and girl have to come back to Sor Tunassi's estate to work off their debt."

"You can't take them like this!" protested Mrs. Lunstrum.

The intruder took a step toward the table. "You filthy pales always stick together."

"Who are you calling pales?" Carl growled. The Lunstrums considered themselves to be Zolyans even if their ancestors came from Svenlund.

Mrs. Lunstrum put her hand on Jilly's shoulder. "Take the boy. I'll watch over his sister. She's too little to—"

"Both work for Sor Tunassi until the debt's paid off."

Kipp stepped in front of Jilly's chair. He did not need a woman's protection. "How long will it take to pay it off?" he asked hoarsely.

The man leaned forward. "That's Sor Saggorn to you, dwiig worm."

Kipp gritted his teeth, trying not to react. Dwiig worms were disgusting. They ate animal feces. "Sor Saggorn, how long will it take, Sor?"

"Oh, years and years by the looks of you." He spat a thin black stream of tobacco juice onto the floor.

Mrs. Lunstrum's neck stiffened.

"My little sister will stay here, Sor Saggorn," said Kipp. Mrs. Lunstrum swept Jilly into her arms and held her protectively, Jilly's bare legs dangling down till they were lost in the ample folds of the woman's skirt.

Sor Saggorn stepped forward and caught Kipp's upper arm in a vise. The sour smell of tobacco and sweat mingled with Mrs. Lunstrum's rich-smelling stew. Kipp's stomach clenched. He twisted, trying to free himself.

"Let go of my brother!" cried Jilly.

Kipp stared up at the dark stubbly chin. He would ask differently this time. "I will come quietly, Sor Saggorn. Just leave my sister here, please."

But neither Kipp nor Mrs. Lunstrum could talk the man out of his mission. He ordered Kipp and Jilly onto the front porch, where he made them don their coats before he tied Kipp's hands behind his back.

The Lunstrums stepped out the door and stood watching while the hired man patted Kipp down. Kipp's breath quickened as the searching hands came down past his waist and paused at his coat pocket.

"Wait," Kipp cried as Sor Saggorn pulled out the potion jar.

"What's this?" he asked, holding it up to his eyes. The thick purple-black liquid in the glass jar looked even darker against the man's heavy turquoise ring.

"It's nothing," said Kipp. *Ahyuu, don't let him throw it away. Don't let him break it!*

Jilly cleared her throat.

The man began to unscrew the lid. Kipp tensed. Would the magic escape? Would he be defenseless against the Gwali? *Say something! Anything!*

"My . . . my sister's cough medicine," Kipp blurted out suddenly.

Jilly gave a helpful cough.

The lid came off with a pop. A sickly odor filled the air. Sor Saggorn wrinkled his nose at the gooey contents. He screwed the lid back on, jammed the potion jar back into Kipp's coat pocket, and continued his search. Kipp curled his toes. His knife was sheathed in his boot just above his ankle. The large-knuckled hands did not dip inside where it was hidden.

Satisfied with his search, Sor Saggorn pressed Kipp down the steps. "Which one's his horse?" he asked. Carl pointed and Sor Saggorn hefted him onto Cassia's saddle. He lifted Jilly up next. The Lunstrums moved to the top step but did not leave the porch.

Jilly whimpered, but she did not cry. "It's all right," Kipp said.

But there was more. The hired man grabbed Jilly's wrists and tied her small hands to the saddle horn.

"You don't have to do that," snapped Kipp. Sor Saggorn slapped him in the face, the rough silver edge on his turquoise ring drawing blood.

"How many animals survived the fire?" he demanded.

"None," Lars said from the steps.

"Don't lie to me!" Sor Saggorn sent Lars after the Corwins' livestock. Lars blushed an angry red as he crated the chickens and took the cow from the pen. "You will follow us and bring the Corwins' animals. They belong to Sor Tunassi now."

Lars did not move.

"Lars!" cried Mrs. Lunstrum. "Do what Sor Saggorn says."

Carl and Jon stood on the bottom step, arms crossed. The Lunstrums had worked hard to be an accepted part of Zolya's community. The family would not want to offend a powerful landlord like Sor Tunassi.

The first star appeared as they left the Lunstrums' farm. Sor Saggorn rode ahead, leading Cassia by the rope. Hens flapped in their crates. Tish lowed, complaining on her tether. Lars rode sullenly behind, clucking his tongue to keep the cow moving.

In the bouncing saddle, Jilly leaned her head against Kipp's chest. "You're a brave girl," he said to the top of her head. "You didn't even cry."

"Don't leave me," she said. "Don't ride off again."

"I won't. I promise." He wanted to wrap his arms around her, but the man had tied his hands behind his back as if he were a criminal. Worse than that, he had tied Jilly's.

Detch! Kipp cursed silently, his gut churning. Aside from the Gwali, he had never hated anyone as much as he hated Sor Saggorn.

Just up ahead, the man's tall figure was etched against the twilight. He whistled between his teeth, a sound like wind through a crack in the wall. Kipp recognized the tune. It was "Plenty." Jilly sat up a little straighter, knowing her favorite song before Kipp caught the melody. To cover it up, to keep Sor Saggorn from ruining the tune forever for his little sister, Kipp sang to her under his breath.

Beyond the fence the Lunstrums' cows flicked their tails at the flies, keeping time for him and Jilly.

> *"You will have horses running wild and free*
> *And coppers for racing and cakes with your tea.*
> *Sing high for the highlands,*
> *Sing low for the low.*
> *You will have plenty wherever you go."*

CHAPTER EIGHT

I AM NOT A SLAVE," Kipp whispered. Lying on the top bunk, he held his arm up to the star he could see through the hole in the ceiling. "I will not stay here with Jilly long."

For now he had to work in Sor Tunassi's orchards. Jilly's cough had hung on, and she wasn't well enough to leave. Then, of course, there was the detching family debt. He'd have to think of a way to pay it off before he could get out.

There were eight bunk beds in the shack. Jilly slept on the bottom bunk below him. If it weren't for her, he would have stayed in one of the young men's shacks, but Jilly was still afraid after the fire, and she wanted him nearby. So he'd agreed to stay in the shack with the orphans in the care of two older tribal women, Sa Wikk and Sa Minn.

He was a man and didn't need watching over, but the women were good with the younger children and kind to Jilly. Escuyan people, old and young, had come to join other Zolyan farm laborers to work the kora harvest. Like many nomads fleeing the drought, these women would return to their tribe when the season ended. Hardship drove the nomads to farmwork; love for the wandering life drove them back to the Farlands. It was their custom not to stay in one place too long.

"*Escuyan* means 'wanderer,'" Sor Joay once said. "All Zolyans once wandered this land together. But long ago some people left the Farlands to settle down. These people say they own the land, but they have lost the freedom of the wind. They have forgotten the sky is our roof, that our home is everywhere under our feet."

Jilly coughed in the bunk below. Three weeks had passed since the fire, and her lungs still hadn't healed. The sickness did not leave her in the heat of the day when they picked kora berries in the orchards, nor in the cool of the night as she lay sleeping. *She won't die,* Kipp thought. *It is only a cough.* Still he worried over her.

"I know this." He moved his hand covering the star. "The Gwali won't take Jilly or anyone else I love ever again." He did not whisper Zalika's name, though he would protect her from the Gwali, too, if he could.

Zalika was just a quarter of a mile away from him in her father's estate house. But Kipp had not gone near her house since the day Sor Saggorn brought him and Jilly here. Nor had he let her see him in the orchards. He didn't want Zalika to know he was one of her father's kora pickers now.

Zalika should remember him the way he was a year ago. He'd been free the day of the Napulo Town Fair, and she had been free, too, though it was only for few hours. He saw her face before him now with silver water droplets running down her cheeks and into her open, laughing mouth. How smooth her skin was, rich and dark as roasted kora. She'd left her father's box seats at the racetrack to play cards in the women's tent, or so she had said, but Zalika had heard children swimming in the Sway and gone to the riverbank instead.

Royan had abandoned his pole to swim with the other little boys, so Kipp was fishing alone when Zalika came down the bank, slipped off her shoes, and waded in beside him.

Her finely embroidered skirt and top were bright red silk, and she had many sparkling bracelets. He knew it was not considered right for a wealthy Zolyan girl to be seen with a pale immigrant from Gare, but he stood at a bend in the river where no one was watching.

She introduced herself formally, as if they were meeting in an ordinary place and not wading in a river. He was startled by her last name, Tunassi—as the landlord's—and realized he'd caught a glimpse of her before, when he'd come with his father to pay the quarterly land fee.

He liked the sound of her voice, which was deep and a little rough for a slender girl, and he liked her friendly manner;

still, wouldn't she get into trouble for wading in the Sway and wetting the hem of her skirt? Sor Tunassi wasn't the sort of man you would want to anger. Just then Zalika plunged her hands in the water and pulled out a turtle. Her bracelets caught the light as she held the little creature up.

"Don't be afraid," she said, speaking to the turtle, who'd withdrawn into his shell.

"He knows better than to come out," said Kipp.

"Why?"

"A giant has him in her hands."

She laughed, and he liked the sound so much he wanted to make her laugh again. He wondered why she had come down to the river, when most of the Zolyan girls, especially the wealthy ones, were sitting comfortably in the shade sipping cold plum juice or playing cards in the ladies' pavilion. He liked her daring.

She ran her finger along the turtle's shell. "Your braid is long."

"It grows steadily," he'd answered proudly.

Suddenly, he wanted to tell her how he'd earned his braid-bead for helping Sor Joay capture and train a wild horse, but an honorable man was not supposed to boast.

Zalika released the turtle with a little splash. They watched it swim under a rock. Water droplets hung from the curls of her short black hair.

Kipp glanced down. "He is glad you let him go."

"I wouldn't have hurt him." She looked directly at Kipp,

her eyes dark as wells. "Where is your family from?"

"Gare," he said. "It is a peninsula on the western edge of Hexium."

"From the northern continent. So you are a refugee from the war?"

"My family owned an estate and rich farmland in Gare until the war." He suddenly wanted her to know his people had once been as wealthy as her family. Zalika arched her brow, but she wasn't listening to what he said; she was looking past him at the water.

"Will you help me capture another turtle?" she asked.

"Why?"

"It is better than playing cards with chatty girls," she said.

He abandoned his pole and they caught three more turtles over the next hour. She gave them names—Tuito, Manny, Isty—and they talked to each other, holding the turtles up as if the creatures were speaking. It was a silly game but he lost some of his shyness and learned much about Zalika. She liked to ride horses, though her father only let her ride sidesaddle. She was an excellent archer and had won second place in the women's archery competition at Goba City Fair.

Sure tales of his father's kora farm would bore her, Kipp told Zalika about his hunting trips with Sor Joay, his rides to the Pinnacles (though he did not speak about the dragon cave), and his expedition to the Stone Giants.

Zalika seemed to like his hunting stories. "I am only

allowed to shoot targets," she said with a sigh. "Never game."

He did not tell her Sor Joay took him hunting because his family needed the meat. They had never hunted for sport the way rich people did, but this girl had diamond earrings, an estate house with servants. She didn't know hunger.

"Your hair is the color of wheat." Zalika's bracelets tinkled as she reached out her hand. Kipp drew back, insulted. It was not right for a girl to touch a man's braid unless they were pledged and there was an understanding between them. He looked down at her bare feet in the river. His heart pounded in his chest now, remembering her smile. The landlord's daughter could defy custom with an ease that shocked and delighted him. He had not known what to think or how to act around her that day last year, but he'd never forgotten it.

What would Zalika look like now? Her feet would not be smeared with river mud from capturing turtles. She would wear silk wrap skirts or colorful kirifa dresses, and slippers with little round mirrors like other wealthy Zolyan girls. He was going against strict Zolyan custom to even think of trying for such a girl.

The children in the shack slept peacefully, their soft sighs barely heard against Jilly's rough breathing. Smoke lung, Sa Minn called it. How long would it be before she was well again? Kipp's eyes drank in the only bit of sky the roof hole allowed. His wrists ached from harvesting kora. He rubbed them, closed his eyes, and saw what he always saw when his eyes were closed. Fire. The memory still burned his skin. It came upon him like a fever each night and at unexpected moments in the day, when the sun's rays scorched his back.

Why? he asked silently.

His parents believed in Ahyuu. People all over the world prayed to the maker of all things seen and unseen. But if Ahyuu made all, ruled all, why had Ahyuu allowed the titaun dragons to give human beings such a dangerous thing as fire? Why did people have to die?

He didn't know what he believed anymore. And though he wanted to, he could not pray.

CHAPTER NINE

"TRY HERE, JILLY." Kipp carried her basket to the next kora bush. He stood above her, picking the berries out of her reach and trying to shade her from the blistering sun. Sa Minn plucked the bush at Kipp's right. She scooted closer and leaned her bulk in to expand the circle of shade.

"Taka, Sa Minn," said Kipp.

She nodded. Kipp reached through the green leaves. Each day the landlord's plentiful red berries ate away at his spirit, the kora's stark, sweet smell haunting him. If the storm had broken sooner, he would have been harvesting his father's orchard today with Royan. He wouldn't have been driven to go after the wild mare, wouldn't have given Royan the tinderbox, wouldn't have lost everything to Techee.

Kipp swallowed a dry moan and quickly turned his mind away from the wall of fire to the scratchy kora bush.

Below him, Jilly coughed. He stooped to give her a drink from his water pouch.

"I'm hungry," she said, her large blue eyes looking up at him, pools of water in a pale desert face.

"We will eat soon," he said. It would be another two or three hours before they stopped work and took their meager evening meal in the camp. But *soon* was a word that could mean anything from minutes to hours to a young child. He was satisfied when Jilly seemed to accept his answer.

They moved on to the next bush. Sa Minn stooping on one side, Sor Twam picking berries on the other. Like so many nomads, the Escuyan elder, Sor Twam, had been driven here by the drought to work side by side with poor Zolyan farm laborers in the rich man's orchard. Sor Twam was a storyteller and reminded Kipp of Sor Joay, though he was much shorter, bowlegged, and his words were wind-filled due to a few missing teeth.

The workers in the next row sang as they picked, their hands moving in rhythm to the song. *"Tuma tuma hay so ehya. Tuma tuma hay so ya!"*

Half a mile down the dirt road, the estate house wavered in the heat, the high white walls rising three stories up to the dark tile roof. There were four windows on each story. Zalika might be in one of those rooms looking out toward the orchard. His fingertips were stained red, the color her skirt had been when she waded into the Sway. How long ago that was—a year ago, when they were both sixteen. Another life.

He wiped his face on his sleeve and took a swig of water. He'd worked away from the road since coming here, knowing Zalika passed the orchard a few times a week on her way to her riding lessons. He wanted to see her. He did not want to see her with his braid cut, his hands stained with kora.

"Tuma tuma hay so ehya. Tuma tuma hay so ya," Kipp sang over Jilly's bare head. The sun beat down. He should let her wear his hat. But the young men in the orchard gave him trouble when he took it off. The one called Swego had tugged his short hair and called him "little boy." He'd punched Swego for the insult. Sor Saggorn flogged Kipp for starting a fight his first day out, and he was not given any dinner.

Sor Saggorn was universally hated among the pickers. They called him Sag Eye behind his back for the scar that crossed his face. Sag Eye was brutal and overly fond of his whip. He spared no one. Many pickers young and old had scars on their backs to prove it.

Sor Twam cleared his throat. Jilly was eating a berry. The kora berries were bitter, nearly inedible. They were grown for the seeds that were roasted to make the rich, dark drink. Sag Eye would whip Jilly if he caught her eating kora.

Sa Minn gently pressed Jilly's hand away from her mouth.

"She is hungry," Kipp said under his breath.

Sor Twam said, "Eat no more of that, child, and I will tell you more of my story." Yesterday, he had begun the tale of his Lostwalk—the ritual journey nomad boys took at age fourteen before they were allowed to braid their hair. If the harvesters sang another work song loud enough to cover his words, if Sag Eye didn't ride close enough to hear his tale and make him stop as he had the day before, he would take the risk to tell them more.

Sor Twam's fingers moved deftly through the kora leaves as he spoke under his breath. "It was on the fourth day of my Lostwalk I saw the titauns."

"Dragons?" said Jilly.

"Yes, they are the same. The sky was pale green when they soared over the land."

Sa Minn jiggled her basket. "Titauns do not live in our time."

"They are not here," he agreed. "They cross through time. But I had walked outside of time," he added proudly.

"You must have been drunk on mebe juice." Sa Minn laughed.

Sor Twam shrugged. "I had not eaten in four days but my eyes were clear. These titauns came to answer my prayer. They led me to a place of water, so I lived."

"What did they look like?" Jilly's voice was loud with excitement.

"Hush," Kipp warned. He kept his hands moving swiftly so Sag Eye wouldn't notice their conversation and split them up. He watched Sor Twam drop more kora berries in his basket. Inside the elder's voice, he could swallow without his throat aching, blink without the flames growing tall again behind his eyes. For minutes at a time he could forget the Gwali appearing through the smoke with his black soul sack, could forget the loss of that one night.

"The titauns' scales were as shiny green as these kora leaves." The bush rustled and the leaves trembled in the sunlight. "Their chests were golden as the sun. Their wings were wide as two tents."

"Were their wings silver like the dragon paintings in the cave?" Kipp asked. Oh, he'd promised Sor Joay he would never mention that.

Sa Minn huffed. "When did you see those? Foreigners do not go there!"

Kipp's neck stiffened. He didn't like being called a foreigner, though it was better than being called a pale. "I heard about it once. That is all." When they left the Pinnacle Mountains, Sor Joay told Kipp he must not tell about their visit to the sacred cave.

Kipp reached over Jilly's shoulder and pulled more berries. He'd promised Royan he would take him to the Pinnacle Mountains one day, though he would not show him the cave. The Pinnacles were a five-day ride from their old farm, but a great river snaked through them.

"I'm making a new fishing pole," Royan had said proudly the last time they'd whispered their secret plans. They were lying on their backs in bed, Jilly sleeping soundly across the room.

"I'll catch a river trout this big!" Royan had spread his arms out wide, the back of his hand falling hard across Kipp's nose.

Kipp dropped more berries into the basket and rubbed the ridge between his eyes. Had it only been a month since Royan accidentally struck him there? Kipp had socked him for it and they'd both laughed so loud, Jilly woke up and jumped onto their bed squealing, "What's so funny? Tell me. Tell me."

The work song had ended. Sor Twam did not speak as the overseer rode along the orchard rows. Kipp thought of the way Sag Eye had tied Jilly's small wrists to the saddle horn the night he'd brought them here. *What's so funny? Nothing. Nothing, Jilly.*

A thin high cloud shadowed over the orchard, turning Kipp's arms and hands brown, the berries black. An open carriage passed along the dirt road beyond the orchard fence. Kipp looked up briefly. The landowner's wife, Mistress Tunassi, was out for her afternoon ride. There was another woman at her side, but he could not see her face.

Kipp's basket was nearly full; he gave two handfuls to Jilly. If she did not fill enough baskets today, she would not be given any onions or millet in her dinner bowl.

A dust cloud rose up along the dirt road. Someone shouted. Then Kipp heard Sag Eye calling, "Kipp! Twam!"

Kipp spun around and dropped his basket. He squatted, hissing between his teeth as he shoved the rolling berries back inside the wicker mouth.

"Stop that, ya stupid dwiig, and come here!"

Kipp and Sor Twam hurried up the orchard row, passing bent workers, their baskets bouncing at their sides. Sag Eye peered down at them from his mount. He jabbed his thumb back in the direction of the dirt road and the tilting carriage.

"Wheel's in a rut. You two help the driver get them unstuck. And be quick about it."

Kipp laid his basket aside and jammed his hat farther down on his head. Zalika's mother did not need to know that he was shorn.

He was over the fence and at the wheel before Sor Twam could reach the road. In the open carriage, Mistress Tunassi was huffing like a steaming kettle. A white parasol covered the face of the woman on her right.

"Ready?" called the driver, who was standing beside the horse, reins in hand. The chestnut stallion at his side was peacefully chewing the dry grass sprouting along the roadside.

"This won't take long," Kipp promised. He'd freed Papa's wagon wheels from ruts plenty of times. It was easily done as long as you didn't startle the horse. The driver encouraged the horse forward as Kipp and Sor Twam pushed against the backside of the carriage.

"Oh! Oh!" Mistress Tunassi whimpered.

"You can get down, Mother, if you need to."

"No, I'll stay," said Mistress Tunassi. The white parasol was flipped back now, revealing Zalika in a bright green blouse and colorful wrap skirt. Kipp quickly bowed his head to shield his face. He pushed the carriage with all his might, hoping to get the job over and slip back into the crowded orchards before Zalika discovered him.

Zalika stood up. "This is taking too long. I will help you push."

"No," said Kipp in a gruff voice that was not his own.

"Sit down, Zalika!" Under the brim of his hat, he saw Mistress Tunassi tug her daughter's skirt.

Kipp was suddenly aware of his sweaty shirt, his singed pant leg that blew in tatters when the wind swirled around his ankles. He shouldered the carriage again and heaved, grunting beside Sor Twam. The carriage rocked harder but the wheel wouldn't budge.

"Why don't you use a piece of plank?" Zalika suggested.

"Good idea, Mistress." Sor Twam went off to fetch a plank. The sun baked Kipp's back as he waited. He should have taken the chance to run off for the wood. He felt Zalika looking down at him, though he could not glance up to make sure. Nervously, he made his way to the chestnut, making sure to keep his back to Zalika.

The driver leaned against the fence, waiting for Sor Twam to return with the plank. A snake darted out of the dry grass and slithered across the dirt road. The chestnut, startled, reared back and whinnied.

"Easy now!" Kipp leaped for the flailing reins, but as soon as the stallion's hooves hit the dirt, he sprang to a gallop, racing with such force that he pulled the entrenched wheel free.

Mistress Tunassi screamed as the carriage lurched forward.

Kipp and the driver chased the carriage, which swung wildly left and right across the dirt road. Gathering more speed, it tipped onto one wheel, nearly spilling the women onto the road.

The driver fell back, too out of breath to keep up the pace. But Kipp ran faster. He felt a stitch in his side, and his lungs began to burn. Drawing close, he threw out his hands to grip the back of the carriage, missed, ran harder, and grabbed hold the second time. Inside the careening carriage, the women had been knocked from their seats onto the floor. Swinging himself onto the back, Kipp climbed over their huddled bodies and pulled himself toward the driver's seat. The floorboards bounced beneath him.

Knees bent, arms out, Kipp leaped from the seat onto the chestnut's back. He would have fallen off if he hadn't been lucky enough to catch the long, brown mane in both hands. Pulling himself forward, he managed to grab the flying reins. His body tossed violently up and down as the horse bounded beneath him.

Dust roiled around them in waves. Kipp clung tight and pulled the reins back. He did not yank hard. That would only make it worse. Beyond the fence the orchards became a green blur. Ignoring the screams from the carriage and the hot wind hitting his face, Kipp became one with the stallion, easing him from his mad gallop down to a canter, then finally to a trot.

Kipp sucked in a relieved breath. "Good boy," he said, patting the chestnut's sweat-soaked neck. The road, white-brown in the heat, still seemed to move in the wavering air, but the horse had stopped and was huffing with exertion.

"It's all right," Kipp said.

There was laughter behind him. "That was the best carriage ride ever," Zalika said breathlessly. Kipp glanced back, startled by the happy remark. Zalika stood in the carriage, the dust cloud settling on her hair, shoulders, and blouse. It took her only a moment to recognize him. She said his name, soundlessly, so he saw rather than heard it.

Her mother did not see—and would not have believed if she had—the look that passed between them.

CHAPTER TEN

IN THE LANDLORD'S empty kitchen, Kipp sat on a stool in the corner nervously jiggling his leg. Rain made a welcome pattering sound on the large window above the sink, good for the kora, the land, the soul. He'd entered through the servants' back door with his hat on. He told himself he would take it off only when pressed and not at all if Zalika were around, though he was sure Sor Tunassi would not tolerate any defiance from an orchard hand.

Kipp stood. Sat again. Wiped a spot of mud off his boot. How much longer was he supposed to wait? He'd been told to come here straightaway, so he'd had no time to wash.

The door swung open. A middle-aged servant in immaculate white gloves motioned to him. "Master Tunassi will see you now."

He led Kipp across the hall and nodded toward the open study door. Kipp was acutely aware of his damp clothes and old work boots as he stepped onto the richly patterned rug.

At the far end of the spacious room, Sor Tunassi sat before his large desk, a tall, dark, heavyset man. He had a round stomach, what Sor Joay used to call a "wealth belly," used to too much food. The scent of steaming kora filled the air. Kipp's mouth watered. He'd not tasted kora in a very long time. The two cups and cream jug on the landlord's food tray made him hopeful.

"Remove your hat." Sor Tunassi was plainly affronted by his insolence.

"Sor, I—"

"What are you waiting for?"

Kipp sighed and took it off.

The landlord's eyebrows rose in surprise. "You have broken the law, I see."

"No, Sor. I was not publicly shorn. I lost my braid in the fire." He worked to make his expression convincing. If Sor Tunassi knew he was lying . . .

"Well, you are not much older than a boy anyway, are you?"

Kipp's neck flushed with heat. "I'm seventeen, Sor."

"Sit." Sor Tunassi's voice was gravelly and firm.

Kipp took the chair, shaking with anger. The landlord carefully adjusted his long braid. Nine jeweled braid-beads of varying colors shone in the wet light falling through the study window. The beads were supposed to honor the man's achievements, but Kipp knew some wealthy men did not have to face trials to acquire them.

"All Zolyan boys used to go on Lostwalks," Sor Joay had said. "Now many stay in town and test their strength in the arena to earn their first bead. And grown men will pay for more braid-beads. They are not earned the old way. It is not the same thing."

In the hard chair, Kipp tucked his worn boots under the legs. The landlord sipped his kora, then opened the jam jar on his desk and eyed his tray of biscuits. Kipp waited anxiously. Sor Tunassi had called him here. Was he about to hear the full extent of the debt he owed? Or was there another humiliation planned for him?

The landlord studied the papers on his desk as he ate a biscuit whole, his cheeks popping out as he chewed. Kipp could see nothing of Zalika in this man. Except for his bulging belly, he was all in squares—square head, square shoulders and chest, even his palms were square. Zalika was long, flowing lines like river water.

He looked through the window where rain pattered the large backyard fountain. Sor Tunassi buttered another biscuit, read some more. Kipp tried not to fidget.

In the painting on the wall, Sor Tunassi stood proudly beside his best racehorse, Tempest. The painter had been kind to the landlord, brushing away his bulging middle.

Sor Tunassi flicked a crumb from his shirt. "I'm sure you're aware that, because you are Keith Corwin's son, you—"

"I *was* his son," Kipp said. "*I'm* the man of the house now." He regretted his answer as soon as it left him, floating vacant and stupidly across the fragrant air. Man of the house? There was nothing on the land now but charred timbers and ash. He tugged a hunk of his short hair and waited for Sor Tunassi to point this out, but the man surprised him with a laugh. "You are your father's son indeed," he said. "Keith was defiant by nature."

Kipp frowned. It was true. No one and nothing could turn his father from his course once he'd decided upon it. The ache in his throat returned, but he would not show any emotion to this man.

"Tell me where you learned to ride," said Sor Tunassi.

"What? Oh, I learned on Cassia. My horse—"

"Not yours," corrected Sor Tunassi. "Mine. All you have is mine now."

Kipp froze in his seat. Everything was the landlord's. Even Cassia, but somehow he'd not included her in his losses. He'd thought of her waiting for him down at the stables. When Jilly was well enough, Cassia would be their way of escape.

Sor Tunassi dipped a spoon into the thick red jam.

"My daughter told me what you did." He dropped a glob of jam on a biscuit. "I would not have believed her story if my wife hadn't confirmed it. Pales do not handle horses that well."

Kipp blushed on two counts. First from Zalika's praise, second from the landlord's obvious scorn. He wanted to leap across the polished desk, get the man in a neck hold, drag him outside to his showy backyard fountain, and dunk his swollen head under the bubbling water.

"What I want to know is who taught you to ride?" Sor Tunassi said around a biscuit.

"An Escuyan elder, Sor Joay. He also taught me to capture and break in a wild horse when I was fourteen." He'd lost the braid-bead honoring his achievement and wished vehemently he had it now.

"I see," said Sor Tunassi. "A Zolyaman taught you."

"The men of Gare can ride, Sor." Kipp tried to keep the edge from his voice but he didn't succeed.

"Can they?" Sor Tunassi snorted.

Had the landlord called him here simply to taunt him? Tell him he owned nothing in the world, was a useless pale, a squatter in Zolya?

Kipp stood suddenly.

"Sit."

Kipp didn't take his chair, but he didn't leave, either. Outside rain pocked the water in the fountain. Already the garden plants seemed greener, richer for the rain.

"You have been picking kora for me. My daughter thinks I should shift you to my stables. Tell me why I should do this."

Kipp's head swam. So that was what the meeting was about. He wanted to turn the man down just to spite him, but he was already sweetening to the idea. Sor Tunassi was often at the track. Everyone knew how much he loved his racehorses. If Kipp did a good job, he might be paid enough coppers to gain his freedom and Jilly's. He breathed in the idea.

"I can train your horses to win, Sor."

Sor Tunassi slapped his knee, laughing at the idea. "A pale train one of my beauties?" His mouth was wide, showing half-chewed biscuit.

"So you want me to clean the stalls for you?" His tone was sharp. He should get out of the room before he lost his temper.

Zalika burst through the door and half-fell into the room. She must have been listening in on their conversation. Standing before her father's tall bookcase, she said, "Let him work with the horses, Father. You promised me. I've never seen anyone handle Rauley as well as he—" She stopped suddenly, seeing Kipp's short hair.

"Kipp, I—"

Shame roared through him. He felt naked in front of her. "I lost my braid in the fire," he said lamely.

Her eyes widened before she glanced away, but her father caught the look, like a dog picking up a scent. "Zalika, did you know this boy before he stopped the runaway horse?"

"We met once at the fair, Father. That is all." She returned to her argument. "Kipp leaped onto the carriage, then onto Rauley's back—"

"As you said before." Sor Tunassi added cream to his kora mug.

Zalika crossed her arms. "Rauley was crazed, Father. Mother and I could have been killed!"

Sor Tunassi snorted. "I doubt that. You see how my daughter argues for you, Kipp?"

Kipp looked out the window at the stone dragon spewing water into the fountain. He felt choked by their attention, coiled tight between them.

"He will switch over to the stables," said Zalika. "Promise me, Father." She said this last bit more softly, as she toyed with the lid of the jam jar.

"All right. For a trial period." Sor Tunassi tapped the biscuit against his plate. "These biscuits are too dry." He glared at Kipp. "Go off to the kitchen, boy, and tell them to make me fresh ones. Dismissed."

Kipp hurried from the room, jaw clenched. Now he was a kitchen boy? Zalika caught up with him in the hall and stopped him by the stairwell. "I heard about that fire. You lost everyone in your family." There was concern on her face, or was it pity?

He did not want to talk about it. "I have my sister Jilly."

"Where is she?"

"With me." He would say no more. "I have to go." He

shoved on his hat and started down the hall again.

Zalika followed him to the kitchen door. He did not want her to go in and see him order more biscuits for her father. He waited for her to leave, to go up the stairs.

"Father makes me ride sidesaddle," she whispered. "I hate it. You will teach me to ride the right way, Kipp. No one else will show me how."

Kipp turned. "You don't mind falling onto your backside?" He was still too bitter from the meeting in the study to be happy with his new position.

"You wouldn't let me fall." He heard the slight tremble in her throat as they stood by the closed door. A woman's neck and ears are her most beautiful features. It was why Zolya woman wore their hair short and adorned their heads with silken scarves. He could reach out now, touch Zalika's slender neck, run his finger up to the tip of her earlobe just below the diamond earring. He was standing close enough. But they were not free, standing ankle-deep in the river as they'd been a year ago. This was her father's estate house. Kipp would not dare do such a thing.

CHAPTER ELEVEN

KIPP RAN HIS HAND down the racehorse's muscular leg, grasped the ankle, and made a clicking sound, the stallion's cue to raise his hoof.

"There now, good boy." Cradling the hoof between bent knee and hand, he used the pick to remove the debris from the frog and clefts. He'd worked two weeks in the stables under Sor Jaffon's stern eye. Picking the hooves was one of the never-ending jobs.

The racehorse leaned into him as he cleaned around the rim. Kipp pressed back, straining his muscles. He finished the left hoof, moved over to the right foreleg, and stood a moment with his hand on the stallion's brushed shoulder to look out the knothole again.

Zalika was nearly finished with her riding lesson, sitting sidesaddle on her chestnut gelding, Obi. Her fitted black shirt clung to her sleek form; her red-and-gold wrap skirt fluttered in the hot wind. She passed beyond view as the stable master, Sor Jaffon, led Obi on another lap around the riding ring. It was only then Kipp realized he'd been holding his breath.

It was another hot day. Kipp hoped Sa Minn was making sure his little sister drank enough water in this heat. He had been uneasy about leaving Jilly working in the orchard with the Sa, but he could not bring her here. *She will be all right*, he thought. *I'll sing her to sleep tonight and make sure she's well.*

On Kipp's first day here, Sor Jaffon said, "An immigrant should not be allowed to handle Sor Tunassi's prize horses." He had worked hard to please the stable master but the man had not changed his mind. Kipp was cleaning a sorrel stallion's hooves in the next stall when Zalika entered. Bent low as he was, he could just see her soft leather boots, the hem of her bright skirt swishing as she walked.

Sor Jaffon removed Obi's saddle, hung it on the corner rack, and stepped outside. The small round decorative mirrors along the saddle's edge sent bright reflections along the walls. They were white silver, the color of the dragon's wings he'd seen in the sacred cave.

Zalika was still nearby. Kipp felt her rather than saw her. Head low, hat on, Kipp scraped a dirt clod from the sorrel's hoof. Zalika's bracelets tinkled as she led Obi into the next stall. The scent of jasmine rose from her skin as she latched the gate.

Don't look up. Work.

She spoke to Kipp's back. "You are busy. I will curry Obi."

"Sor Jaffon will expect me to do that."

"No one ever lets me do anything. I like brushing him."

Kipp moved to a back leg, turned, and slowly ran his hand down the horse's flank. Zalika marched across the straw-covered barn, swiftly overturned a bucket, and stepped on top to take the curry brush down from the shelf. Her blouse wrinkled as she strained upward, silky black as Kwaja. Kipp blinked against the image. No, the Gwali's soul sack had been much darker.

The tiny mirrors from the saddle played across Zalika's head, back, and skirt as she went on tiptoe to grip the brush. It was like the play of sun on water, and he saw her for a moment the way she'd been with him down by the Sway last year—laughing as she plunged her arm in the water to pull out a startled turtle.

Sor Jaffon reentered the stable whistling to himself as Zalika jumped down from her perch.

"Mistress Tunassi," he said. "You do not have to curry your horse!" He waved at Kipp, shouting, "What were you thinking, boy? Were you raised up with pigs?"

Kipp went to Zalika and held out his hand for it. Zalika crossed her arms and tightened her grip on the brush. "Let him be, Jaffon. I want to curry Obi today. Kipp already tried to talk me out of it."

"Are you sure, Mistress?" He pursed his lips, uncertain.

"I am sure."

Sor Jaffon left. He had come in whistling. He was not whistling now.

Kipp took a drink from his water pouch. He'd wanted Zalika to come inside and stay a little longer than she had the day before, but her visits were making his stable job more difficult. He respected the stable master's knowledge and might learn much from him if he could only prove himself, if Zalika would stop interfering with his work.

He wanted to tell her this now. Zalika's brown arm moved in a small arc along the horse's shoulder as she brushed. The gesture erased his words. He was taken with her presence here in the stall where the dim light crowned her head.

"You are left-handed," he said.

"I can curry all the same."

Kipp hung the water pouch over his shoulder. He felt as if he were all arms and legs. How was he to speak to her? He began to wish he had stayed in the orchards. At least there he could be close to Jilly, could listen to Sor Twam's tales.

The sorrel mare behind him flicked Kipp's buttocks with her tail as if to goad him on. Zalika stopped brushing, bent down, and peered up at him from under the chestnut's neck.

"Will you come out tonight?" she asked in a hushed voice. "Father will not let me learn anything but sidesaddle. It is impossible." She stepped in front of Obi and rubbed his nose gently with the flat of her hand. "We can meet beyond the kora orchard. Bring Obi and saddle up another horse of your choosing."

"Are you asking me or telling me?"

Zalika laughed. "Both. But I will only ask if that is better."

He cleaned the dirt from the hoof pick. Sor Jaffon would whip him if he were caught taking the horses out without permission, or worse, the stable master might call him a horse thief and have him locked in a cell in Napulo. He couldn't afford to take such a risk, not only for himself but also for Jilly, who needed him here. As it was, he worked the stables dawn to dusk and only saw his little sister at the evening meal just before her bedtime.

Zalika's eyes were on him, dark and cool as a night wind. He found a small stone in the sorrel's back hoof and carefully removed it.

"I'm not sure, Zalika. It would be difficult."

The stable master whistled an Escuyan work song out in the riding ring.

"We cannot talk here with Sor Jaffon coming inside every other minute," she said. "Meet me out by the cork trees tonight. We can talk more about my plans then."

"I won't be bringing horses."

"You do not have to this time. I only mean to talk. Will you come?"

He thought a moment, then nodded.

"Good." Zalika rubbed the white star on Obi's proud forehead. Going up on tiptoe, she leaned in and kissed the animal.

Kipp noticed the curve of her neck as she pressed her lips to the horse's nose.

"Beautiful," he whispered.

Zalika patted Obi. "He is, isn't he?"

CHAPTER TWELVE

S TARS SALTED THE night sky, but Kipp had not yet made it to the cork trees to meet Zalika. Instead he'd anxiously watched Sa Minn mix herbs for Jilly. The Sa felt Jilly's cheek, shook her head, and spooned eana-twig mash into her mouth.

"Swallow," she whispered. Jilly's eyelids fluttered. Sa Minn brushed back Jilly's curls, whispering words Kipp could not make out. He stepped outside. He should be with Zalika by now. She must be wondering why he had not come to her. But he could not put on his boots. Not yet.

Kipp looked east toward the hills and listened. He was sure he'd heard the Gwali's hounds and surer still after hearing Jilly moaning in her sleep that they were howling for her. That was why he'd dug up the potion jar he'd buried in the dirt under Jilly's bed, why he'd awakened Sa Minn. Jilly was in danger. He had to stay here and stand guard.

Sa Minn came outside and stepped into a pool of moonlight.

"Why did you wake me up?"

Kipp trembled. "Jilly's sick."

"She is not ill, Kipp."

"But she was moaning in her sleep."

"A bad dream passed by. The eana twig will ease her back to sleep."

Sa Minn turned and squinted at him as if he were hard to see, though he, too, was standing in moonlight. "Jilly's cough is better now. You hover over your sister. A plant does not grow well in shadow. Jilly will not grow well under yours."

"I am not hovering. My sister is in danger," whispered Kipp. "I think she will die tonight if I don't guard her."

"How do you know this?"

Kipp curled his naked toes against the cold earth. "Sa Minn." He blew out a breath. "You are an Escuyan elder. You know there are"—he paused—"spirits in the world."

"What are you saying to me, Kipp?"

He had to tell her. He needed help from someone who understood who he was fighting, someone with more knowledge of the spirits than he had. "I heard the Gwali's hounds tonight."

"It is wrong to speak of these things. It was nothing.

A dream." She clapped her hands as if to say that was all. It was finished.

"But I have to say it, Sa Minn. I have to tell someone. I don't know what else to do."

"Pray to Ahyuu. Ask Ahyuu to turn death's messenger away. Say you did not mean to call him."

"I didn't call him . . . I said I heard—"

"Boy? I am telling you what to do."

"I will pray," he said, wrapping his fingers around the jar in his pocket.

Crickets sang in the long dry grass.

"There is something else," said Sa Minn.

There *was* something else. Few people could draw the words out, but Sa Minn was a woman with some healing powers, and Jilly was in trouble. He would risk the truth.

"The night our farm burned. I was away when the fire began. I was up at Titaun Koy chasing a wild horse."

"A boy your age should have already gone on his Lostwalk," she said gruffly. "Then he would not chase horses that do not belong to landholders." Kipp knew the Escuyans caught and trained only enough horses to add new blood to their own herds, and let the rest run free. The nomads did not think landholders should touch the free herds.

He felt her irritation but did not let it stop him. "I could not capture the horse."

She nodded, satisfied. She would not have expected a landholder to catch Lightning.

"I rode home to find the farm on fire. Papa rescued Jilly from the house. He handed her to me, told me to get her away from the smoke, and ran back inside for Mother and Royan. I raced back into the burning house once Jilly was safe, but Carl Lunstrum pulled me out before I could reach my family. Then the roof caved in."

"I know the Lunstrums came," she said.

He started. "How?"

"People talk."

Kipp thought a moment. Lars had brought the farm animals over to Sor Tunassi's barns the night they were brought here. He must have spoken to someone then, told the story of the fire.

"What else have you heard?" he asked cautiously.

"That you went wild and started screaming at invisible spirits."

"I didn't go wild."

"Whom were you shouting at?"

"I heard the Gwali's hounds. I saw their shadows on the ground." He noticed that she was frowning, but the words were coming out of him rough and hard, a pelting of stones. He'd held them in too long. "The Gwali . . . he rode in on his ghost mare. He came after my papa and mother and . . ." He couldn't say "Royan." "I tried to fight him off. I grabbed his soul sack, Kwaja."

Sa Minn put her hands out in front of her; her dark fingers made the diamond shape to ward off evil. "Only those with Naqui powers can see spirits. You cannot have this magic. You are a pale."

Pale? Kipp tensed reflexively. He'd not heard her use the insulting term before. He'd thought they were friends. She'd been kind to Jilly and had helped him protect her from Sag Eye. *She's frightened*, he realized. *Frightened of me.*

He stepped back, as if to walk away from himself, from the tale he'd just told. His heel hit a stone. He fell onto the ground, caught himself with his hands, then sat up quickly, feeling for the jar in his coat pocket to make sure it was not broken.

"I don't know if I have Naqui powers, Sa Minn. I only know I saw him as well as I can see you now."

She leaned over him, swaying a little. "Men and women with these powers see more than we can see, they hear more than we can hear. Sometimes they sense what is to come. You tell me you heard the hounds, and you saw the—" She stopped herself before she said "Gwali." "And you say you touched?" Again she seemed afraid to say "Kwaja."

Kipp shuddered. "It doesn't matter." He brushed dirt from his trousers, wishing now he hadn't told her what was in his heart. He was terribly ashamed. If he hadn't gone off after the detching horse . . .

He'd come home too late, hadn't been able to save anyone but Jilly, and that was only with Papa's help. The burning he felt whenever he remembered this came to him again. He looked at his pale hands hanging as limp from his wrists as wilted leaves. He used to think he was strong. He could work as hard as any man. But who had strength enough to fight Techee? Who could outrun the Gwali?

Sa Minn huffed at him. "You say it does not matter. I say do not give in so easily. I do not think your father raised you that way." She reached down and dug a sharp bloodstone from a clump of weeds. "I do not know what you have seen, but if you plan to sit here all night guarding your sister, take this." She handed him the stone.

"What is this for?"

"Pray for peace and do not let war enter your hut."

"Sor Joay used to say that."

"Um." She shook her head. "You are a strange boy. It will be hard for you to find a place to build your hut."

He knew what she meant. He was not Gare, Zolyan, or Escuyan. He had grown up shadowing Sor Joay, wishing he were not an immigrant working a small farm, wishing instead that he could live free and move from place to place the way the nomads did. His father's farm was gone. Dust swirled through the ashes of what was and could have been. He was only lightly tied to the world now by the love he had for Jilly and for Zalika.

If it weren't for them . . .

He looked skyward, letting his mind reel out and out, beyond the mountains, the far-off sea, his childhood home of Gare in the damp and freezing north, beyond the earth where he'd known little happiness in his seventeen years of life.

In his mind he was flying through silent space where dragons soared, a place beyond the tether of time.

"There you go," said Sa Minn, as if she were seeing right into his dream.

She left him there with the bloodstone in his hand and the witch's jar in his pocket. A rock and a small glass jar of sticky magic potion, all he had against the power of death.

CHAPTER THIRTEEN

ZALIKA GRIPPED HIS arm and drew him to the corral fence. "Where were you last night?" she demanded. "I waited and waited." Her black eyes sparked like flint.

"I had to guard my little sister, Jilly."

"Against what?"

Sor Jaffon led Zalika's chestnut gelding, Obi, outside and looked at Kipp suspiciously. "Is this boy causing you worry, Mistress?"

"Yes," she answered.

"You are dismissed to the stable, boy."

Kipp pivoted on his heel and was heading for the dark entrance when Zalika said, "I want Kipp to lead Obi today."

Why ask for that? Hadn't she just admitted his presence was troubling her? Kipp paused in the open frame of the stable door, his body half in heat, half-swallowed by cool shadow.

"Are you sure?" asked Sor Jaffon.

"I'm sure."

Kipp hesitated, then took Obi's reins from Sor Jaffon. The stable master cleared his throat angrily as Kipp led the horse into the riding ring. He wasn't sure if Zalika meant this to be an apology or a punishment. Sor Jaffon sat on the fence, filled his small pipe with dried sanuu leaves, and lit up. If Zalika was testing his stable boy, Sor Jaffon would smoke awhile and watch.

The small mirrors edging the saddle stung Kipp's eyes as he cupped his hands to help Zalika up. He felt awkward as she placed her soft leather boot in his hands. He had not touched anything but her wrist before this, and that was a year ago down by the river. Now she was so close to him he could hear her breath as she stepped up and mounted Obi.

Zalika gripped the saddle horn and sighed. "I hate riding sidesaddle," she said to Kipp under her breath. Kipp didn't look up, didn't answer. Zalika's boots peeped out from under her long yellow skirt.

She tried again. "You said you had to guard Jilly. Guard her against what?" They were partway around the riding ring now, out of Sor Jaffon's earshot.

"I would have come if she hadn't been ill." He wrapped the lead line around his hand. Jilly had moaned in her sleep, and he was sure she was in pain. But Sa Minn said it was only a bad dream. Was Sa Minn right that he was too protective of Jilly? Had he stationed himself outside all night with the potion jar and the stone for nothing?

"Does she need a doctor? I can send for one." He dared glance back and saw that Zalika's face had softened with concern.

"You don't even know her," Kipp said, picking up the pace.

"She's your sister, Kipp."

He waited until they had passed Sor Jaffon, smoking on the fence. "Jilly won't need a doctor. She's much better."

His little sister had awakened refreshed and hungry. She chattered over their small bowls of porridge about her strange dream, riding to Titaun Koy with Kipp, clapping her hands and calling down the rain. "And I sent the rain to our house and it put out the fire and the house grew back up again like a tree does and Mama and Papa and Royan were inside and Mama was calling us to dinner. . . ."

"You moaned in your sleep."

"I sang down the rain," Jilly insisted.

After breakfast he'd crept back into the bunkroom and buried the potion jar again.

Kipp's mouth tasted of dust. His shirt clung to his back. The sun was low on the horizon, but the heat of the day had not died. They rounded the ring a third time. "Don't swing your feet, Zalika. Hold still."

"I have to move."

"You don't."

"I cannot stand this pace. Go faster, Kipp."

"You are not secure enough for that."

"I will hold on. Do it."

Kipp sped up. Obi began to trot. Zalika laughed, bouncing up and down on her pretty saddle. The laugh told Kipp she had forgiven him for making her wait last night. His heart lightened.

"Hey," shouted Sor Jaffon. "Slow down, boy!"

"She wants to go faster," called Kipp.

Sor Jaffon threw himself from the fence, grabbed the reins, and whipped Kipp across the mouth. "I said stop!"

Kipp's face stung. He covered his mouth, tasting blood.

"Get back to the stable, boy. You will feel my whip again!"

"Leave him be!" screamed Zalika.

"You do not know what's good for you, Mistress. I have my orders."

"Your orders? Let go and give Kipp the reins."

Kipp stepped out of Obi's shadow, his back pressed up against the fence.

Zalika grunted angrily, kicked out her feet, and leaped off the saddle. It was an uncalculated move and she pitched forward, falling facedown on the dusty ground before Kipp could catch her. When he helped her up, the gash on her cheek was bleeding.

"Zalika?"

"Step away, boy!" shouted Sor Jaffon. Kipp did not listen. He gripped her arms, holding Zalika up.

She swayed a little. "Sorry," she said. She was laughing, and he laughed, too, out of awkwardness and some fear. She'd scraped her elbow. It was sticky with blood in his cupped hand.

Zalika pressed her hand against the cut on her cheek. Blood seeped between her fingers and ran down her knuckles.

He let go of her. They were inches apart.

"Take me back to the house, Kipp," she said.

Sor Jaffon pushed Kipp away. "I will take you home."

"I want Kipp to take me."

Zalika had no idea the awkward position she was putting him in, but she was hurt and he wanted to be the one to help her. Damn the stable master, he would go.

As Kipp led her through the riding ring and out the creaking gate, Sor Jaffon shouted from behind, "Sor Tunassi will hear of this, you detching boy. You will not be allowed back in my stables after this!" Sor Jaffon had never wanted Kipp there to begin with. He was a cropper, a pale, and shouldn't be allowed to work with such noble horses.

Kipp licked the blood from his cut lip. "Does it hurt, Zalika?"

"Yes," she said. "My face and my knee." She was walking with a limp and did not mention her scraped elbow, but then he wasn't talking about his cut lip, either.

"Why did you jump down like that?" he asked. "If you wanted to get down, Sor Jaffon could have—"

"He whipped you. He threatened to whip you again back in the stable. I can't stand the way he treats you!"

She'd flown off the saddle in protest of his beating. Knowing this sent warmth down to his heart. Zalika was strongly favoring her right leg. He'd seen her limp a little before when she was tired and had wondered at it. Was it an old injury, worsened by her fall?

"Your leg," he said. "Is it very bad?"

"It's just a little scratch," she snapped.

Kipp's stomach tightened. Why snap at him? He was only asking out of concern. He bit down his desire to snap back. *She's hurt. She's tired. That's all.*

He was beginning to feel much too exposed here on the dirt road. They were nearly to the orchard. He did not want Sag Eye or the pickers to see him with her. They would notice the blood, pry into his business.

"I'm telling Father what Sor Jaffon did to you."

"Don't, Zalika."

"But he lashed you in the face."

"Let it alone. Promise me you will." No matter what she said, he was likely to be blamed for her fall. They walked side by side, but they lived in two worlds. Zalika didn't see the danger she had put him in when she reprimanded Sor Jaffon in his defense. But she was bleeding now. He shouldn't be thinking of himself. He took her upper arm to help her along.

"We have to think of a good story," she said. There were

96

bloodstains down her blouse and splashes of red on her yellow skirt. Rounding the last stable, she veered to the left and crossed the stubbly grass.

"Where are you going?"

"I should wash the blood off before returning to the house." He waited for her by the water trough and turned his head when she pulled up her skirt to bathe her injured knee. It was not right for him to look at her knee. They were not children. They were old enough to be pledged.

"Is it deep?" he asked, his back still to her.

"I will be all right. You can turn around now," Zalika added.

The gash on her cheek was still bleeding steadily as she rinsed it with cold water.

"My boot caught in the saddle when I was dismounting," said Zalika hurriedly, pressing her clean hand up against her cheek. "You ran to catch my fall but it happened too fast, and I asked you to help me home."

"What?"

"That is the story I will tell Mother and Father."

"Oh." There was no mention of Sor Jaffon. He would have his own story to tell.

Minutes later they passed under the stone arch and onto the rich green lawn.

"This never would have happened if you had met me last night," she scolded.

"I told you my sister—"

"I know." She sniffed and for a moment he thought she

was crying, but he saw that she was not. They'd nearly reached the house. "We will try to meet again tomorrow night to plan the riding lessons. Mother will have the doctor out for these cuts today, knowing her, and she will be hovering over me."

Hovering over . . . Sa Minn said he'd been doing that with Jilly. Kipp stepped into his own shadow. He had not decided yet about the secret riding lessons she wanted. He had to think. Zalika was not complaining at all, though bright red lines traced the backs of her fingers again and she was still limping. *She is beautiful and brave,* he thought. His throat ached knowing it. A man would be proud to be with a girl like this.

Zalika's mother was coming down the stairs in a green silk gown and copper-colored sandals when they entered the front hall. Seeing Zalika's bloody gash and stained clothes made her scream. She bounded forward, wrapped her arms around her daughter, and hurried her down the hall.

Zalika protested, "I am all right, Mother," but Kipp heard Mistress Tunassi's words "terribly hurt" and "doctor" before the door shut firmly behind them.

Kipp stood a moment in the empty hall, feeling himself shrinking under the glare of the family portraits lining the stairwell. His lip was beginning to swell. He stooped and used his sleeve as best he could to wipe the spots of blood off the tiles.

There was a commotion behind a door down the hall:

shouting, banging, scuffling. He wanted to rush in but knew he could not. He stood in the brightness of the open front door, and shook off the feeling of foreboding. This was not a matter of life and death. There was no need for him to run for the buried potion jar. Zalika had only a few cuts and scratches from her fall.

He felt a surge of anger for the way she'd jumped down so unexpectedly. If she'd startled the horse, she could have been trampled. She was too impulsive. Unpredictable. He hated that about her. He loved her for it.

As he crossed the gravel drive outside, he saw Sor Jaffon marching toward the big house. Darting through the gate on his left, Kipp sped around the backside of the estate. Beyond the low garden wall the Tunassi kora orchards covered the rolling hills for miles along the Sway River. Some patches were empty; others teemed with pickers. The setting sun cast an orange glow over all. Kipp crept closer to the fountain. The study curtains were drawn shut; no one peered out at him.

Cool water spurted from the stone dragon's mouth atop the fountain. He slipped his hands under the surface of the pool. Ripples spanned out in ever-larger rings. As his hands came clean, the water around his wrists turned pale pink with Zalika's blood.

CHAPTER FOURTEEN

ZALIKA HAD SAID they should meet by the cork trees the following night. But they did not meet the next night or the next. Kipp was not sure how he could give her secret riding lessons now, anyway. After a sound whipping from Sor Jaffon, he'd lost his place in the stable and was back with Jilly, working the sweltering kora orchards. The pickers buzzed like switflies with their endless questions.

"How did the mistress fall?"

"Was she pushed?"

"Why was she made to walk to the big house after the accident?"

"How deep was the wound?"

"How much did she bleed?"

Rumors spread in hushed whispers. Mistress Zalika was gravely injured. She would live but have a facial deformity and be a monster. She would die, and either Kipp or Sor Jaffon or both would be thrown into the deepest, darkest cells in OnnZurr.

Kipp knew how tales tended to spread, so he tried not to worry. Still he felt a cold place growing in the pit of his stomach as the doctor was called to the mansion day after day. Had the cut gone deeper than he thought? Was she truly in danger?

The fourth night after the fall, Kipp could not bear the tension any longer. Risking capture and punishment, he crept to the landlord's house. He had to know if Zalika was all right. It worried him to see the doctor's carriage still out front as he crept silently along the hedge, though the stout man's silhouette in the second-story window helped him locate Zalika's room. In the dark garden below her back window, Kipp kept vigil in the rosebushes.

An hour later, when he heard the front door close and the doctor's carriage wheels crunching against the gravel drive, Kipp found a toehold and began to scale the thick green vine growing up the wall. His fingers scraped against the stone house, but he managed to climb about seven feet before the vine gave way under his weight. With a yelp he tumbled back into the thorny roses.

The sound brought Zalika to her window. She poked her head out, saw him sprawled below, and laughed. He smiled, relieved to see her up and well. He was scratched up, covered in prickles, and bruised. He hardly noticed.

"Zalika." Her name tasted good to him. He pulled a crushed rose from under his backside and held it up though she was far too high to reach it.

"Shh!" she warned. "They will catch you."

Kipp stood and began to pull out the prickles. The thorns near the witch's knife mark stung the most. "Are you all right?" he whispered.

"I am terribly injured, Mother says." She fingered the bandage on her cheek. "She has me caged up like one of her songbirds. If I don't fly soon I will die!"

"Where would you fly to, Zalika?"

"Somewhere. Anywhere. Meet me on the next full moon. And bring Obi when you come."

"What you ask for . . . I don't work in the stables anymore, Zalika."

"Hush. Someone is coming," she warned. "Please, Kipp, will you do it?"

He saw her anxious face above. She'd jumped from her horse in protest after Sor Jaffon whipped him. She was always so daring, so unafraid. He wanted to be more like that.

"I will."

"Yes?" She looked delighted. "Oh. Here they are." She drew her head in and shut the window. In her well-lit room, two female figures—Zalika and her mother, he guessed—began a kind of circular dance, one trying to hold on to the other's shoulders, the other pulling away. Zalika's movements were jerky as she tried to break free. A girl like that could not be kept inside forever. She would have to fly. She would fly to him.

A week later, on the night of the full moon, Kipp and Jilly sat under the eucalyptus tree with Sor Twam. Nearby other pickers gathered around small fires, talking in low voices. Someone played a skree pipe. Jilly laid her head in Kipp's lap. It was early yet, but when Sor Twam's tale was done and Jilly was in bed, he'd sneak out to meet Zalika. For now he wrapped one of Jilly's curls around his finger and listened.

"The titaun cave is in a secret place," Sor Twam said. "It is deep in the Farlands."

"Where?" asked Jilly.

"I cannot say this."

"Why not?"

"Hush, Jilly, let him speak." Kipp knew the nomads kept the location secret. Only those who practiced the old traditions went there. Sor Twam was showing a good deal of trust in them by even speaking of the dragon cave.

"This was the same year I took my Lostwalk. I saw the titauns painted on the cave wall. The silver wings were the color of the Sway River in bright sunlight. *Their wings are like water,* I thought inside the cool cave. I did not say this to my father. I was just a boy with only one braid-bead."

Kipp leaned back against the trunk, remembering. Sor Twam did not know he'd been to the sacred cave. He had just earned his first braid-bead himself when he found the titaun cave at age fourteen. It had been a long and hungry journey to the Pinnacles. They'd fought a sandstorm and were later drenched in mountain rain. But Sor Joay had been with him, and a boy's Lostwalk is taken alone, so the adventure could not really be called a Lostwalk.

Jilly scratched her ankle. "Tell us more about the dragons." She pressed her tongue against her loose tooth, wiggling it in and out. "Not drawings of them," she added. "Real ones."

Sor Twam laughed. "You have hungry ears, little one." He drew up one knee and folded his hands over it. "I will tell you of a place my father used to speak about when I was a sweeper."

"A sweeper sweeps with a broom," said Jilly knowledgably.

"Yes. I earned money as a boy sweeping the cellblocks in OnnZurr."

"They let you in the prison, Sor?" Kipp had never heard of this.

"Every day they let us in at dawn to clean, and they gave me a dimi coin when I was done."

Kipp let out a low whistle. "What was it like?"

"Now you have questions for me, too. How can I tell my story?"

"Sorry, Sor."

Sor Twam cleared his throat and began. "There is a high cliff at the end of the world where three towers stand. This place is called TeySaaNey, the singing towers."

He looked up at the rustling leaves in the eucalyptus

tree, black now with the dark. "The wind at the end of the world blows through the hollow towers of TeySaaNey." He lifted one hand and stirred the air. "Songs swirl inside the towers and come out again. One tower is Past, one is Present, one is Future. Beyond these towers and their song of time, the dragons fly."

Jilly squirmed. "Why do they fly there?"

"Have you not heard before, Jilly? Dragons fly outside of time. They exist beyond past remembering, beyond present thinking, beyond future dreaming."

"Where do they live then?"

"Some say they dwell with Omaja, the Daughter of Time, in a place we cannot see, little one."

"But you saw them on your Lostwalk," protested Jilly.

"Child, you cannot listen with your mouth," he said.

Kipp put a finger to his lips. Jilly's questions were childish but he was partly glad for her boldness. He wanted to know these things himself.

Sor Twam continued. "I was outside of time when I saw the titauns. They led me to water. When I drank and fell back into time, the dragons were gone." The old man sighed. In the cool of the evening, the air was sweet enough to drink. Kipp let it wash over his skin and chill him where the sweat was still moist across his arms.

"When I take my last Lostwalk," said Sor Twam, "I will go as far as TeySaaNey. I will hear the towers singing and see the dragons once more."

Jilly sat up. "Will you take us with you? Kipp and me?"

"I will take you with me here." He pointed to his heart.

Jilly laughed. "There isn't enough room for us there."

"There is room for everything there, Jilly. You will learn that someday if you are lucky."

Kipp toyed with a bell-shaped eucalyptus seed, putting it to his nose to catch the pungent odor. Some women strung these into necklaces. He would make one for Zalika if she would wear it. He was not sure she would.

Just then, Sa Minn came toward them, her bright skirt brushing through the long dry grass, *swish, swish.* "This child is ready for sleep," she said, holding out her hand.

"One more story, Sa, please?" asked Jilly through a half yawn.

"One more and one more and one more," said Sa Minn with a chuckle. "There will never be enough stories for your ears."

"Come on, Jilly." Kipp helped her up. "I will tuck you in."

Jilly nodded at the elder still sitting by the tree. "Taka, Sor Twam." Kipp was pleased to see that she remembered her manners.

"Ee-tak," Sor Twam replied.

In the shack, Sa Wikk was sweeping the hard-packed dirt floor. Kipp's heart quickened as he went to Jilly's bunk. Had the old woman swept under it, seen the place where he'd buried the potion jar? He glanced at Sa Wikk's orange skirt.

No telltale dust marks around her knees. She could not have gotten the short-handled broom that far under the bunk without kneeling.

Sa Wikk put away her broom and stepped back out into the night.

Sa Minn untied the small bag of medicinal salve she had mixed for Jilly's cough as the child crawled onto her thin mattress.

"Breathe deep," she said, rubbing the salve on Jilly's chest.

"Sor Twam won't take us with him." Jilly screwed up her face.

"Take you where?" Sa Minn had come over too late to hear the story.

"The singing towers at the end of the world."

Sa Minn huffed, then said, "You will learn this. People go places where they cannot take another."

Jilly coughed.

"Yes," said Sa Minn. "Let the medicine work."

"Mama and Papa did not take me." Jilly's eyes welled up. "They took Royan. Not me."

"Hush now, child. Everything will be all right."

Kipp couldn't bear to see Jilly crying. "Do you want me to sing to you now, Jilly?"

Sa Minn hung up the salve bag and pulled up the worn blanket. "We will say the night prayer." She helped Jilly wipe her nose. Then they closed their eyes and opened their hands.

"Quiss." (Live.)

"Quiss eatuya." (Live now.)

"Quiss eatuya Ahyuu Youm." (Live now in Ahyuu's Love.)

"Your sister is ready for the song now," Sa Minn said before stepping outside.

Kipp sat on the edge of her bunk, and Jilly placed her small hand in his. The chipped nails were dirt-rimmed, but her fingertips were still round, still a little girl's. He began the song with the second verse. Words of comfort he could no longer take for himself. Lies he desperately hoped Jilly still believed.

"Neither a master nor servant you'll be,
For you are a child of the high country.
Sing high for the highlands,
Sing low for the low.
You will have plenty wherever you go.
You will have plenty."

Jilly was asleep when he slipped out the door and crept along the fence toward the stables.

CHAPTER FIFTEEN

H E THOUGHT TO free Zalika if she were a bird
trapped, a girl who needed flight from everyone who
caged her. But as they stole away together to ride in the early
autumn nights, Zalika freed him. Bit by bit she took away
the fire burning behind his eyes, lifted the looming specter
of the Gwali, and slowly filled him with her infectious wild-
winged laughter.

It was no easy thing to fetch the horses, but Kipp knew
the layout of the stable even in the dark. He was aware of
the hut where the new stable boy slept and knew which
path to take to avoid being seen with Obi and Cassia. They
mounted the horses in a hidden spot behind the cork trees.

On the nights they met, they rode along the Sway, following
the path below the line of trees that ran along the main road
lest they be seen. Tonight was their fourth night together in

as many weeks. Zalika's soft leather breeches gave her the freedom to straddle Obi and abandon the constrictions of riding sidesaddle. Kipp soon discovered that she was a natural rider, moving in time with her horse, and guiding him when needed.

He watched her from behind as she cantered beneath the trailing willows.

"Do you want to take a rest?" he asked.

"I'm not tired. I could ride forever, couldn't you?"

"We'll have to get back sooner or later, Zalika."

"Don't talk about that yet."

He heard the longing in her voice as he rode alongside her, his hat casting a shadow across her face. The river mirrored the waning moonlight and turned it into a long white road. Kipp wished he could ride with Zalika atop the shining water, take that road wherever it led them. He wanted to stay out longer, too. Zalika made him see beauty everywhere; even the ugly kita thorns that grew in crooked patches along the river seemed full and richly patterned. A man had to complete arduous rites within a pledge year to earn the white braid-bead of marriage. This girl would be worth every rite.

"When will you teach me to jump, Kipp?" asked Zalika.

"Later. You have only just learned to ride."

"Sor Jaffon trained Obi. He's a good jumper."

"But you are not ready."

Zalika clicked her tongue. "You hover over me like my mother."

"I am a man." Kipp tugged the reins, affronted. "I do not hover." He'd begun to hate that word.

She let out a sudden whooping laugh and playfully slapped Obi's flank. "Then come on!"

They raced along the water's edge till both horses were in a lather and the riders were out of breath. At a small sandbar edged with trees, they dismounted and let the horses rest.

The cool night air was rich with the scent of life swimming in the river, the smell of ripened kora berries where they grew in wild patches by the Sway.

"I have something for you."

"What is it?" Kipp was surprised. He wished now he'd made her the eucalyptus bell necklace.

Zalika walked backward across the river sand and drew a small white rubber ball from her pocket. She threw it in the air, tossing him the moon.

He caught it and squeezed it in his hand. They played catch in the cool darkness. She laughed when he missed.

He tossed the next one short just to see her lunge. They both laughed when she fumbled the catch.

"That doesn't count, Kipp," she said. "You have to throw it all the way to me."

"You play catch like my sister, Jilly," he said. "She makes up the rules so she can be sure to win."

"I like the sound of that," said Zalika.

When they stopped, she made him keep the ball.

As Kipp's sweat dried, he felt the chill. Zalika's riding cloak was thin. He gathered a few sticks, made a small sand pit in the river stones, and started a fire.

"Where did you get that?" Zalika asked, admiring the oblong tinderbox.

"A man I once knew made it for me." Kipp crouched and blew at the kindling pile, coaxing the thin stream of smoke to a small finger of fire.

"Did he carve this tree on the lid?"

"Yes." Kipp eyed the box. He did not like seeing Sor Joay's gift in her hands. The last person who'd cradled the tinderbox with such care had misused Techee. Thinking of Royan, his throat tightened. The smoke drifting up from the ground smelled of burnt flesh. He wished now he hadn't lit the fire.

Zalika sat looking at him, her large dark eyes housing golden sparks as if she were Techee, as if she held the flaming spirit within herself. "Tell me about the fire."

"We should go now." He stood. "There is nothing to tell."

"We are friends, Kipp. You should tell me."

Friends. Was that all? He held out his hand. She returned his tinderbox, and he slipped it into his pocket. Zalika had brushed her curly hair across the small scar on her cheekbone to hide the crescent-shaped mark, but the wind had blown her hair back. Kipp took in the graceful slope of her shoulders, her slender brown neck, her shapely ears, each soft lobe encircling a diamond.

"You do not want to hear about what happened, Zalika."

"I do. And if you don't tell me, I'll ride home alone." She stood, waiting.

Kipp sat again and hugged his knees to his chest. He would never forget how his family burned, but when he was with Zalika, the pain of the loss lessened, if only a little. He could breathe more easily. Now even that was changing.

A water rat paddled past, his nose poking up from below the surface. Kipp motioned for Zalika to sit, and she settled so close to him he could smell her fragrant skin. Jasmine and salty sweat combined into a scent that was Zalika.

He felt his heart beneath his ribs, surrounded with bone, skin, silence. She was waiting for him to tell her what had happened to his family two months ago. He adjusted his seat in the sand and began with the tinderbox, leaving Royan in bed with Sor Joay's gift as he rode to capture Lightning. The story blazed through him, the words scorching his mouth. It was all fire and heat and death. Just before he reached the part where the Gwali rode in on his ghost mare, Kipp stopped. What would she think of him if he told her that?

They had not spoken about such things before. Kipp knew Zalika's family rode to Napulo to worship in Ahyuu's temple. He assumed they were like most Zolyans who believed in the Maker, Ahyuu, and in the First Beings like Omaja, the Daughter of Time. Still, Sor Joay warned him that many modern Zolyans had lost the old traditions. Many no longer believed in a Death Catcher or in witches. They said these were shadow tales from their nomadic ancestors, things better left out in the wild lands.

Zalika traced a spiral in the sand. "When did the fire burn your hair?" she asked.

"What?" Oh, that's right. He'd told everyone that was the way he'd lost his braid.

"It must have been when I went back in after Royan."

She looked at him suspiciously. "There is something you are not telling me, Kipp."

"What do you want?" His words were angry. He'd told her how his family died. Did she want him to put his head on her shoulder and weep like a girl?

Zalika frowned. "I will give you something of mine."

"What is that?" She had already given him the ball. But it was not a thing he could hold in his hand this time.

"You know my father gambles, and he bets on the horses."

Kipp snorted. "Everyone in Zolya knows that."

"But you do not know that last year he was in such debt to Sor Litchen that he nearly lost our house and our land."

Kipp was interested now. "How did he pay it off?" He'd heard of Sor Litchen, one of the richest and most powerful men in Zolya, but he had never seen him.

Zalika looked down at her hands. "Sor Litchen had seen me when he came to dinner at our house. He was . . . he wanted me to . . . My father agreed that I would marry him if he forgave the debt."

"What? When you weren't even pledged? Did he perform the rituals first and earn the right to—?"

"He was married once before, Kipp. He'd completed those rites years ago to earn a white braid-bead of marriage."

"To win another woman! Not to win you!" He leaped up. "How old is this man?"

"About forty."

Kipp grabbed a stone and hurled it into the river. He threw in more, the water making deep gulping noises as each stone broke the surface. He did this until he could speak without shouting.

He sat down beside her. Zolya women often married around age sixteen. They joined with men who had completed the rites, showing their worth to the girl's parents and larger community, but this detching man was forty! He'd been married once before! Kipp tried to soften his voice as he said, "But you did not marry him, Zalika."

"I would have been made to do it, but the man invited me to dine once too often at his house. Do you know the one in Napulo? It is the great house on the hill."

"I've seen it from the market square." The white-roofed mansion with its lush gardens and large bathing pool was hard to miss.

"My parents took me to his house a few times," said Zalika. "Father had not told Mother or me about the bargain he'd made, so Mother approved of the match. She was overjoyed to know such a wealthy man wished to marry her daughter."

"Even though he is forty?" Kipp argued.

She ignored the outburst. "I did not know what sort of man he was until the last night I dined at his house. My parents could not come that night, so they sent our servant, Sa Wenday, as my chaperone. Sor Litchen made sure Sa Wenday drank enough mebe juice to intoxicate her. She fell asleep in the sitting room. That's when Sor Litchen said he wanted to have me"—she glanced at Kipp—"as a man has a woman. I would not let him."

She did not speak but pulled up her trouser leg. A long puckered scar ran up her right calf and disappeared under the cloth above her knee. He could tell it had been deep, had cut into the muscle. It explained the times he'd seen her favoring that leg.

"We fought. There was a knife. I cut him, and he took the blade and slit my leg from top to bottom. He damaged my leg so no man would ever take me."

"Why wasn't his braid cut off for that? Why wasn't he publicly shamed and imprisoned in OnnZurr?" Kipp shook with fury, thought of ways he could punish the man himself, whip him the way Sag Eye whipped the pickers.

"My father said he would tell no one what happened if Sor Litchen forgave the debt. I didn't marry. We didn't lose the house or land. That was how it was done."

She turned to Kipp. "My mother does not want anyone to know about the deep scar on my leg. She says a woman's skin is her beauty. That is why she made the doctor treat the cut on my cheek day after day. There must not be a scar on my face."

Kipp wanted to say he liked the little scar. It was a mark of their friendship: she'd leaped from her saddle to protest Sor Jaffon's treatment of him. He wanted to touch the scar with his finger, the small crescent moon in the night sky of her skin.

He could not say the things that were close to his heart, but he could talk around them. "If a woman can pierce her ears and put diamonds in the lobes, why worry over the scar on your leg? Why fear the small cut on your cheek?"

"I do not fear it. My mother does." Zalika grabbed a branch and poked the fire. "My parents bargained with my enemy. Because of what they did, I hate them. I will not stay in their house any longer."

"Where will you go?"

"That's a secret." Her eyes twinkled. "I need enough coppers of my own to go. First I'll win the Women's Archery Competition at the Goba City Fair." She said this as if it was a fact.

He'd heard of the yearly competition held in Goba City, though he'd never been to see it. Goba was said to be a beautiful place nestled in the Wygoba River Valley, but the city was more than six hundred miles to the east. "How do you know you'll win?"

"I came in second last time. I'm much better now."

He had not seen her shoot, but he recognized the fixed

stare on her face. She was already there in her mind, winning the competition, picking up her prize money.

She spoke again. "I have my diamond earrings I can sell if I need to. Also there is a man I trust who bets for me at the track. When my purse is full I will be gone. This was why I needed to learn how to ride, Kipp."

Kipp's neck stiffened; she'd used him. Now she would leave him. "You should go soon," he said angrily.

"I will!"

Kipp touched her clenched jaw, drew her close. He would taste her lips once before she left. It was an angry kiss. But Zalika did not push him away. Her mouth was soft and sweet.

She drew back at last. "You have made it hard for me to go," she said in a choked whisper.

He should say he was sorry for that, but he was not. He was still floating from the kiss. "I'll go with you, Zalika. I can protect you."

"I don't want protection. Men think that about women."

"I know you're strong, but the world is hard. We can go tonight if you have enough coppers."

The water rat left the river and scuttled into the bushes. "What about Jilly?"

She was right. How could he forget his sister? The kiss had driven everything from his mind, everyone but Zalika. But he couldn't leave Jilly. "We will bring her along."

"No, Kipp. One person might get away from my father, but three? And one of them a child?"

Kipp didn't want to consider the complications. He wanted to kiss Zalika again. She stood suddenly and went down to the Sway.

He followed. Dared to stand behind her and wrap his arms about her.

"I will go alone," she said.

"Then I will meet you later, Zalika."

"Don't."

"I will."

"If my father catches you, he will have you paraded through the town. He will see that you are imprisoned in OnnZurr."

Kipp felt the weight of the threat. No one imprisoned there had ever come out again. "I'll run to meet you anyway, Zalika."

She turned and kissed him again, pouring the night and all it contained into him.

At last she pulled back. "I will leave soon, but we both have to return tonight. Tell me the rest of your story as we ride back."

He could not refuse her.

CHAPTER SIXTEEN

S TARLIGHT SPARKLED ON the river as they
headed home. How strange it was to speak of the Gwali
while riding with Zalika by the Sway. *There are two worlds,*
Kipp thought. *One holds pain, anger, and revenge; the other is full of
beauty and laughter. One is but the shadow of the other. The true world
is the one I share now with Zalika.* He surprised himself thinking
this; despair had bound him for so long. His world had
been dark except for the small happiness he'd felt with Jilly.

Zalika listened well. She clicked her tongue to urge Obi
forward, but she asked few questions and was silent when
Kipp needed her silence most, when he told how the house
collapsed after Carl had wrestled him outside, how the
Gwali rode in with his hounds and drew his mother's, his
father's, and Royan's souls into his evil sack.

Kipp had relived the scene so many times when he was

alone, wondering what he could have done differently if he'd arrived home earlier and rushed back with greater speed after he brought Jilly to the well. If he'd twisted Carl's arm, scratched his face, forced him to let him go so he could save his family. But the questions knotted in his belly could not be undone. The scene always ended with the burning house, the deaths, chasing the Gwali up to Titaun Koy.

The thing that came next, facing the witch to demand power over the Gwali, was but a secondary dream hitched on to the true and lasting nightmare of that first night.

Owls circled above, hunting for cheewiis in the dark sky. Zalika halted Obi. She reached out and touched the tips of Kipp's shorn hair just below his ear. At any other time, this would have shamed him to the core, but as her fingers left his hair and traced the scar on his neck from the witch's knife, the touch spoke a language too private to be said aloud. *We are both scarred.*

Dozens of quick-winged cheewiis flew past all at once like bright sparks. Zalika raised her hand in the air as if to catch one, but they were too fast for her. Still her gesture made four males circle over her head in a swift golden crown before flitting off again with a dark-winged owl in chase.

The hour was late. They urged the horses to a gallop and sped along the Sway. Turning a bend in the trail, they approached a fallen tree. Kipp had made Zalika ride around it on their way in. This time Zalika kicked Obi. "I'll take it now," she called triumphantly.

He could not stop her. "Duck your head," he shouted. "Cling with your knees and keep your weight down low!"

Obi thundered up the trail and jumped. He was an agile horse, but in the dark his hind hoof caught on a short branch protruding from the log. There was a loud crack. Kipp raced ahead shouting, his heart leaping up into his throat as Obi pitched sideways and tumbled hard onto the path on the far side.

"Zalika!" Leaping down, he scrambled over the log. Zalika was pinned under Obi. The horse rolled back and forth on top of her, trying to get up.

Kipp strained, pushing against Obi's side, but couldn't budge him. "Ahyuu!" he screamed. "Help me now!"

Zalika's blood darkened the sandy earth. Her eyes were rolled back, the whites showing under her half-closed lids.

Grabbing the bridle, he tugged with all his might. "Move, you detching brute! Get off her!"

At last Obi struggled onto his feet. As soon as he was up, the terrified horse whinnied and fled the scene.

Kipp fell onto the ground by Zalika. Her body was strangely twisted. He put his ear to her mouth, listening for her breath. It was shallow, but still there. He tore a strip of cloth lining from the bottom of his coat and wrapped it around her head. Her hair was soggy with blood.

"Zalika? Can you hear me?"

He had to get her home, but she was too badly injured to lift onto his horse. He picked her up and started running.

Heart pounding, feet pounding, he raced for the higher road, Cassia following behind.

"Zalika," he cried aloud, as if the sound of her name might keep the small spark of life in her burning just a little longer.

In the stark night wind, the call he heard above his own was not a human sound. It came from the hills or from the river, he could not tell which. Suddenly the howling was all around him, before him, and behind as he ran with Zalika. He knew the strange baying sound of the shadow pack: he'd heard it the night he lost everything in the fire. Kipp raced through the hollow sound, pitching down the hounds' dark throats, hearing the Gwali's dogs everywhere and nowhere in the shadows.

Even with the bandage, there was so much of her blood streaming down his arm. He ran, holding her, trying to press her head against his chest to stop the flow. He feared even as he ran that the life was draining out of her, that her skull was broken.

His lungs ached as he crested the hill. *Don't stop to take a breath. Go faster.* Two more hills and he would see the outlying orchard workers' shacks. The howls grew louder. He couldn't outrun the Gwali and his hounds bearing Zalika's weight, but the potion jar was under Jilly's bunk. It was the only power he had to stop the Death Catcher.

"Ahyuu!" he screamed again. Cassia ran up behind him. He decided: he would leave Zalika by the road and ride home to get the potion. He couldn't bring her. The jolting ride alone would kill her.

Gently laying Zalika in the tall grass, he kissed her, his mouth salty with tears and blood. *"Quiss eatuya."* Live now.

He threw himself onto Cassia. To the beat of her pounding hooves, he said the prayer again and again: *"Quiss eatuya.* Live now."

Flying past the kora orchards, Cassia came to a sudden halt outside his shack. Kipp's heaving breaths flooded the shack with dark wild waves, but the sleepers, weary from their day's labor, did not waken as he went down on his belly, dug in the dry earth, and grabbed the witch's jar.

Live, Zalika. Live long enough for me to get back to you now.

Outside he mounted Cassia and rode hard, the glass jar clenched tight in his hand. Speeding by orchards and stables, he galloped back up the road.

Already the hounds were circling their master's prey, as the airborne Gwali descended on his white mare.

The sight of the Gwali stripped away Kipp's courage. He could not remember what the witch had told him to do with the magic potion. Was he to smear it on one hand or both? No time to think it through. The dogs were sniffing Zalika's legs, her shoulders.

"Get back!" screamed Kipp.

The ghost mare landed soundless on the ground before him. He could not see a face under the Gwali's dark hood. No face, no heart to plead with. *Deysoukus.* Devil. The black sack was in his hand, its mouth hanging open.

"She is not going to die tonight!" Kipp ran Cassia at the

dogs, herding them like sheep, but they split apart, and gathered again into a menacing black team. Leaping down, he threw himself between them and Zalika, kneeling quickly to check if she were still alive. The hounds snarled, drawing closer.

Kipp felt Zalika's cheek. It was cold. "Keep breathing, Zalika. You are going to live." He put his palm above her lips. No breath. Nothing.

Too late! The Gwali must already have her in his hideous sack.

The Death Catcher towered over him on his white horse.

"You can't take her!" Kipp screamed. "She's mine!"

He was small against their combined power. They were not of this world; there was no telling what they might do.

Kipp smashed the jar against a rock. Glass and sticky potion covered his right hand and, leaping up, he flew at the Gwali, grabbed Kwaja, and clamped down hard on the sack. He screamed as the glass shards sliced into his palm and fingers.

High in the saddle, the Death Catcher pulled and pulled, but Kipp held the sack fast. The Gwali lighted down, his hood drawing back a few inches as his feet hit the ground. Enough to see the Gwali had a face, not just a shadow or bones, though the night was too dark to see more than that. The Death Catcher gave a mighty tug and turned on his heels, swinging Kipp around with such force that his feet went out from under him. Kipp spun out like a flag, legs flailing in the air.

The hounds barked under Kipp's soaring body, all noise and teeth and rage. He had Kwaja in both hands. Letting go with his left hand, he swung by one arm over the hounds, turning upward so he spun beneath moon and stars, the frenzied dogs snapping at his back.

The soul sack held fast in Kipp's right hand as the swinging slowed and Kipp fell onto his feet. The dogs scattered and returned in a growling wave. The Gwali yanked Kwaja with renewed force. Kipp felt as if his arm would be pulled out of its socket.

"Cassia, come!" She raced for him. The hounds leaped at her, snapping and snarling. Cassia whinnied, went up on her hind legs, front legs flailing only inches from Kipp's shoulder. The startled roan kicked the Gwali's back, knocking him facedown. Kipp pulled with all his might, freed the sack, and darted away seconds before the whining dogs swarmed around their master. Now the hounds were between him and Cassia. He couldn't get to her fast enough, so he bounded to the Gwali's mare and leaped into the saddle.

Zalika.

He turned the white mare back toward the place where Zalika lay at the side of the road and opened Kwaja wide as he cantered past her body. Kipp leaned over so far he nearly fell from the saddle, but he was sure he saw something soft and shining fly out of the sack.

Live.

He grabbed the reins with his free hand and circled her

once. She was partly curled up as if in sleep. Her torn shirt fluttered. He circled again. Her arm moved. Wasn't it moving? It had to be.

Live now.

Five hounds left their fallen master, who was still facedown, and rushed toward him in a snarling mass. Kipp kicked the white mare to a gallop. The dusty track shone dimly in the moonlight. Trees loomed black to the left and right. He took a quick glance behind and saw the Gwali rising.

"Run!" He flicked the reins, riding one handed, his right hand clenching his prize. Rounding a corner, he heard the sound of pounding hooves. The Gwali was riding Cassia. Poor, terrified Cass careened left and right, dogs and dust roiling all around her.

The ghost mare was all muscle, a born runner. But he could sense that she was holding back. She knew her real master was riding behind her. If Kipp couldn't get control of her, she'd let the Gwali overtake them. Wrapping the reins about his right wrist, he drove his boot heels into her side, shouted for her to go faster.

The road widened near Sor Tunassi's landholding. Someone had to go after Zalika, get her off the road, find a doctor. In a wild gallop past the stable yard, he spied Sor Jaffon trying to quiet a stormy Obi. The horse must have bolted home after the accident.

"Zalika's hurt!" Kipp screamed as he raced past. "She's near the roadside! Get a doctor now!"

The last words he shouted might well have been lost on the man for he could not slow down. Did Sor Jaffon see the Gwali and his hounds or only Kipp riding an unfamiliar horse, Cassia galloping not far behind with no one on her back?

It didn't matter. Sor Jaffon was already mounting Obi to go after Zalika. Now all Kipp had to do was keep the Gwali's sack away from her long enough for help to reach her. *Quiss eatuya,* Zalika.

Veering from the main road, he drove the mare into the grasslands. Behind, the Gwali chased him with his hounds.

Night sped under the stars. Galloping east toward the rolling hills, Kipp glanced back many times. The Gwali and his pack were never far behind. He prayed for Cassia to fall back, for her old bones to give way under the strain. *For once, old Cass, just this once, do not obey your rider.* But she was a good horse, too good.

His hand pulsed painfully from the broken glass where he gripped Kwaja. *Run quickly once you have what you desire, for the sticking spell will not last long.* The witch had not told him how long. An hour? Two? The potion oozed black between his bloodstained fingers. Even now he could feel his magic hold on the sack beginning to loosen.

CHAPTER SEVENTEEN

H E'D RIDDEN ALL night through barren grassland when he spotted sanuu trees in the distance
and steered the ghost mare up the hill. Small rocks tumbled
down the hillside behind her scrambling hooves. The potion
had lost its power and useless black goo and blood stained
his fingers. His cut hand was excruciating; still he hadn't let
go. Thinking of Zalika, he dug his fingers deeper into the
sack, holding Kwaja's mouth closed.

Sor Jaffon must have carried Zalika home by now. The
doctor would already be at her bedside. She might live if
Kipp could keep the Gwali away.

Through the thick sanuu woods he rode, hoping to lose
the Death Catcher in the forest. The sky over the distant
mountains was pale green with the new day. Reins in his
left hand, sack in his right, Kipp turned the ghost mare

around in a small clearing, and spotted the Gwali entering the woods below.

Deysoukus! How had Cassia made it this far without a rest? She was old and should have given out by now. He hated the Gwali for driving her so hard, his hideous dogs for swarming about her hooves, for frightening her so. Poor Cass.

The dogs began to bark. Kipp turned around and booted the white mare. Her mane flew up in waves as she galloped across the clearing.

Just before they plunged into the trees again, he glanced back and saw the shadow pack splitting up around the trunks; Cassia and the Gwali weren't far behind. In his hand the sack began to move. He felt it tugging hard against his grip. Did the Gwali have some power over the sack? Now that the potion had worn off, could the Gwali call Kwaja?

Kipp lowered his head. "Faster!" he screamed. "Fly!"

The white mare's hooves pounded the forest floor. Thick-leafed trees bled together into a long streak of black and green. Then the drumming sound beneath him disappeared as the chaotic jolting ride sped into creamy smoothness.

The ground teetered below him. What . . . what was happening? The mare was rising over the treetops, flying the way he'd seen her fly with the Gwali.

Wind sang in Kipp's ears as they soared above the sanuu trees. A shout erupted from his mouth. He was terrified. Elated. How had he gotten her to fly? It couldn't just be the words he'd screamed. It was magic—his or hers or Kwaja's? It didn't matter. He didn't care. He was above the Gwali. The yelps and howls increased as the Gwali's angry dogs jumped up, snarling and snapping the air.

The Death Catcher looked up, his dark cloak fluttering in the wind where he raced below. Would he work his magic, leap into the air, and fly after him? Cassia couldn't fly, but what might she do under the Gwali's power? The ghost mare whinnied. Her muscular legs moved soundlessly in the air. Far below, the trailing hounds and the speeding Gwali were growing smaller and smaller, still earthbound, the howls fading now as Kipp rose higher. He let out a whoop when he lost sight of the figures among the trees. He was freed into the morning sky, and Zalika was safe.

The Zolyan dawn spread white-gold over the mountains, as the mare sped over the hills and into the white.

High up in the air, the ghost mare covered half a day's ride in three breaths. Speed beyond knowing. Kipp barely held on. The reins seemed useless in his hands. How did a man ride the sky?

"What is your name?" he shouted. The mare must have one but he did not know it. *Lightning,* he thought as the wind swept her white mane across the backs of his hands. He'd not caught the white horse he'd been after, but this one was stronger, faster; this one could fly. Not just lightning, then, he'd call her ChChka, the Escuyan word for lightning!

"I name you Sa ChChka! Madam Lightning." A mile ahead he could see the Sway River snaking across the land. The mare turned and sped above the sleek bright water toward the dark green orchards; Sor Tunassi's estate. Kipp watched his shadow skimming along the dirt road below. No body lying alongside the road where he'd left Zalika. He heaved a sigh. *Thank you, Ahyuu.* Sor Jaffon had taken Zalika home. Had the doctor helped her? Would she be all right?

As they flew over the kora rows, one of the pickers looked up. Another did the same, took off his hat, wiped his forehead. They talked and laughed down below. They had looked right at him, had not seen him. *I am invisible up here.*

ChChka blazed through the sky, a part of the white heat of day that drove down on the pickers' sweaty backs. Jilly's blonde head appeared between the red berry bushes.

He thought of calling out to her. But it would frighten her to hear his voice, to look up and see nothing but sky.

The mare flew toward the estate house. She circled the roof and pulled up outside Zalika's upstairs window. Sheer yellow curtains fluttered through the opening. Kipp gasped at the sight of Zalika covered by a thin blue sheet on her four-poster bed. Was she asleep or . . . ?

"Zalika," he called.

ChChka bucked midair. The unexpected jolt sent Kipp tumbling off her back and through the open window. He landed on his backside and lay, arms out, trying to catch his breath. Zalika hadn't moved. He tucked Kwaja into his belt and poked his head out the window. ChChka nibbled on the grass below. Good horse, kind horse. She'd followed the secret pulling of his heart and brought him here to see his girl.

No one was here with Zalika, but she wouldn't be left alone for long. Kipp crept to the bedside. Zalika's eyes were closed. The bandage around her head looked ghastly against her smooth dark skin. She breathed in little birdlike starts.

"Zalika?" He touched her shoulder. His right hand was still smeared with the last remains of the sticky potion and specked with dried blood. He pulled his hand away.

The sweet metallic smell of blood filled his nose. His heart tightened. He could see that she was badly hurt. If she opened her eyes, he would kiss her lips. Bring back their sweet reddish-brown color. He would tell her what he had done for her and say that she was safe. The Gwali would not come.

A door slammed. He heard the muffled sound of a woman crying. Kipp stiffened, listening to the heavy footsteps coming down the hall. He was about to bolt for the window when he heard the footsteps thumping down the stairs.

Kipp jiggled her shoulder gently. "Zalika, wake up," he whispered. "It's me, Kipp."

Her chest rose and fell under the blue sheet. The hours by the Sway came back to him.

When my purse is full, I will be gone, she'd said. He'd been angry at that, told her she should go soon.

"Not like this," Kipp whispered. "I didn't want you to go away from me. I couldn't say it at the river." But she'd understood that, hadn't she?

Her room was full of beautiful paintings, books, flowered vases, and a vanity with a great oval mirror. She had plenty of things, but her parents didn't love her the way he did. Her father had lost her by gambling and given her to Sor Litchen. Her mother wanted Zalika to have perfect skin, but only so she could marry a wealthy man.

Last night they'd made a plan to run off together. He still needed that plan for her, for himself and Jilly.

Kipp breathed over Zalika, wanting to give her his breath. A morning wind blew through the window. He felt Kwaja move against his thigh and stepped away from the bed, alarmed. The sack had pulled against his hand just before ChChka flew, or had he only imagined that? Another gust lifted the sheer yellow curtains at the window. Kipp heaved a sigh. For a moment he'd thought . . .

A monarch butterfly flew in, alighted on the silken sheet covering Zalika's slender body, and opened and closed her orange-and-black wings. In that brief second the sack pulled free from Kipp's belt and drifted over Zalika's head.

Sucking in a terrified breath, Kipp jumped for it and caught it in both hands. The black sack was woven in a light material and he should have been able to drag it down easily, but Kwaja would not budge. Putting his boot against the side of the bed, he gave another enormous tug. Still it slipped away and undulated higher. The tie cords loosened, opening the black maw.

"You cannot have her!" Kipp's whispered shout startled the butterfly, and it darted back out the window. Voices down below. Would someone come up the stairs and find him here?

"I stole you with my potion," he said vehemently. "I own you!" He didn't want to own Kwaja, only to get it away from Zalika. *Become the master of the sack. Become the master . . .*

Using the bedpost to pull himself up, he stood on the bed, his boots inches away from Zalika's pillow. Catching the bottom corner, he strained against the weight. It was like dragging a heavy tree trunk, but the sack began to come his way.

Kipp jumped down and looped Kwaja's cords around his waist. He tied knot after knot to firmly hold it in place.

Beside him, Zalika's finger twitched. Life. Hope.

Kwaja gave another strong pull against its cords. Kipp pressed the sack to his side. The soft black fabric shuddered as he bunched it in his hands and tucked it inside his pant leg.

The sack wrapped around his thigh and clung to him like a leech. Kwaja's embrace startled him as much as the pulling, maybe more, but he had no time to think about it. He poked his head out the window and clicked his tongue. ChChka raised her head below and shook her long mane as if to say, *Are you done already?* She flew up.

Footsteps. Someone was coming down the hall.

". . . until she comes out of her coma," the doctor's voice said from behind the door.

Kipp hurled himself out the open window onto the saddle. He stole one last look at Zalika before the mare took off, engulfing him in a stream of warm air as the roof grew smaller and smaller below ChChka's hooves.

The hills and plains sped by below. The land was dust-red here, golden there, green along the tree-lined gullies where streams ran after a good rain.

Miles away, the mountains capped the edge of the horizon. "I don't see the Gwali anywhere," Kipp called. "ChChka, you are mighty!"

He eased back in the saddle. Wind washed through the mare's mane, across his arms, his chest, his face. Kipp opened his mouth and swallowed it whole, let the power course through him, fill his body, expand his lungs. He would burst with it. Spread his light across the sky.

"I am Kipp!" he screamed.

"I have stolen Kwaja!"

Who could hear him? The sculpted rocks below, the bushes almost black in sunlight. Snakes, lizards, the circling buzzards. ChChka flew toward the highlands.

CHAPTER EIGHTEEN

L ATE IN THE day, white clouds rolled over the
countryside, staining the earth below. This part of the
grassland was flat as a griddlecake. A small herd of impalas
raced below. Kipp watched the delicate brown-backed females
and the horned males running past boulders and scattered
shrubs.

ChChka followed the herd from above. They would put
as much distance between Kwaja and Zalika as they could in
one day. The impalas reached the dunes and headed downhill
toward a watering hole. It was large, though likely very
shallow—a gift from the recent rain. The pool was crowded
with hundreds of flamingos. They took flight as the impalas
approached, their pink wings flapping wildly as the animals
trotted to the water's edge. Kipp laughed as the flamingos
encircled them, stirring a small hot wind. It was like being

showered with pink rose petals, except for the raw honking sounds.

Down below a leopard suddenly burst from the tall grass. The startled impalas darted to the right, broke into two groups, and rejoined a moment later, bounding across the land with the leopard in chase.

The watering hole wouldn't be deserted for long. ChChka landed at the edge. Kipp hopped down, removed his coat, and searched the Gwali's saddlebags for a water pouch. When he pulled the leather skin out, a necklace of tiny red and blue beads came with it. He tucked the necklace back in the saddlebag with his coat. Whose necklace was it? Where had the Gwali gotten it? He gave an involuntary shudder. He didn't want to know.

He drank in great thirsty gulps, filled the water pouch, then dipped his hat in the water to wash the cuts on his hand. The remains of the witch's dried black potion came away with the encrusted blood. He filled his hat again, dumped the cool water on his head, and shook like a dog. ChChka stepped back and snorted.

"Sorry. I can't help it," he said, but he did it a second time. The third time he filled his hat, ChChka nosed him hard, knocking him on his side. "All right, all right. I'll stop."

He was still laughing when he noticed the ground shaking. He turned in time to see five elephants tromping toward the little lake, trunks swinging, ears billowing. Kipp threw on his wet hat, grabbed the water pouch, and mounted ChChka.

The mare skittered to the side, splashing through the shallows to get out of the elephants' way. She was bolting through the tufted grass just a few yards from the pool when the herd reached the water. ChChka kept to a gallop all the way to the dune where kwik bushes rattled in the hot wind. Kipp glanced downhill at the elephants wading in the pool below.

"Why didn't you fly, ChChka?" He patted her neck. Couldn't she fly whenever she wanted to? There was so little he knew about her. He clicked his tongue and they descended down the far side of the dune.

An hour later, Kipp was scratching his leg where the cloth sack rubbed against his thigh, when ChChka suddenly sped to a canter. Veering around a termite hill, she plunged into the air. "Now you fly?" he asked. "With only termites challenging us?" Again he didn't understand, but he was grateful to leave the dry land below for the feel of the cool air rushing against his body.

At sunset they passed over an Escuyan village. The dying day spread pale purple light across the grass-roofed huts. He had visited some villages with Sor Joay when they hunted in the Farlands. Villages like this were not permanent, though each tribe kept their village name and took it with them wherever they went. The grass huts were built, lived in for a few seasons, and later torn down. The nomads had always moved across the land like the wild horses they loved.

There were twelve horses in the corral near the baobab trees: some red roans, a few chestnuts and bays. Each spring, men journeyed to the mountains to bring back a few two- and three-year-olds. The nomads took only what they needed from the wild herds, letting most roam free. They kept some horses, but most were trained and sold.

Just outside the encampment a group of Escuyan women danced in a circle near an isolated hut. Hands clapping in rhythm, their voices rose up in song. Kipp saw no men in the encampment. They might still be out hunting.

ChChka's shadow passed over the ground outside the circle where the dancers were swaying in their colorful kirifa dresses. The song they sang sounded familiar but he could not remember where he'd heard it before. The women threw their heads back and lifted their hands to the sky. It looked as if they were calling to him, asking for something, a blessing, rain, but Kipp knew they could not see him.

A spicy smell rose up from the village. His mouth watered, and his stomach rumbled. He wanted to land and approach the villagers to ask for food, but how could he do this with Kwaja tied to his side? ChChka seemed to make her mind up for him. Circling back, she descended slowly and landed behind one of the huts. Kipp was unsure what to do next, but the mare urged him forward with her nose. He began to lead her around the hut, hoping to think of a good plan. He was too hungry to leave without some food. As he came around the front, the dancers saw him and drew back into a protective huddle.

CHAPTER NINETEEN

KIPP WAS ALMOST as surprised as they were that they could see him. He quickly adjusted to the idea that he and ChChka became visible again once they touched the ground. Stepping forward, Kipp cleared his throat. The nomads did not see many light-skinned immigrants traveling through the Farlands. Still, he had visited a few villages as a boy, and Sor Joay had taught him how to behave. If he greeted the Escuyan women respectfully they might offer some food. Kipp put his hands out, palms up in an Escuyan greeting. "Aum."

An elderly woman in a bright green turban that matched her kirifa dress stepped away from the circle.

"Aum, traveler." She eyed the cuts on his right hand.

Kipp knew his open-handed greeting told the Escuyans he carried no weapons. He removed his boots and stepped back a few paces. The elder nodded at the hunting knife sheathed in the high leather boot top. Accepting his honest gesture, she did not take it from him. Boots back on, Kipp still kept a respectful distance from the women.

The elder had not given him her name nor asked for his. Her eyes covered his dusty clothing, his sweat-stained hat, his pale skin.

"There is no one in our village looking for farmwork." She spoke in common Zolyan, guessing correctly that he did not know enough Escuyan words to serve him here.

Wealthy farmers sometimes sent men out to the villages at harvest time to hire extra pickers. He'd ridden in alone. She must have assumed he worked for a landholder.

"I did not come here to hire pickers," said Kipp. "I am . . . traveling."

Two of the dancers laughed behind their hands.

The nomads' customs were tricky, especially between tribal women and male outsiders. He could easily say the wrong thing, make a foolish mistake, and go hungry.

"You travel with no goods," said the elder. Her eyes narrowed. "You left in a hurry." She stared at the scar on his neck and the place where a young man his age should have a braid touching his shoulder. Was he an outcast?

"You have a fine horse," she added. He could read the growing suspicion in her face. He was dressed like a poor laborer. He was shorn. He had a magnificent horse. These things did not go together.

A rattling sound came from the tent beyond. Kipp heard a man's voice chanting.

"Our hunters will return soon," said the elder. "You will leave us."

"I am hungry," said Kipp. "May I have some food, Sa?"

Two women turned their backs and whispered to each other. Detch! He had probably asked it the wrong way. They would have offered him food if they had approved of him. The elder had decided he must be an outcast and she'd dismissed him. He stayed put, ravenous.

A woman with a striped kirifa said, "He is just a boy."

A younger girl in a pink headscarf with a fine heart-shaped face bit her lip to control a smile. The half-hidden smile showed an even row of small white teeth.

"He lost his braid," the elder argued. She turned back to Kipp and crossed her arms. "What did you do?"

"Do?" he choked. "To lose my braid?"

She waited, frowning. The group gathered behind her like cubs behind a lioness.

"I traded it to . . ." *Don't say to the witch of Sanuu Wood.* "To save my little sister from harm." It was the truth, and he held her gaze.

"For medicine?"

He nodded, unable to say yes. He couldn't truthfully call the sticky potion medicine.

"And did you save her?"

"Yes." He could feel Kwaja moving against his skin in

protest, but this was the truth. He had saved Zalika, and if he could keep the sack away from the Gwali, today, tomorrow, forever, Jilly would be safe, too.

The elder took a small step. Her ankle bracelets jingled. "Do you have this medicine with you?" she asked. Her face was anxious, hopeful. Someone in the village was sick. It would explain the dance of supplication, the rattling sound coming from the isolated hut.

He thought of the sticky black glue that had helped him steal Kwaja. "I do not have it anymore, Sa."

The anxiousness stayed on her wrinkled face; the hopeful look fell away. She turned and snapped her fingers. The girl Kipp had noticed earlier scurried into one of the larger huts, came out again, and gave the elder a clay bowl of goat's milk and a husk cone filled with yellow root mash. Kipp knew it would not be right for an unpledged girl to offer food to a young man.

The elder passed the food and drink to Kipp. He tipped his head to thank her. "Taka, Sa."

She replied with the formal, "Ee-tak." But she did not nod back, as was the custom. Her head remained erect. Her neck was noticeably stiff.

There was no hope of being invited into a hut to sit on a rug and eat. He'd taken a meal that way when he'd traveled through the Farlands with Sor Joay. But these women did not trust him enough to invite him in. He was lucky to eat and go.

Kipp drank the warm goat's milk and chewed the red-flecked

mash. The chopped spices in the meal burned his tongue. His eyes watered, but he finished the food and thanked the women as he handed back his empty husk and bowl. It was polite to offer a gift for a meal. Kipp frowned, thinking, then reached into the Gwali's saddlebag and pulled out the necklace he'd found earlier.

The elder took it with a nod. Kipp sighed. He had done the right thing. He would have mounted and ridden away then if it weren't for the sudden convulsive tug under his pant leg. He lunged to the side and before he could right himself, he was stumbling toward the isolated hut.

"What are you doing? Stay away from there!" the elder woman protested. She did not touch Kipp, but as he was dragged closer to the hut, her voice rose in warning.

"Do not go in. There is a sickness inside." She halted, unwilling to come any closer.

"Sa," Kipp called, "I am sorry, Sa," before he disappeared through the door flap.

Smoke stung his eyes. He blinked in the dim light trying to take in the scene. A man in an orange-feathered cape sat cross-legged waving a burning bundle over the girl on the blanket. Ten white stones encircled her body. Three smaller stones made a triangle on her belly. The green stone on her forehead kept slipping off. The healer replaced it with the hand that held the bundle and shook his rattle over her.

Kipp was drawn toward the girl's feet. She wore copper ankle bracelets like the dancers outside but her wrap skirt was a soft plum color. Her face had the same heart shape as the girl outside who'd brought him food, likely her older sister. But this girl was very thin. Her bony face was moist with sweat. Her mouth opened just a slit and she moaned quietly, her voice going up and down in rhythm with the rattle.

"Go away," said the healer. Like the elder woman outside, he spoke to Kipp in Zolyan.

Kipp lurched forward again, so forcefully he nearly fell atop the girl. He struggled, grunted, reeled back. Step-by-step he pressed himself toward the door flap. He was halfway out before he was propelled inside again.

"I told you to go away," the man snapped. He was still rattling, still waving the smoke bundle.

Kipp's stomach turned. His flesh felt slippery. "I do not want to be here, Sor."

"Then why have you come?" The man glared at him in the half dark.

There was no time to answer as he battled with the sack. He pressed both palms against his thigh trying to keep Kwaja down. It struggled under his hands like a wild ferret.

"Get out." The healer held up the smoking bundle like a shield.

"I'm going, Sor."

But even as he said this he was pulled forward with such violence that he stumbled. In seconds, Kwaja forced its way out from under his pant leg and wrenched apart the knots he'd tied so firmly to his belt. Kipp groaned as it flew toward the girl. The wavering cloth was blacker than crow wings.

The healer's eyes grew wide. "Deysoukus!" He made a sign of the devil. "You have brought death into my tent," he shouted, leaping to a stand. Kipp threw his arms around the softly undulating sack and tried to wrestle it to the floor.

"Get out!" The healer had reverted to the Escuyan language, but Kipp understood him well enough.

"I don't want to hurt her. The sack wants to take her soul. Help me capture it, please, Sor. I will take it away."

Kipp had tackled Kwaja and pressed it down; still it wavered nearly a foot above the dirt floor, floating toward the girl.

"Grab it if you want to save her!"

The healer dropped his bundle and rattle and pounced on the sack.

Kipp tore off his shirt. "Tie it around me," he gasped.

Together they fought the sack, cinching the top, then shoving it under Kipp's right arm. The healer brought one tie around Kipp's back, the other in front, and knotted the cords over Kipp's left shoulder. Kipp sucked in another breath and pinned the sack under his arm. Kwaja whipped and flailed like a flag in a storm.

"More rope!"

"What spirit moves this thing?" The healer's deep voice croaked with fear. He tore off his hemp belt, wrapping it around Kipp to keep the writhing sack in place.

The belt was too tight around his chest but Kipp didn't dare loosen it. When the knots were secure, the man threw

Kipp his shirt and pushed him roughly toward the flap.

"Go!" he shouted. "Now!"

"Taka!" Kipp called behind his back. "She will live now, Sor."

Outside the dancers had tightened their circle. They moaned and drew farther back as he ran out. The elder stood before them protectively. Hands up, she made the diamond shape to ward off evil, shouting some spell or prayer as Kipp threw himself into the saddle. "Go, ChChka!"

The mare didn't budge until the healer rushed outside and slapped her on the rump. Breaking into a canter, she passed the wide-eyed women and darted between the huts.

"Now I know why we came here!" Kipp shouted angrily. ChChka whinnied as she sprang to a gallop. She was firmly on the ground and running fast. Kipp reveled in the feel of her pounding hooves coming down in a hard rhythmic pattern against the earth. The harsh jolting motions kept pace with his rising anger.

"I can't live this way. I'm not going to let this detching sack pull me around. I'm not going to serve death. Do you hear me?"

The first star appeared over the high blue ridges of the Botswi peaks. Kipp headed east for the jagged hills where the Botswi ranges made their first foothold. A pattern was emerging and the knowledge hit him like a blow to his gut. He thought he'd flown to Zalika to check on her and see that she was safe, that they'd stopped in the village for food. But as he reeled back through the day, Kipp saw it was not his wish or ChChka's power that had made them fly. It was Kwaja. The sack had drawn them first to Zalika, then to the Escuyan girl. Kwaja's power made them fly to the next dying person and the next.

Become the master of the sack. He remembered the witch's crusty voice. He heard the taunting words now for what they were, a curse. How could he master such a thing? He could almost see the witch's face in the air before him, her head coiled with the snake braids of all the men she'd enspelled, cheated, or killed.

ChChka slowed to a trot. Kipp did not urge her into another gallop. Where could he go? What would he do now? Twilight fell from the sky and cupped the grasslands. Wind swept the last of the day away, blowing in the cool of night.

He'd saved Zalika from the Gwali last night. This morning he'd mastered the sack again in her room and flown out the window with it, but his strength had failed him in the village. The girl would have died if the healer had not thrown himself across Kwaja and tied it to Kipp's body.

What have I done? he thought wretchedly. *This thing is beyond my power. I am human. I am not a devil or a god.*

Kipp adjusted his seat where the saddle grazed his thighs. His joints ached from endless riding.

Tied down. The soul sack strapped to his body. His body bound by the sack.

He feared he would fail the next time.

CHAPTER TWENTY

K IPP COULD NOT keep Kwaja any longer. He would not let the dark power draw him and ChChka to another death. He rode on and on to find a way out. Let himself get lost in the bare Farlands. Prayed to Ahyuu.

Two nights later, the moon curved slim and white as an ox horn as he entered a lone place where sandstone towers rose from the red earth like a colony of disfigured giants. Some were nine feet high, others more than twenty. Kipp pulled the tired mare to a halt.

"What do you think of this place, ChChka?"

Sor Joay had brought him here to camp in the shadow of these towers when he was ten years old. That day he'd pointed to the giants and told Kipp their ancient names. He couldn't recall the names now, though he remembered peering out from behind the giant stones seeing the Far-lands spreading out for miles.

Kipp looped ChChka's tether about a narrow standing stone. He kept himself moving as he gathered kindling beneath the nearby stunted trees.

"Do you know the story of these stone giants, ChChka? You'll like the story because it's about beautiful horses." As he set up camp, he told ChChka the tale he'd learned from Sor Joay the first time he came here, concentrating on the words to keep his mind inside the story and away from what he was about to do.

"Long ago these giants were called from the deep earth to protect the ancient king, Mbasu Ejanuu, from a people who wished to steal his magnificent horses. The giants drew together and made a great wall to keep his enemies away. The wall they formed together was a living thing. It moved about, shook the enemies off, and threw them down.

"When the enemy fled at last, and King Mbasu Ejanuu's proud horses were safe, the giants drew apart again. They had been away from their underworld for a long time. They had grown used to the vast Farlands. They loved the open sky above their heads, the sun, the moon, and stars. They did not want to return to the dark underworld, and so they lived and died here and turned into these stones. When you love a king, you will fight for him. When you love a land, you want to live there. That is what Sor Joay said."

Kipp ran his hand along the rough stone tower with a

hunched back and a huge leering head. The giants were still considered guardians. "Will you watch over me and my proud horse tonight?" he whispered.

After drinking from his water pouch, Kipp put on his long black coat against the night cold. He was glad for the old guardians. He would let them witness what he had to do.

In the Gwali's saddlebags he found a tin cook pan and poured some of his precious water in for ChChka. The pan was just wide enough for her to drink. When she was done he rubbed the hand-shaped marking on her neck, put his face against her side, and breathed in her scent. "I need you. Will you stay with me when this is done?" He did not say what he planned to do. The sack was like a living thing. It had a will, so Kipp kept his plan tucked under his tongue.

Near a stooping stone, Kipp broke the longer branches, which he'd gathered earlier, over his knee and stacked a small woodpile. The third stone giant in the circle was small and squat compared to the others, only about six feet high. It looked like a fat laughing baby. He'd called this boulder the Jilly giant when he was ten, though it had another ancient name. Jilly was just a baby back then, plump and happy in her mother's arms.

Kipp's throat ached. His little sister was more than a hundred and fifty miles away. He'd promised not to leave her again. What would she think of his word now? He rubbed his smarting eyes and took out Sor Joay's tinderbox to light a fire.

Flames licked the branches. Kipp leaned down and blew on them to encourage Techee before adding more kindling.

"I do not know what I am doing," Kipp said to the fire. He missed his old teacher. He needed his wise eyes, his questions that turned the world upside down, shook things up, let new ideas tumble out.

Lifting his shirt, he carefully untied the hemp rope and loosened the cords. "I can't let the Gwali catch me. I don't know what else to do."

Kipp held Kwaja before him. Black. Limp. Before he dropped it in, he crushed it in his hand. So light. It seemed empty, but was it?

Throw it in. No, check first. Make sure the sack is empty.

Slowly, Kipp tugged the drawstrings and opened Kwaja's mouth. Too black to see inside. He would have to reach his hand in. Trembling, he slipped his fingers in one inch, then two. He'd seen his parents' and Royan's souls sucked into the dark. They couldn't still be inside, could they? The sack was too light for that. But if they weren't in Kwaja, where had the Gwali taken all the souls he'd stolen?

By the stooping stone, ChChka whinnied uneasily and pressed back her ears.

"It's all right," he said, though his heart was pounding and his knees felt weak. He sat on a small boulder and reached a little farther in. The woven cloth at the mouth was kitten soft. It was cool, not warm as he expected. Kipp walked his fingers down toward the bottom seam. Nothing there. Frowning, he peered into the black and reached inside up to his elbow. Nothing. He sucked in a breath. Kwaja was no bigger than a tote bag. Where was the bottom? *Pull your hand out, quick. No, keep it in. Keep going.*

He explored a little deeper, up to his shoulder, and still felt nothing at the bottom except a stirring inside, like a cool breeze. He couldn't see his arm, his hand. He waved his arm back and forth frantically. Where were the sides now? He couldn't find them. Kwaja was a hole; it would swallow him up.

"Ahyuu! My God." Kipp leaped up and wrenched his arm out. He quickly felt along his flesh, shoulder to hand. For a moment he thought he'd lost his arm. He held the sack away from his body, trembling.

"What . . . are you?"

There must be a bottom. He had to find it. He turned the sack inside out. Kwaja was empty. *All the souls the Gwali took, where are they now?*

"Where is my mother?" He shook Kwaja, both hands tight around it now, strangling the top. "Where is my father? Where is my little brother? Where did the Gwali take them?"

He crushed the empty thing into a black ball, held it over the flames, and dropped it in.

ChChka's eyes grew wide. She reared back, fighting against her tether.

"Quiet, ChChka!"

Kipp turned to the flames. "Techee, fire, eat." He piled

the two thickest branches on top of the sack to keep it in place while it burned. Techee's yellow tongue licked the wood. Sparks flew up. The crackling logs made the sound of snapping teeth.

The mare shook her head, her mane flying, her lips curling. Kipp went to her, rubbed her neck, and spoke softly in her ear, keeping an eye on the fire. Whatever power the sack had over her, it would be gone soon. He would try and keep her settled until the thing was done.

Inside the ring of stone giants, the flames engulfed the logs covering Kwaja.

"Wood is Techee food and so is cloth," Kipp told the mare. "She will eat what I feed her."

Wind swirled the smoke over the giants' heads.

ChChka stopped stamping her hoof and began to ease. "That's it," Kipp said. He sat again on the small boulder and leaned up against the stone hunchback. The fire blazed bright. When the sack was nothing but ashes, he would be free. It shouldn't be long now.

His arms and body felt lighter. He was almost floating as he thought about the days ahead. *I'll go back to Jilly and Zalika.* He sighed and cleaned the dirt out from under his nails.

The heat from the flames tightened the skin across his arms and face. His coat felt too hot, but he did not remove it. A new idea was growing and not a comfortable one. How could he explain everything that had happened? Wouldn't Sor Tunassi think he had deserted Zalika after she fell, that he'd stolen Cassia and run away because he was afraid he would be punished?

Kipp spat in the dirt. He would hate himself if he'd done that. Then again, Zalika had been too badly hurt to know what had happened after she fell. Would she think he'd deserted her, too? That he was nothing but a detching coward?

He scuffed the dirt with his heel. He couldn't stand the thought of her believing that, not even for a moment. But what could he say or do to prove otherwise? Sor Tunassi would probably order Sag Eye to whip him as soon as he showed his face. After that he'd likely be arrested.

ChChka turned her head and gave a loud snuff. The wind had changed direction, blowing smoke her way. She blinked and flicked her tail. Kipp checked the logs. Kwaja was still trapped underneath, burning. He pulled off his coat and used it like a fan to redirect the smoke.

"You see, ChChka? I will take care of you."

The mare huffed again, but not so loudly this time.

When the wind moved from south to east, Kipp slipped his coat back on.

He could not think what to do now. Once Kwaja was destroyed, Zalika would be out of danger, but returning to her and Jilly would mean endangering himself. Still he had to go back. Now that the rest of his family and Sor Joay were gone, he had only those two. There was no one else in the world he cared for, no one else he wanted to be with.

Firelight painted the surrounding giants yellow and sent their shadows across the ground. The shadow from the giant Jilly stone fell lopsided at the stooping stone woman's feet. The stooping stone now had a wavering black stream to drink from. It made Kipp happy to think that.

Open your eyes, Sor Joay used to say. *Tell me what you see.*

"I see the fire destroying my enemy," Kipp said proudly, as if Sor Joay were standing right beside him. "I see the shadow from that fire easing an old woman's thirst."

He stepped closer, squatted, and took up a long stick. More than half an hour had passed. It was long enough for the thing to have burned. He would check to make sure. Pressing his tongue against his teeth, he poked one of the logs aside.

His eyes were on the fire and nowhere else. Techee was eating. The flaming branches glowed red. Cracked and bright as cheewii lizard scales, they throbbed with heat.

Open your eyes. Tell me what you see.

"Sor," he whispered. "Sor. The sack is not burning."

Kipp leaped from stillness to action, like a leopard springing out of grass ready to kill. He jabbed the fire to roll the log back on top of Kwaja. Too late, the sack escaped and began to rise. It hovered in the air, encircled with flame, but the cloth was not on fire. Kipp grabbed a longer, thicker stick from the reserve pile and swung it hard against the floating sack.

Kwaja wavered in the air unsteadily, like an animal

awakened from sleep. Haloed in flame, Kwaja began to spin slowly in the air like the captive things he'd seen inside the witch's jars: the insects, the flowers.

Kipp jabbed the sack. It folded over the stick and spat it out again. Silent, light as a leaf, it swam in the air. Swearing, Kipp slashed through the burning circle nine times, ten. Kwaja gave under every blow, but each time he raised his weapon up to strike again, the sack billowed back to full size and hovered waist-high in the air. The circle of flames around it sizzled and crackled. But the sack was not burning and he could not bash it back down into the fire pit.

Kipp fought till his arms ached, his shirt soaked in sweat, till he was choking for breath, till he could no longer lift his arm.

Surrounded in golden flame, the soul sack spun slowly, perfect and untouched.

Techee was hungry.

She had it in her mouth. She would not swallow.

CHAPTER TWENTY-ONE

TEARING KWAJA FROM the fire, Kipp shook it as if it were an animal and he was trying to break its neck. He sat, unsheathed his knife, and stepped on the bottom of the sack. Stretching it tightly between hand and boot, he jabbed it with his blade. The point didn't pierce the cloth. He stabbed it again and again, and ran the sharp point from mouth to bottom. He would shred the detching thing!

Kipp's knife would not impale, stab, slit, or shred the Gwali's sack. It didn't alter a single woven thread. Breathing hard, he slid the blade back into his boot. The fire still burned brightly. He kicked dust into the flames and watched them sputter.

Pulling the healer's hemp belt from ChChka's saddlebags, he bared his chest, pressed Kwaja against his skin and carefully wound the rope around himself from top to bottom. He knotted the sack's cords to the hemp in three places, continued to encircle his body, and tied the rope at the base of his rib cage. Kwaja covered his front like a warrior's chest plate. Soft and black, it weighed less than a handful of feathers. It weighed as much as sorrow. Kipp stumbled with the weight.

The next day, he left the stone giants and rode out into the bush in search of a waterhole. He'd ridden less than an hour when he felt Kwaja stir beneath his shirt. Kipp jumped down from the saddle.

"I will not let you fly ChChka and me to the dying," he said. "Not anymore."

He grabbed the reins. Head bowed, knees bent, he tried to walk with ChChka against the mighty pull. It was like trying to press through a heavy sandstorm. Kipp grunted as he moved two steps forward, three steps back. He knew the force would ease if he obeyed Kwaja, mounted ChChka, and let the sack fly them where it wanted to go.

He wouldn't mount, but he walked in the direction of the pull. ChChka whinnied and eyed him uneasily.

"It's all right, girl. It will pass."

It did pass, but the battle strained the muscles in his back. By the time Kwaja gave in and was still, Kipp was drenched in sweat. He raised his fist and whooped a victory cry. It was a half-exhausted feeble cry, but he had won. Still he waited another hour to be sure he was truly out of danger before slipping thankfully into the saddle. Head down on ChChka's neck, Kipp dozed off riding under the sun.

The drama happened daily over the next three weeks. It wore him out, wore him down, but he kept fighting Kwaja's pull and never let the sack draw him and ChChka back into the air. In the dry Farlands he caught rabbits and snakes, and chewed tangy kwick-bush leaves. When that failed he survived on grubs and grasshoppers. By the time he reached Namibo, hunger drove him into the town.

The day's heat had been chased away by thick, moving clouds when Kipp dismounted and passed Ahyuu's temple. On the top step, a blue-robed priest was ordering a younger novice to line the worshippers' discarded shoes into a neat row. Kipp stopped to gaze up at the turquoise spire pointing to Ahyuu's heaven. It was beautiful but he favored the large open pavilion to the right where people worshipped nightly under the starry sky.

It was an hour before dusk, and the market would be closing soon. ChChka's hooves clip-clopped behind him through the busy town square. The fruit seller's oranges and pomegranates were stacked into fine, bright pyramids, and there were baskets heaped full of sweet brown dates oozing with sugar. Kipp's mouth watered but there were no coins in his pocket. First he had to sell his rabbit skin and snakeskin.

He passed a small crowd gathered around a bone thrower, who sat cross-legged on a colorful rug. His long braid was coiled into a ball at the end, and his beard was also braided in the fashion of bone throwers. An old woman had just paid him for her fortune and closed her money pouch, looking satisfied.

Kipp frowned. If he hadn't been so hunger-driven when he'd hunted the coral snake, he would have remembered to save the skeleton. This bone thrower might have paid good money for it, especially if the skull and fangs were intact. He'd been foolish to kill his prey so clumsily by smashing a rock against its skull. He'd do it differently next time, if there was a next time.

A ragged group of men and women, with skeletal arms and legs, huddled near the cloth merchant's stall.

"Get away," the merchant warned. "I have nothing to give you."

Kipp watched the vacant-eyed people move on to the flatbread stall where they were sent off again. "What is the matter with them?"

"They are sigurun, very sick. They should all be dead by now."

Kipp tried to swallow but his throat was too dry. Had he kept Kwaja away from these people? The sack was not stirring now, but he decided to do his business quickly and get out of this town.

"Tie your horse there." The merchant pointed to the hitching post beside his stall. Kipp tethered ChChka and drew two rabbit pelts from the saddlebags. The merchant ran his dark hand over the soft gray fur, then turned it over and scratched it with his long thumbnail.

"How much will you give me for these skins?" Kipp asked.

"I will give you a dimi."

"Five dimis for both skins." Kipp knew the merchant could sell them at a good price. Zolyan women liked to give rabbit skins as a gift to new mothers. The soft fur was sewn into little booties. Older children prized them, too. A year ago his mother had made a pair of rabbit-fur slippers for Jilly. His sister loved them. They were gone now along with everything else on the farm. He gripped the skins. "Five dimis," he demanded again.

A gentle drizzle fell, jewelling the potter's glazed plates and cups at the next stall. Kipp longed to feel the cool drops on his head but he would not take off his hat to show his shorn head in public. The old man offered two dimis for each skin. Kipp accepted it and carefully took out the coral snakeskin and laid it out on the table. The colorful red, yellow, and black segments shone brightly even in the gentle rain.

The cloth merchant's eyes popped before he tried to hide his interest by wrinkling his nose in distaste. But Kipp had seen his first reaction and knew the vendor wanted it. Kipp ran his finger along the snakeskin. Behind him the tanner rode his cart through the market. The wheels hit a puddle, spattering ChChka's long white legs with flecks of mud.

"One dimi," the man said, drumming the table with his long fingernails. Kipp began to put the snakeskin away.

"Two," the merchant snarled.

After more bargaining, they settled on four dimis. He might have sold the skeleton for double the price. Kipp went straight to the fruit stand before it closed and loaded up on oranges, plums, and pomegranates. At the next two booths he bought onions and peppers, some dried meat, and a small bag of grain.

Clouds tugged across the sky, and the rain came down in earnest now. Kipp put on his coat and ate a plum. It tasted almost as sweet as the jam his mother used to make. Sucking out the juice, he remembered the time Jilly dunked her hand in a jam jar when Mother wasn't looking and licked her sticky purple fingers. Kipp laughed but did not say a word to Mother. Jilly was only three then, and her cheeks were still plump. He stepped away from thoughts of Jilly. He'd promised never to leave his little sister again, but he'd had to go away this time. He wondered if she would ever understand why.

Dropping the peel in hunks onto the wet cobblestones, Kipp jammed half an orange into his mouth, letting the sour sweet flavor sting his tongue as he stopped to read a poster tacked to the side of the tanner's stall.

Goba City Fair
Horse Races. Rope Rides. Jugglers.
Fire Eaters. Women's Archery Competition.

Kipp sucked the orange, remembering what Zalika said on their last ride together. *I'll win the Women's Archery Competition at the Goba City Fair.* She planned to use the prize money to get away from her mother and father and start a new life on her own.

I'll go alone, she'd said.

Then I will meet you later, Zalika. He'd felt so bold saying that. Kipp read the words again, his heart racing. The fair was a month from now. Would Zalika be fully recovered by then? Would she be well enough to take the long carriage ride to Goba City, strong enough to compete? A plan began to form in his mind. He would find a way to get rid of the Gwali's sack before the fair, then he'd go to the competition. When she won the prize and was finally free to leave her father's house . . .

"Boy?"

His thoughts were broken by the vendor's call.

"You. Boy." The butcher shouted again, waving his thick arm. Kipp left the sign and headed for the man's stall. The stout butcher was balding on top, though he still had a thin braid and four braid-beads woven into the sparse hair that ringed the lower half of his head. His apron was smeared with blood. Behind him a tall woman plucked a dead hen. Feathers fell at her feet. Some caught the wet wind and swirled through the crowd.

Kipp removed a small hunk of white feathers from ChChka's mane and chewed the rest of his orange hungrily, waiting to learn why the butcher had called him over.

"Your father's servant is looking for you."

Kipp swallowed the orange chunk, nearly choked, then coughed and said, "My . . . father?"

"He came here yesterday to tell you you can come home. Your father is not angry with you for taking his best horse." He cut over the chicken thighs and chopped off the wings.

Kipp's head spun. He pressed the bit of peel between finger and thumb. "I think you are looking for someone else, Sor." Even as he said this, his mind was racing down two roads. One led to the Gwali. The Death Catcher had come here looking for him. The other road led to Sor Tunassi. The angry landlord wanted to see Kipp punished and had sent a hired hand, probably Sag Eye, out to scavenge the country-side for him. The Gwali. Sag Eye. It could be either one.

The rain rolled off Kipp's hat and coat. ChChka stomped her hoof and nosed his back as the butcher continued.

"You are the right boy. Your father's servant described you right down to that scar on your neck. And he said the missing horse had a dark mark on her neck no bigger than your hand."

He wiped the cleaver with his apron as he eyed ChChka. "She is fine. I can see why you were tempted to steal her."

Kipp wanted to turn and leave but he stepped a little closer just as the cloth awning dipped under the weight of the rain and sent a waterfall between them in a thin clear sheet.

The Gwali was riding Cassia when he last saw him. If the butcher had seen his old red roan, Kipp would know the rider. He spoke to the man behind the waterfall. "What did this man's horse look like?"

"Which one? He bought a new horse here in the market before he left."

Sag Eye might have decided to change horses. Kipp bit his lip. It was said only people with Naqui powers or those about to die could see the Gwali unless the Gwali wanted to be seen. But Kipp had discovered it was Kwaja who gave the power of flight. And he was also sure it was Kwaja who made you invisible when you flew. Could it be the same for the Gwali? Was it Kwaja's power that made the Gwali and his hounds invisible? If so, they were out in the open now.

Ask again. Make sure. Kipp's heart beat so loudly in his ears he found it hard to think. "This man. What did he look like?"

The butcher had gone back to chopping up the chicken. "A tall man. Not much meat on him. I was working when he came and did not look up until he offered . . ." The butcher paused less than a second. Long enough for Kipp to gather the "servant" had offered him money.

A small stream of dirty water ran past his boots, caught a bit of his dropped orange peel, and sped it, boatlike, along the cobbles toward the cloth merchant's stall.

"I have delivered the message now," the butcher said behind the streaming water. "Now I have a message for your father. The servant he sent caused trouble. I lost some of my best soup bones when he came. Tell your father the next time you run away, he should not send a servant after you with so many detching dogs!"

167

CHAPTER TWENTY-TWO

KIPP FLED THE marketplace riding to the out-skirts of town. *It's not me the Gwali's after,* he reminded himself. *It's the detching sack! I have to get rid of the thing.* They passed a garbage dump where the bony people he'd seen begging in the marketplace were digging through the trash—*sigurun, very sick. They should all be dead by now.*

"Come on, ChChka." A longhaired black-and-white dog abandoned the fly-infested hill and ran to the muddy road.

"Get away!" Kipp shouted, waving at him. "Go on. Get!"

The dog with a white patch around one eye was still padding along behind them when ChChka overtook a rickety wagon. Kipp steered ChChka off the road and was about to pass by when he caught sight of the red roan hitched to the front and took a startled breath.

Cassia, beautiful old Cass pulled the wagon. Kipp peered at the driver. The bone thrower sat on the driver's bench, his sandaled feet exposed to the rain.

"Sor?" Kipp said through the rain. "Where did you get that horse?"

The old man turned stiffly. "I bought her in Namibo yesterday. I was told a tall man with many dogs traded her in for a stronger horse." The bone thrower held the reins loosely in his knuckle-swollen hands. "This good horse is strong enough for me, I think," he added.

Kipp couldn't speak for a moment. Cassia, his sweet Cassia, was pulling a bone thrower's wagon.

"I . . . know that horse," he said in a thick voice. "She used to be mine."

The bouncing wagon made the bone thrower's braid sway, the coiled ball at the end pounding the old man's thigh. "A horse can have many masters in his life, but a man should not let himself be mastered by anyone."

His keen eyes were on him. Kipp shivered in his soaking coat. The old man was trying to impress Kipp with his bone thrower's talk, maybe trying to drum up a little business. Kipp was only interested in Cassia. He wished he could take her with him, but he didn't have the coin to buy her even if the price was low, and he couldn't leave the thrower without a horse to pull his wagon.

ChChka rode close enough for Kipp to run his hand along Cassia's red mane. "You will take care of her, Sor?"

"She is my only horse," the thrower said with pride. "What else can I do?"

They rode side by side in silence awhile.

"What did you call this mare?"

"Cassia."

"It is a good name for her," the old man said.

Kipp rode ahead till horse and wagon were out of sight. He had to leave the animal he loved behind. But the one he didn't want, the filthy dog, couldn't be gotten rid of. The stray followed them out of town, into the brush, and trailed them relentlessly day after day all the way to the foothills of the Botswi Mountains.

Late one cloudy afternoon at the base of the jagged peaks, Kipp knelt between two acacia trees, drove a sharp stick into the ground and loosened a clod of earth. A man buries his dead.

Kipp would bury death.

In this hole.

In this hollow.

In this secret place known only to himself.

The week of rain had softened the ground enough to dig. ChChka nibbled grass by the tree roots.

"I'm doing this for us, ChChka."

She turned her head, pressed back her ears, and looked away.

"I couldn't burn it or shred it. I cannot keep it anymore."

She flicked her tail at the flies. The stray dog lifted his

leg and relieved himself on a trunk. He'd kept to the shade since they arrived.

"I could use some help," said Kipp.

The dog panted and licked his snout. If the mutt had a master back in Namibo, the man had let his animal go to bone. On their first night out the dog had crept in closer to beg for food. His long black-and-white fur was tangled but the white patch around his left eye gave him a slightly comic look, and Kipp couldn't turn him down.

That night, the mutt inhaled his meat so fast, Kipp snorted a laugh. "I name you Epopo," he'd said, "who was a prince among dogs." And he'd given him a little more meat as he told him one of Sor Joay's favorite stories.

One day Prince Epopo was so hungry, he hunted many miles from his territory. He left his land unguarded and had to fight to win it back. This prince among dogs nearly lost his kingdom for a meal.

"Come here, Epopo." The dog trotted over. "Watch me." Kipp demonstrated with his hands. Epopo got the idea and helped him dig. His paws churned. Dirt flew between his hind legs.

"That's it." Kipp removed hunks of dirt with his hands, loosened more with his sharp stick, and dug deeper. This had to work. More than four weeks had passed by since Kipp had stolen the sack. He was too worn down to keep fighting its relentless pull. There was another reason to abandon Kwaja. Back in Namibo, he'd discovered the Gwali had picked up his trail. Kipp was sure the Death Catcher and his hounds would continue to hunt him down till he had what he wanted. It was only a matter of time.

The shade from the wide branches cooled his back as he dug beside Epopo.

"Zalika will be well by now," he said to ChChka. The horse turned her head, chewing grass rhythmically. "I've done what I set out to do," he added.

He was talking to ChChka, to Epopo, to himself, keeping his mind off the moment when he would remove his shirt and untie the sack.

"I've done more than that when you think about it." He paused to grunt as he dislodged a particularly stubborn rock and put it on the dirt pile. Epopo sniffed it curiously, then gave it a lick, his pink tongue darkening the white stone.

"If this sack goes missing once and for all, no one will ever have to die." Kipp stood up and shook himself. No. That wasn't really true. He settled on the small boulder between the trees to rest a moment. Epopo stopped digging and curled up in the shade at his feet. Other lands had Death Catchers. His father used to tell stories about the Shonheen. And he vaguely remembered tales about a Catcher who sailed a shadow ship and caught drowned people in his net—the Doolemun or the Doolegon or something? Kipp couldn't recall his name. Papa stopped telling those stories after Kipp began to have nightmares.

Elbows on knees, he gazed at his dirty hands and ran his finger along the scars from the witch's potion bottle. *Of course there is more than one Death Catcher,* he reasoned. *People die every day. There must be many Catchers in the world who gather souls.*

A small yellow bird landed in the branches calling, *Kwiksu, kwiksu.*

Kipp stood again. He'd fought only one Death Catcher, stolen only one sack to save Zalika, still he'd saved more than her. Other Zolyans had escaped death since he took Kwaja. There was the girl in the Escuyan village, and many others he had not gotten close enough to see because he'd leaped down from the saddle to keep Kwaja away.

How many Zolyans were alive now because of him? He'd not counted the number of times he'd fought the sack, but the pull was strong at least once a day. It was one reason he'd kept clear of towns or villages as much as possible, never knowing when Kwaja would stir.

Kipp pulled the water pouch from the saddlebag and took a gulp. If the sack were buried here in this secret place, the Gwali could never find it, never return for Zalika, or capture Jilly's soul, and that was all that really mattered, wasn't it?

He covered the dark spot on ChChka's warm neck with his hand. "It has to be enough, ChChka."

He crouched and pulled small rocks and earth out from between the tangled roots and added them to his pile. When the hole was deep enough, Kipp stood to take a breath and gather courage.

His hands shook as he removed his shirt and carefully untied the sack that had been bound to his chest for a month. It had joined to his skin with the wearing and the sweat. He hated how it clung to him. Ripping it off, he jammed the thing deep in the ground, held it firmly down with one hand, and shoved dirt and small rocks atop it with the other. Kwaja did not fight. It lay still as a dead animal, the woven cloth soft and warm in his fist.

Epopo shivered, tail between his legs. When the dirt was up to Kipp's elbow, he let go of the sack, and used both hands to heap rocks and soil on top. He hopped on the dirt mound, stomping hard with his boots till it was completely flat. It felt good to have buried the evil thing.

Stepping back, he brushed off his hands and went for another drink of water. He was taking the tin pan from the saddlebag to water his animals when he heard a sound behind him and turned to see Epopo digging up the hole.

"Get away, you stupid mutt!" Kipp threw the pan at him with a clatter. Epopo yelped and sped behind a tree. Kipp inspected the spot. He'd only dug a few inches down. Still . . .

He replaced the dirt, stomped the earth, and stepped back, panting from exertion. Then, climbing the nearest tree, he broke off the straightest branch he could find and dropped it to the ground. ChChka shook her mane irritably as the branch landed too near her right hoof.

"It's all right, ChChka. We're almost done." He was beginning to feel elated. He could already breathe more freely with the thing off his chest.

Wedging the branch under the boulder he'd been sitting on, he used it like a pry bar and pushed the high end down. The heavy stone rolled a few inches. The animals watched as he shoved the branch under and rolled the heavy stone again and again until it sat atop the grave.

"Try and get at it now, Epopo."

Epopo sniffed around the bolder, tail wagging. Kipp swept the ground with the leafy end of the branch, erasing his boot prints and Epopo's paw marks along the dirt until he reached the edge of the greener grass where ChChka waited.

They left a moment later and rode toward the mountain peak. Rain clouds were gathering above. It would be good to find a cave or some overhanging rock to shelter under for the night. He chose one of two trailheads at random and started up.

Thick forest skirted the base of the mountain, but there were a few places on the switchbacks where he could still view the valley below and the two acacia trees standing apart from the rest. Even though he never wanted to see the wretched sack again, he felt a need to know exactly where it was.

The sun was setting. Thirty or so miles from the valley and past the rolling hills, Kipp could see a few lone farms. There were no other townships out this way and would be none until he crossed the mountains.

Kipp breathed in the heady mountain air. He felt light and free. He lifted one palm to cup the red-gold light, the last of the day in his hand.

CHAPTER TWENTY-THREE

O N THE ROCKY switchback Kipp heard the distant howling. Hair rose on the back of his neck as
he peered over the treetops below. Far across the valley, a
rider with seven hounds moved down a tawny hill. Kipp
leaped from the saddle and led ChChka and Epopo behind
a nearby boulder to spy on his enemy from above.

The Gwali had reached the base of the hill. The Death
Catcher could have gone any number of ways along the
valley floor, but the dogs must have picked up Kipp's trail.

He leaned his forehead against the boulder. *Deysoukus!*
They were heading right for the two acacia trees! He
never should have abandoned Kwaja! He couldn't let them
get the sack. He had to get there first. Back in the saddle,
Kipp turned ChChka to ride back down the mountain.
She shook her mane and obeyed, but the switchbacks

were too steep and rocky for a good gallop.

Epopo scrambled down the path ahead of them.

"Go on, Epopo! Get down to the valley!" Kipp waved his arm, pointed to the dogs racing for Kwaja, and shouted like a madman. He was sure Epopo didn't understand, but the dog sped up at his command and bolted down the trail.

Kipp's heart sped. He was a detching idiot for burying the sack. He should have known the hounds would sniff Kwaja out and undo what he had done. He flicked the reins desperately. ChChka needed to fly, now! But she couldn't fly without Kwaja's magic.

Reaching the bottom at last, ChChka sped to a gallop. The twilight sky was pale green. Fresh evening wind whooshed through the grass as they bounded for the small stand of acacias. Less than a quarter mile away, he spotted the Gwali riding behind four black dogs. The other three hounds had already reached the acacias. One circled the twin trees; two more hurriedly dug beside the boulder. Where was Epopo?

Kipp looked about for his dog, and saw him rushing through the undulating grass. "Go, Epopo!"

His gut wrenched as he saw one of the black dogs by the tree whose head and shoulders had just disappeared into the hole. A moment later the dog pulled out something black.

"Deysoukus!"

ChChka tore across the land, her hooves digging up chunks of dirt and grass. Up ahead, Epopo leaped on the hound with Kwaja in his jaws.

The hounds tangled into tumbling knots; snarling, barking, yelping, they broke apart, ran, pounced again. Epopo had a corner of the sack clamped between his teeth. His paws dug grooves in the earth as he was pulled helplessly along by his foe. Forepaws on his shoulders, another hound went for Epopo's neck.

"Get off him!" Kipp jumped down and hurled a stone at the hound. It yelped and rolled away. Epopo still had a hold of the sack. Kipp swung his arm back and threw another stone at the dog pulling Kwaja's other end. The stone missed its mark but it was enough for Epopo to get the better of him and he dragged his foe the other way now.

ChChka pranced fearfully on the edge of the scene as the growling dogs circled Epopo and their brother; the bristling black hair on their shoulders standing out like lions' manes.

Epopo lost his hold on Kwaja. The victor raced off with the sack flailing from his jaws. The other two followed.

"Get it back, Epopo!" Mounting ChChka, Kipp tore after the others, speeding through the tall grass.

The sound of pounding hooves grew louder from behind as the Gwali and the rest of his hounds joined the chase. Neck and neck with his opponent, Epopo snapped at the corner of the rippling sack, tore it away from the lead dog, and veered to the right. ChChka hurtled for him. Bouncing wildly in the saddle, Kipp leaned down and just managed to grab the flailing end of the sack. He yanked with all his might to pull both Kwaja and Epopo up into the saddle.

One arm on the reins, he wrapped the other about the faithful dog, who had the sack safely in his jaws.

They rode uphill and down, barking hounds at their heels, and farther back, the Gwali closing in on his stallion. Kipp was wedging the sack safely under his thigh when the saddle stopped its violent jolting and Kwaja's power lifted them all into the air.

Epopo hid his head under Kipp's arm as horse, dog, and master ascended with their prize into the dark blue air, leaving the Gwali and the frenzied shadow pack far below.

Kipp kissed his mutt's furry head. "Epopo! You are a prince among dogs!"

CHAPTER TWENTY-FOUR

WOMEN'S ARCHERY Competition. The words rang in Kipp's ears as he stripped down and waded into the small stream, naked except for Kwaja strapped firmly to his chest. He'd hidden deep in the central Farlands, camping many weeks in the sandstone caves in Kiyu Canyon with only ChChka and Epopo for company. In the canyon, he'd battled Kwaja every day, refusing to mount ChChka and fly to the dying. The struggle sometimes lasted hours when Kwaja's pull was strong.

It was risky, even dangerous, to ride to Goba City knowing the sack might awaken at the crowded fair, that the Gwali or Sag Eye might catch him out in the open, but he could not keep away.

Scraping a layer of encrusted dirt from his arms, he dunked his head in the chill water. The day had come when he might see Zalika again. He would be clean when he did. He would have food in his belly and money in his pocket, his hair tied with a leather strap. This was his plan, though when he left the stream, his wet hair was only just long enough to tie back, his stomach growled, and he was penniless.

Was Zalika here? Would she even come? Kipp led ChChka and Epopo across the crowded fairground, his eyes darting left and right. He refused to tie his mare to one of the many hitching posts where some detching thief might steal her.

Crowds moved in small groups on the sprawling fairground just outside the city. The Goba fair was three times larger than the one in Napulo, with a racetrack set off to the right, hundreds of colorful craft displays and food booths in the middle, and a tournament field far to the left. Kipp avoided the area surrounding the racetrack in case Sor Tunassi was here.

The smoky air was rich with spices. Kipp's mouth watered. *First the money, then the food,* he thought. He had a fittarr snakeskin to sell to a cloth merchant, and the snake's impressive skeleton to sell to a bone thrower if he could find one.

At a game booth children threw pebbles at a target to win a cheewii jar. Spotting the cloth merchant, he sold the fittarr skin, then bought a bowl of spikka and stuffed himself until his mouth burned from the spices. "For you, Epopo," he said, dropping a few choice bits of meat. Epopo inhaled them in seconds.

"You have bad table manners, my prince," Kipp said. Epopo wagged his tail.

Near the ladies' card tent, Kipp spent two dimis on fruit and ate four plums in rapid succession. He could never eat a plum without thinking of Jilly at age three dunking her little hand into Mother's jam jar. When he'd left Jilly sleeping in the orphans' tent, her breath had sounded clear, not congested. Sa Minn's ointment had healed her cough. He hoped the elder was still watching over his sister.

The scent of roasted kora filled the air. The best part of the kora crop was already bound in burlap bags and stacked aboard merchant ships that were heading off to wealthy markets around the world.

"Our kora will outsell coffee in a few years, Kipp," his father used to say. "Then we'll be as rich as kings."

Kipp felt the spot on his shoulder where his father used to pound him while saying that. After a few happy thumps he'd give his openmouthed smile, showing all of his teeth down to his worn molars. His father hadn't lived long enough to see how high the prices had risen this year. A raw taste filled the back of Kipp's throat, as if he'd just swallowed smoke. He quickly pressed down the thoughts about his father.

Far-off skree pipes and drums played, where people gathered around the ritual dancers. The Women's Archery Competition would start in just over an hour. There was still time to sell the fittarr bones for the coins he needed. A sigh from a small crowd ahead drew him to the edge of the circle.

"Sit, Epopo." The dog obeyed, his wagging tail sending up puffs of fine dust.

The bone thrower was on his rug beneath a eucalyptus tree. His white shirt, trousers, and turban were covered in the fine red dust blowing across the fairgrounds. Bone throwers drove their wagons from town to town; still, Kipp was surprised to see this was the same thrower he'd passed in Namibo. Where was Cassia? He peered beyond the eucalyptus and caught sight of the thrower's wagon. Cassia stood nearby, swishing her tail at the flies. The old man had kept his word. Kipp was relieved to see her looking so well.

The tip of the bone thrower's braided beard touched the rug as he leaned forward, gently sweeping the animal bones into a single pile. Kipp had just missed a bone reading. The girl on the rug pulled a half-copper from her waist pouch, smiled, and dropped it into the brass bowl with a clink. As she turned to go, her bright pink headscarf blew back, revealing her short dark hair and delicate heart-shaped face.

Her green kirifa dress and patterned belt looked Escuyan. Kipp frowned to himself. He had seen her somewhere before, but where? She left the thrower, talking happily to an older girl, her laughter as light as her tinkling bracelets. The bone thrower must have tossed her a very good fortune.

Kipp nodded to the thrower, who began to stir the bones. He tied ChChka to the tree behind the thrower, where he could watch her closely. He paused a moment to run his hand along Cassia's neck before turning back to take the bedroll from ChChka's saddle. Holding the blanket, gingerly he stepped up to the bone thrower's rug.

"What do you have?" asked the thrower.

"Bones to sell," Kipp said quietly.

The thrower waved his hand at a new group of onlookers who had gathered around his rug. "Leave me now," he said. "This will be a private reading."

Kipp turned to watch them go and shuddered. Sigurun, all of them; one of the walking skeletons gazed back with empty eyes as he stepped through the red dust.

"What did they want?" Kipp asked.

"The same thing I want," said the bone thrower. "Peace. An end to their suffering."

Kipp checked his pant leg. Kwaja was not moving. Not yet. He placed the bedroll on the bone thrower's bright rug and carefully began unfolding it. He hadn't come here for a reading, but he was glad to see the small crowd disperse. Untying the leaf bundle, he gently laid out the fittarr bones. The thrower sighed as he uncoiled the skeleton. It was perfectly intact and at least nine feet long, an amazing specimen.

The old man turned the braid-stone in his beard thoughtfully. Kipp knew this snake was a rare find. He'd been lucky enough to kill it before it killed him. Fittarrs were large and poisonous enough to bring down a lion. The thrower gently fingered the triangular skull that was bigger than a man's fist, with long, curved fangs. His leathery fingers were as dark as roasted kora, and the knuckles were very swollen. Some of the elderly field-workers had large joints and bent backs like this man. His father had hired some, expecting little work from them; he'd offered short days, rest, food. Papa had been a big-hearted man. It was one of the reasons he hadn't prospered here in Zolya.

The thrower looked up. "I will pay nine dimis for this."

"Five coppers."

The man's brows went up and he tugged his ear. His earlobes were large and round, a mark of beauty on a girl, but not good for a man. "A copper and two dimis," he countered.

"Four coppers and two dimis."

"That is a great deal of money."

"I know what fittarr bones are worth," said Kipp.

"Four coppers and I will throw in your fortune."

"I did not come to hear my fortune."

"But you want to hear it," argued the old man.

The girl's half-copper glinted brightly in the dish. "You will not be able to make me smile as much as the girl who was just here."

The old man said, "Her older sister was in the way of her pledge. I told her not to worry. She will marry soon."

Kipp knew a younger sister could not be pledged to a man if her older sister remained unmarried. "How did you know her older sister would marry, Sor, and not stand in the way of the girl's happiness?"

"The older sister will not marry. She will die."

Kipp felt a slight rustling movement on his chest. He put

his hand against his rib cage, remembering now where he had seen that face. The girl had been one of the dancing women in the village. She was the one who'd brought him food and goat's milk. Her older sister was the girl who had lain dying in the isolated hut. He'd seen the resemblance between the two at the time and thought they might be sisters. How could this thrower say she was going to die? What gave him that kind of certainty? Kipp had beaten Kwaja down with the help of the healer. He'd prevented her death.

He was suddenly thirsty. "Did you tell the girl her sister would die?"

"I did not tell her that, only that she would marry soon."

"How do you know her sister will die?"

The thrower swept his open hand over the neat pile. "The bones told me this."

"What do you expect the bones to say?" Kipp argued hotly. "Bones know nothing but death!"

The thrower's eyes narrowed. "My bones give a true reading."

"They were wrong this time."

"If you do not believe my bones, why bring me the fittarr?"

"I need money."

"And that is all?" He wiggled his finger at Kipp. "I say you want a reading and are too afraid to ask for it."

"I am not afraid of bones!" Kipp shivered, remembering

his long-ago dream of sweeping human bones into a sack. The old man chuckled.

"Pay me first, then throw your bones," Kipp demanded. "I dare you to read my fortune." He felt the power rising up his spine. If this old man only knew what he wore beneath his shirt. This thrower had never met a man strong enough to steal the Gwali's sack. Let him try to read *his* future.

"First the fortune. Then I will pay you for the fittarr. It will only take a few minutes," said the thrower.

Kipp carefully moved the skeleton closer to his place on the rug, out of the thrower's reach. He would not let him touch it again before the money changed hands. The field beyond the fence to the right was vacant. People had not yet begun to gather for the archery competition. Before it started, he'd need to find a good spot beneath the trees to view it without being seen.

"All right," he agreed, "but hurry. I have somewhere I must go."

Epopo crept closer and tried to put his head in Kipp's lap. Kipp shooed him away. The red-patterned carpet was half in the sunlight now. The old man began to stir the bones. Some had black slits across one side, letters or numbers in some script Kipp didn't recognize. The smaller bones were from birds, lizards, and other Farland animals. Throwers did not use human bones. The old man finished stirring and gave half the pile to Kipp.

"Choose three to toss," he said.

Resting his chin on his hand, Kipp fingered through his pile, took two tiny bones and one with black marks, and placed them in the middle.

The thrower closed his eyes, scooped up some of his share, and threw them on top of Kipp's. Five bones landed *clitter-clatter*. He held up three fingers.

"Three more?" Kipp asked. He wanted to get the reading over with. Zalika could be here even now, preparing for the competition. He tossed in the first three bones his fingers touched.

The thrower raised his brows, then repeated his toss. He held his open hands facedown over the throw, like a man warming himself by a fire.

"Hessua Sa Omaja la." He rocked as he sang. His chant to Omaja, the Daughter of Time, trailed away as he studied the bones, pointing here and there as if he were simply counting them.

It is all an act, Kipp thought.

"You are a man of good fortune," began the thrower. "You love your family very much."

These were uncomfortable words. This man could not possibly know anything about what happened to his family.

"Especially your sister."

"Which sister?" Kipp could not hide the irritation in his voice.

"Your younger sister. The only sibling you have left."

"What do you mean by that?" Kipp had to sit on his

hands to hide the uncontrollable trembling. What did he know about Jilly?

The thrower tipped his head and pointed to a small bone at the top of the pile. "Everyone who is born will die. You must understand this. A man cannot fight Omaja, the Daughter of Time."

"Shut up!" Kipp lurched forward, scattering the bone pile, then jumped up and ran for ChChka.

"I did not pay you for the fittarr bones," called the thrower.

Kipp hurried away. Let the lying bone thrower have the detching snake bones! The man was evil. How dare he talk about his family, about his little sister, Jilly?

Epopo ran up and gave him a pitiful look.

"What are you staring at?"

The sudden angry shout sent the dog scurrying with his tail between his legs.

CHAPTER TWENTY-FIVE

PEOPLE WERE beginning to gather at the tournament field. Shading his eyes, Kipp scanned a line of trees to the left of the field, looking for a safe place to tether ChChka. He planned to scale one of those acacias and hide in the branches above to watch the archery competition.

"One hundred coppers for your horse."

Kipp turned and took in the portly man standing a few feet away from him. The short man was fastidiously dressed in a loose silk shirt and pants. His long, oiled braid was studded with glass beads. Too many men from cities and townships had started to buy and wear braid-beads as ornamentation. They were not placed in the hair to signify valorous deeds as the Escuyan tradition demanded. A man like that did not even deserve to have a braid.

"My horse is not for sale," Kipp said. He'd left the

thrower without any dimis, but he'd never sell ChChka.

"Come on, girl." Kipp tugged the reins with his sweaty hand. He was too exposed on this side of the tournament field. If Sor Tunassi were here to watch Zalika shoot, or if one of his hired hands like Sag Eye was somewhere in this swelling crowd, he needed to take cover fast.

The fat man stepped directly into Kipp's path and pointed to the proud-looking man sitting on a cane lawn chair. A small boy was cooling him with a peacock-feathered fan.

"My master will offer you a good price for your horse. He lives in the largest mansion in Napulo."

"The mansion on the hill above the market?" Kipp stopped himself from saying anything more. So this was Sor Litchen, whose great house crowned the hill above Napulo—the man who'd won Zalika gambling, who'd viciously cut her leg when she would not become his mistress. Kipp felt an intense wave of anger rising up his spine. Had the wealthy bastard come here to watch Zalika? Had he followed her here?

The servant looked pleased. "You know of him, I see. Shall I tell him you accept his offer for the horse?"

"I do not accept his offer." Epopo was sniffing the servant's hand. Kipp called his dog and tried to step around the man.

"Wait." The servant caught hold of Kipp's sleeve.

Kipp shook him off. "I don't have time to wait."

Kipp continued walking as the man scurried back to his master. He'd like to march over and give Sor Litchen a few fresh slices of fist pie. Three or four big slices should flatten the detcher.

The servant returned. "My master will give you a hundred and sixty coppers. This is very generous. It is his final offer."

"You can tell your master to go to hell!"

Kipp hurried off with ChChka. He would have liked to stay and see the look on Sor Litchen's face when the servant delivered his reply, but the drum roll on the field announced the beginning of the tournament.

Half an hour later, Kipp peered through leaves as the last mid-rank competitor took her final shot. Zalika hadn't appeared yet. His pulse raced and his ears rang with anticipation. *Be here. You have to be here.*

He finished the last plum he'd bought earlier at the fruit stand, flipped the pit in his mouth, and leaned against the trunk. ChChka nibbled the grass below; Epopo rested by the roots nearby. He was lucky to have grabbed this spot so close to the field. The family making use of the shade below did not have the view he had up here in the branches. Best of all, he was well hidden from the crowd.

Kipp held his breath and parted the leaves as the top-rank shooters entered the field with their bows. He quickly scanned the blowing headscarves that protected the girls from the afternoon sun, stopping at the bright yellow scarf at the end of the line. Zalika? Yes, it was she.

He leaned out farther, nearly fell out of the tree, righted himself, and looked again. He wanted to be closer, to touch her cheek, catch the scent from her skin. He wrapped his fingers around the branch.

Zalika looked strong and healthy as she twanged her bow and laughed with the girl on her left. He couldn't hear the laugh through the noisy crowd, but he could remember the sound, a deep rich laugh that was surprising for such a slender girl.

One of the top-rank competitors was taller than Zalika, but she was not as poised, and she did not walk as gracefully as Zalika when they were told to break into two lines.

Zalika was golden sunlight that is warm but does not burn. She was the most beautiful girl in the competition, at the fair, in all of Zolya, and he had saved her from the Gwali's sack.

Kipp quickly searched the audience for Sor Tunassi. If he was at the fair, wouldn't he leave the racetrack long enough to watch his daughter compete? Scanning the section filled with comfortable seats, he spotted Sor Litchen under one of the orange parasols. Kipp had found a good tree to watch the competition, but it was a little too close to Sor Litchen's seat. He hadn't liked the man's offer to buy ChChka. He didn't like the way Sor Litchen was pointing at Zalika now as he bantered with the man on his left. Kipp bit down on his plum pit so hard his jaw ached.

"Ladies, ready your bows," the announcer shouted through his bullhorn. Zalika's target was on the right—closest to Kipp's tree, closer still to Sor Litchen's seat on the far right of the field.

The archers narrowed down to six, then four, then two.

One was Zalika. Her squarely built opponent had taken the higher score in the previous round and was still in the lead. The girl tied down her green scarf, and stepped up to the line to take her last three shots in the final round.

The crowd hushed as she hit the inner red circle not once but twice, for sixteen points. The girl's final shot made the center gold, keeping her firmly in the lead.

Kipp's hands began to sweat as Zalika stepped up to the line. A soft hot wind blew across the crowd, stirring the red dust underfoot. Zalika had six shots to go. She drew her bowstring and released the arrow, hitting the center gold. Ten points. That was more like it.

A dog barked as she took her fifth shot. It was the high-pitched sound of a smaller dog; still Kipp scanned the crowd. *Not one of the Gwali's hounds. He wouldn't dare venture into such a mob, would he?* The arrow had struck the blue. Zalika frowned and shielded her eyes, looking for the disruptive little animal.

"Unfair," a man said from down below, "she should be allowed to take the shot again."

The yapping continued. Sor Litchen stood and stepped out from under his parasol. "Silence that detching mutt!"

Kipp heard yelps, someone kicking the mutt, no doubt. Sor Litchen laughed and spoke to the man in the next chair. "It doesn't matter. The slut won't win."

The dog's sudden silence exposed the cutting words to everyone within earshot. Kipp nearly choked on his plum pit. He coughed, spat it out, and glanced across the field.

He could see by look on Zalika's face she'd heard it, too. The word *slut* seemed to hang over her head in the heated air. A low murmur followed as heads turned, people whispered to one another behind their hands.

Across the field the men and women in the judges' box held a quick conference. After a few minutes, they ruled that the abrupt disturbance from the stray dog had come after the arrow had been released. Zalika would not get the chance to repeat the fifth shot. One arrow left.

Zalika looked uneasy as she faced the target. Seemingly still shaken by Sor Litchen's remark, her fingers slipped as she tried to place the notch at the base of her last arrow on the bowstring.

Sor Litchen was still on his feet, watching Zalika from his place just beyond the fence.

"Don't think about him," Kipp whispered. "Don't let the bastard make you lose."

The crowd went silent again. Kipp noticed Zalika adjusting her stance to favor the leg Sor Litchen had sliced with his knife. Was she overtired now? People wriggled impatiently as Zalika discarded one arrow for another and readied her bow. There was a sureness in the way she drew the bowstring back. His heart swelled. She was in control again.

High in the branches, Kipp nervously flipped the plum pit over and over in his mouth. He would get rid of the Gwali's sack somehow, rescue Jilly, and follow Zalika after she won the prize and had enough money of her own to run away.

The stray dog escaped his master's hold and barked as she let fly. Zalika's last arrow sped past the target, hitting a man in the crowd. Kipp heard a panicked cry from below as Sor Litchen toppled over backward, breaking the chair with his fall. He gripped the branch, couldn't believe what he was seeing.

Shouts of horror and disbelief swept through the crowd.

"He's dead!" someone cried. "She killed him!"

Kipp leaped down and rushed into the throng. *She shot him. Zalika shot him. This can't be happening.* Somewhere ahead a man shouted, "Out of the way! Get out of the way, I tell you!" Others yelled, "Somebody get a doctor!"

The mass swarmed around Sor Litchen. Kipp tried to push his way toward the fence. "Zalika!" He made it only a few yards from the tree before he was sucked into the frenzied mob. On the field, Zalika had dropped her bow.

Kipp put his hands to his mouth and called again. "Zalika!" He tried to fight his way out of the pressing, shouting horde.

Zalika stood as if in a trance, hands hanging at her sides. Encircled by the roaring crowd, she was the only one standing still. The judges marched across the field toward her. Why didn't she move?

Kipp tried desperately to push his way through. The mob lurched forward, knocking him down.

"Zalika!" Even as he screamed her name, he recognized too late the force that was dragging him relentlessly toward Sor Litchen's body. It wasn't just the uproarious crowd. The black thing under his shirt was moving.

CHAPTER TWENTY-SIX

S TAND BACK!" a man bellowed into his bullhorn. "Let the doctor by!"

Kipp tried to pull away as he was swept to the front of the shouting, swirling mob. On the ground, Sor Litchen was sprawled on his back across the chair he'd broken in his fall. Had Zalika meant to shoot him or had the sudden barking from the unruly little dog thrown off her shot?

The pink-feathered arrow was lodged in Sor Litchen's chest, near his heart. How near, Kipp couldn't tell. He reared back against Kwaja's mighty pull, to drive himself deeper into the crowd. He needed the throng to suck him in again, to engulf him and drag him away.

Kipp groaned and dug in his heels. His arms swam in the air. He was desperate to get his hands on something stable to hold him down. The ropes under his shirt strained, dragging him closer to Sor Litchen. It was like trying to push down a great stone wall, only the wall was bound to his body.

After another mighty heave, Kipp crumpled to the ground and rolled onto his back. He drove his fingers into the dirt and tried to hold on as he was pulled toward the man's sprawled body, where a physician now knelt.

The crowd shouted directions and encouragements at the physician. People circled the scene like a moving curtain around a play. Only this was real, the arrow was real, the blood at the base of the arrow shaft, and . . . could anyone else see what Kipp was seeing now, a dim pearl-colored glow no larger than a man's hand, rising out of Sor Litchen's chest? It glittered in the sunlight, floating straight for Kipp.

The top of the sack began to wriggle out from under the tight rope beneath his shirt. Kipp's fingers were raw from scratching the dry earth as he was pulled along. He tried to get a firm enough hold to roll over onto his stomach and crush the sack.

Sor Litchen's soul was drifting closer. Kipp groaned. Half of him wanted Kwaja to win this time, wanted Sor Litchen dead for what he'd done to Zalika, but he'd stolen the sack to put an end to death. If he let the man's soul in, Zalika would be accused of murder and would end up hanging from a noose or serving a life sentence in OnnZurr.

The soul landed birdlike on his chest. Strange animal noises leaped from Kipp's mouth as he frantically tried to brush it away.

Someone shouted, "Look. The boy is having a fit."

"I can't go to him right now!" The doctor pressed a cloth against Sor Litchen's chest.

"He's dead," the man beside him said.

The doctor pushed him away. "Clear off and let me do my work!"

The loose soul was trying to burrow under Kipp's collar. "Get off me!" His fingers passed through the spirit as he tried to grab it and hurl it back toward Sor Litchen.

A spectator shouted, "Open the boy's shirt. Let him breathe!" A small turbaned man with long black whiskers started fumbling with Kipp's buttons.

"Stop it. The soul will get inside!" He could see the glistening thing flitting around the man's calloused hands as he undid the second button.

Kipp grasped the man's bony wrists, trying to wriggle away.

"The boy's faking it," a voice called from the crowd. "He's nothing but a detching horse thief!" Sag Eye thrust himself through the gaping mob, wrenched the bearded man away, and planted his boot on Kipp's chest.

"Well, well. I found you at last, dwiig worm!"

The heavy boot staked Kipp to the ground. It also shut Kwaja's mouth. Nothing but that kind of forceful step could have pinned the soul sack down. Kipp looked away from his captor's looming face, shuddering under the weight, a weight he sorely needed to stop Sor Litchen's soul from entering the sack. He was grateful for the pressure and terrified at his new predicament. He watched the spirit circle the big brown boot like a frantic butterfly, still trying to find its way into Kwaja.

Beneath his shirt the edges of the sack fluttered around the leather sole, but the very top—where the strings had fought to loosen themselves and open Kwaja's hungry mouth—was firmly shut.

Sor Litchen's spirit flitted left and right before it seemed to give up the quest. Kipp followed its flight back to the body and saw with relief the bright glittering shape vanish as Sor Litchen gasped a startled breath.

A man hovering near the doctor raised a shout. "He's alive!" He pounded the physician's back. "You saved him. You did it!"

It had all happened in a moment—the soul flitting back, the man's life returning. No one seemed to have noticed it but Kipp. Certainly not Sag Eye, whose crushing weight had made it all possible.

Sag Eye removed his boot and kicked Kipp's thigh. "Get up!"

Kipp sat up dizzily, slowly heaved himself to a stand, and tried to bolt. Sag Eye grabbed his upper arm.

"Not so fast, filthy little dwiig." He spun Kipp around and tied his hands behind his back. Kipp's sweat-stained hat was on the ground by his feet. His leather hair tie had come out, exposing his shameful braidless head to all the onlookers.

"I need my hat," Kipp said through gritted teeth.

Sag Eye kicked it deeper into the crowd as he looped the rest of his rope around Kipp's waist. "Fetch it if you want it," he said.

The turbaned man called, "Hey, what are you doing to that boy?" He was still rubbing his upper arm where Sag Eye had grabbed him to wrench him away from his prey.

"He's a horse thief," said Sag Eye. "You can see by his head he is an outcast."

Murmurs rose from the crowd as Sag Eye yanked Kipp's short hair so hard he wrenched his neck. "I've been hired to find this thief and bring him in to face charges."

Sag Eye led Kipp through the crowd on the end of his rope like an animal. Kipp kept his eyes to the front and held his head up. He was determined not to let Sag Eye win, still he felt himself blushing. A Zolyan complexion would have hidden it, but his own pale pinkish skin fully exposed his reddened cheeks.

Where was Zalika? Kipp craned his neck, trying to spot her through the sea of moving bodies. Dust stirred in small tides as people fanned out around him. He picked up small scraps of conversation.

"Did you hear a girl shot her arrow into the crowd and hit a bystander just above the heart?"

"I myself saw the dying man miraculously restored to life by the renowned physician."

"I saw the boy frothing at the mouth like a wild dog. He was screaming and having some kind of fit."

"His captor said the boy's a horse thief. There he is now."

Sag Eye dragged him past the kora stall, where two men were arguing. The shorter of the two was waving his arms. "I tell you, the girl had perfect aim. Didn't you see her score? It's clear she meant to kill the man."

The other diagreed, "It was an accident. The barking dog threw her off her aim at the last moment."

"Then why did the judges have the girl arrested?"

Arrested? Kipp slowed his pace to hear more but was forcefully yanked away. He noticed a slight swagger in Sag Eye's gait. Was he proud of himself for catching the "horse thief" for his employer? Or was he thinking of his detching reward?

"Get over here!" Sag Eye waved at a pale-skinned, pimple-faced boy about Kipp's age. The boy's red braid flew back as he hurried up to them. Clutching his side, he breathlessly reported, "That man over there said he saw the boy's horse tied to one of the acacia trees by the tournament field."

Sag Eye seemed pleased. "Show me."

Kipp's heart fell as he was dragged to the acacia tree. He never should have hitched ChChka up so close to the field. He scanned the ground behind her for Epopo, but the dog was gone. *Better for him,* Kipp thought. He already missed him.

At the hitching post on the edge of the fairgrounds, Pimple was ordered to untie a chestnut horse and a bay. A moment later Kipp was enraged to see Sag Eye jam his boot in the stirrup and swing his leg over ChChka.

Kipp cursed the detching hired hand under his breath, using every vile word he could think of. ChChka did her best to buck the unfamiliar rider off. She whinnied, slashed her tail across his thighs like a whip, and kicked up her back legs. Sag Eye clung to her like a leech.

ChChka was still stomping her feet and nodding her head in protest when Sag Eye ordered Pimple to help Kipp up onto the bay's saddle. Even with his wrists bound, Kipp managed to get a few backward kicks in on Pimple's shins as he mounted.

"Ow! Watch it, ya detcher!"

Pimple bent down to rub his shin. Sag Eye snorted with pleasure at the injury. The boy swiftly retaliated by yanking Kipp's rope so hard it cut across his middle. Kipp's yelp of pain brought a contented smile to Pimple's face. He knotted the rope to the bay's saddle horn before mounting the chestnut stallion.

From high in ChChka's saddle, Sag Eye pulled the bay's long tether and triumphantly led Kipp out of town.

CHAPTER TWENTY-SEVEN

W**HAT'S THE MATTER?"** asked Sag Eye. "Lizard steal your tongue?"

Kipp had drunk from the water pouch and opened his mouth for a few spoonfuls of cooked beans, but he had not spoken to Sag Eye or Pimple since the cook fire had been lit.

Sag Eye had kept him firmly tied, with his hands behind his back and the rope encircling his waist. The end was knotted to Sag Eye's belt. Pimple had been instructed to feed Kipp his dinner. He'd purposely missed Kipp's mouth so the sticky bean sauce would drip off Kipp's chin. A brown stain was forming on his pant leg. Hungry as he was, Kipp slammed his jaw shut. He'd had enough.

A few yards away, ChChka's white coat stood out in the dark. Sag Eye had chosen this camp spot for the two broad boulders that partially protected them against the night wind, and for the sapling to the left of the smaller boulder. Pimple tethered the horses to the little sanuu tree before making camp. Sag Eye had inspected them a few minutes later and decided the sanuu wasn't strong enough to hold a strong mare and two stallions, so he hobbled the horses' front forelegs.

By the sapling, ChChka's nostrils flared. She'd probably never been hobbled. Kipp's protest over the treatment had gotten him a clout on both ears. His right ear had quieted down during the meal. His left was still ringing.

"What do you think happened to Zalika?" Pimple asked.

His question earned him a clout. Sag Eye was generous when it came to punishment. He was willing to dish it out freely to anyone who needed it. "That's Mistress Zalika to you, pimple face!"

Kipp noted that Sag Eye had landed on the same nickname.

"Sor?" Pimple covered his red ear. His eyes watered, and he blinked to hold back tears. "Will the mistress be jailed, Sor?"

Sag Eye smiled, then took a bite and chewed. "Probably not for long. Master Tunassi will use his wealth to bail her out."

"But what if the injured man dies, Sor?"

Sag Eye shot a glance toward Kipp. "What do you think, dwiig worm? What happens if the man Zalika shot dies?"

Kipp stared at the fire. If Sor Litchen died, Zalika would

be taken to OnnZurr. No amount of money could bail her out.

Sag Eye scraped out the last of his dish. "The detcher's too stupid to know the answer."

Epopo crept up behind one of the boulders. The faithful dog had shadowed them all afternoon and evening, the same way he'd followed Kipp from town a month before, only this time Epopo seemed to understand the importance of keeping out of view.

Kipp would have noticed a stray dog skirting one field, moving tree to tree in another, but Sag Eye hadn't seemed to. And the boy only noticed things he was told to mind.

Pimple had undone his braid and was brushing his long red hair with his fingers. Sag Eye seemed to approve the obvious slight. Pimple had no braid-beads, but his hair fell two inches below his shoulder. *The same length mine would have been by now,* Kipp thought, *if the witch hadn't knifed it.*

Sag Eye took a deep breath and pounded on his chest.

"Is the heart pain back, Sor?" Pimple asked.

"Who said I have pain?" barked Sag Eye. He flinched, gripped his chest a moment, then pulled a pill from his coat pocket, and swallowed it with whiskey from his tin flask. The color had gone from his face. Kipp wondered what ailed him.

Sag Eye recapped the flask, slid it into his pocket, and jingled the small leather money bag hanging from his belt. How much bounty money would Sor Tunassi pay him for collecting Kipp? Would Pimple get any coppers? Adjusting his position in the dirt, Kipp watched the boy clean up after the meal. Pimple was likely caught in the same servile position Kipp had been in before he'd ridden off with the Gwali's sack. But the similarities ended there. The boy had no real pride. He'd proved that through his need to better himself by putting Kipp in his place. Flaunting his long hair had said it all. No matter how wretched Kipp felt, he would not have belittled another man like that.

Pimple was a good name for him, Kipp decided. He was full of pus. The boy took the bedrolls down from the saddles. He was laying his own out by the fire when Sag Eye thumped him on his shoulder. "Let the thief sleep there. You are first watch tonight."

Pimple's eyes narrowed. Kipp was getting the clear impression that Pimple hated Sag Eye as much as he did. Drawing out his knife, Pimple began to whittle by the fire. On top of the thin bedroll, Kipp lay uncomfortably on his side.

Scraping the sharp blade down a thin branch, Pimple peeled the bark as if peeling Kipp's skin from his bones. The boy was trying to scare him. It wasn't working, but he didn't give up. He went on whittling as Sag Eye drifted off to sleep by the fire. The rope around Kipp's wrists and waist was still tied to Sag Eye's belt. The man would feel a tug and be ready to knock down Kipp if he tried to get away.

Two left awake now. Kipp took note of the sharp point

at the end of Pimple's stick and asked, "Do you know the story of Tiatuu's Egg?"

"Never heard it." Pimple cut deeper into the wood.

Kipp was silent long enough for Pimple to grow uncomfortable. "Why did you ask that?" he finally blurted.

"The spear you're making made me think of it."

Pimple's brows went up a moment. "How does that part of the story go?"

Kipp looked into the fire and began. "It was light above and below. The dark of time had not yet come. There was no beginning and no end, only endlessness."

"What does this have to do with a spear?"

"I'm getting to that." Kipp decided to shorten the preamble. This boy did not know how to listen. "In the place of the One World, Ahyuu ruled over many created beings, and one of them was the beautiful Tiatuu. When Tiatuu and Izagun were married, Ahyuu sent a dragon bearing a special wedding gift. The dragon gave Tiatuu a sacred egg with a clear crystal shell and a golden orb inside, and Tiatuu treasured it above all her possessions.

"The dragon told Tiatuu the golden yolk in the crystal shell would always and forever glow for her, and she must never break it. Always and forever meant little to Tiatuu. The First Beings who dwelled in the One World did not know day or night, only Ahyuu's primordial light, for time had not yet begun.

"Now Tiatuu loved the beautiful golden yolk of the egg

on which a tiny emerald dragon fed, so her husband became jealous of the pleasure it gave her. Izagun fashioned a great spear in secret with a point that was exceedingly sharp."

Pimple stopped carving to touch the sharp end of his stick, and whittled a little harder.

"He waited long for Tiatuu to put the egg down in its blue silken box. And when she turned her back, he speared the crystal shell. Thunder and lightning were born with the spearing, and that was not all, for now that the golden orb was free, it rose high above them all. The orb became the sun and the One World was overcome by Day."

"It was a good thing he speared it," said Pimple.

"It wasn't a good thing or a bad thing. It was the end of the endlessness. Not for Ahyuu and the First Beings, but for everyone who came after. It was the beginning of time."

Kipp continued the tale. "After the first day, the golden center of the egg went back down toward the One World to rest again in the silken box. But the box was gone. The silk had become the blue sky, the black box night, and the shards of the broken shell had scattered stars across the heavens. There was no place for the sun to rest; still the sun fell below the rim of the world, looking and looking for the box, and this was the first night."

Pimple had put his stick down. Clutching the knife, he lay by the fire, resting his head on his hand, droopy-eyed. Kipp went on to tell about Tiatuu's first child. "Tiatuu's child, Omaja, who is known as the Daughter of Time, was formed on the first night after the egg was broken. Time grew ever stronger and endlessness was overshadowed by the sunlit beauty of the day and the starry splendor of the night. Ahyuu is too great to be confined by time, so the Great Being left the One World for a new home."

He went on talking in a low, musical voice, waiting for Pimple to lose consciousness, but the boy was fighting off sleep. Each time his head started to droop, he snapped it up again and squeezed the handle of his knife.

"Where did the Great Being go?" he asked, stifling a yawn.

"Ahyuu searched world to world, but all the worlds were bound in time by then. There was no one place for one so great to settle."

Pimple snorted. "Is that the way the Escuyans tell it?" he said bitterly. "Typical of nomads to say that Ahyuu became as homeless as they are."

"This story is not just Escuyan," Kipp argued. "It is told all over Zolya. Why limit the Great Being to a single dwelling place, when Ahyuu's spirit is everywhere? Besides, the Escuyans are proud to live as nomads. They do not say they are homeless, but that their home is wherever they stand."

Pimple laughed. "Those people say anything."

Kipp was getting angrier. Sor Joay had been a nomad, and he'd taught him nearly everything he knew—everything of any importance anyway. When he was still a boy, he'd wished more that once that he could live like the Escuyans and not be tied down to a failing kora farm.

Letting out a slow sigh, he worked to calm his voice. He continued talking in a singsong tone, making up what he could not remember. The story became a strange mishmash that made no sense at all, and this, more than the real tale, seemed to charm the boy to sleep.

Twenty minutes later Pimple was curled up by the fire. Kipp studied his face and saw his pale eyelids fluttering. He waited a little longer and asked Pimple a few questions to make sure he was asleep.

"Do you think the dragon meant for the egg to be broken?"

The fire sent up yellow sparks. No answer from the boy.

"Do you think the Great Being is as near to us as he is far?"

Again no answer.

And last Kipp said in a whisper, "If there were no time, no beginning, and no end, would death disappear?"

The fire hissed. Kipp turned his head and whispered quietly, "What do you think, Epopo?"

CHAPTER TWENTY-EIGHT

EPOPO CREPT around the boulder and padded over to Kipp.

"You are a prince among dogs," Kipp whispered. He continued talking in the same singsong voice, keeping Pimple and Sag Eye safely asleep.

Epopo gave Kipp a few licks across his cheek.

"Your slobber stinks, my prince." Kipp talked on as he curled up knees to chin. He paused a moment to chew the rope that tethered him to Sag Eye. It was the only way he could think to show Epopo what to do, and the dog went at it until the rope frayed and split in his sharp teeth.

Now Kipp could move a little without waking his captor. He stood slowly, continuing his story as he lowered his hands to the back of his knees and stepped back through his arms.

With his bound wrists in the front, he chewed the rope briefly, then lowered his hands for help.

Hands free, he gave Epopo a grateful scratch behind the ear and went to free his horse. Sensing Kwaja stirring under his shirt, Kipp took a breath, and thought a moment. This time he could not refuse a death call by keeping his feet on the ground. He needed Kwaja's power of flight to help them all get away. ChChka gave a soft whinny as Kipp drew his knife and began to slit her hobble cord.

"Shhh."

The whinny must have awakened Sag Eye. Before Kipp could free the hobbled leg, he was grabbed from behind. The sudden movement knocked the knife from his hand.

"Where ya going, dwiig?"

Kipp struggled against his captor.

"Get over here, ya detcher, and bring me some of that rope!" Pimple ran up. "Now help me hold this dwiig worm still while I tie him up again."

Kipp's wrists were already bound when Epopo leaped up, clamping Sag Eye's shirttail in his jaws. The man kicked Epopo hard enough to send him flying past the tree. He yelped and landed, tumbling on the ground.

Kipp cringed at the pitiful sound. "There's no reason for you to kick my dog!" he cried. "He only tore your shirt a little."

"He only tore your shirt a little," Sag Eye repeated in a wheedling voice. Pimple laughed nervously as Sag Eye dragged Kipp over to the tree.

"Bring me more of that rope," he ordered. Pimple hurried to obey. While he was gone, Sag Eye grabbed Kipp's collar and tore the shirt from his body.

"What's this?" Sag Eye used the knifepoint to toy with the ropes binding Kwaja to Kipp's chest.

"You'd better leave that alone," Kipp warned.

"Your money bag, eh?" he snorted. "Looks empty to me." He slit the rope, tore Kwaja from Kipp's chest, and threw it toward his bedroll. "You don't know what you're doing," Kipp warned.

"I know exactly what I'm doing, little detcher." Spinning Kipp around to face the tree, Sag Eye looped the rope around Kipp's waist and tied him to the trunk. Kipp tried to swallow his fear. He knew Sag Eye's fondness for the whip. He heard Pimple give another nervous giggle as Sag Eye pulled the whip from his saddlebag.

Kipp shut his eyes.

"Gonna teach you not to try and get away from me again, ya dirty dwiig."

The first five lashes stung, the sixth went deeper, cutting into Kipp's back. Refusing to scream, Kipp tightened his jaw and groaned with the pain. Epopo came out of the shadows and raced for the tree, barking wildly.

Kipp shouted, "Stay back, Epopo!"

Still Epopo rushed for Sag Eye.

"You want a piece of this?" Sag Eye turned and savagely lashed Epopo's back.

"Stop it! Leave him alone!" It was more a sob. Kipp's own searing pain fueled the plea.

Pimple was laughing hysterically. Sag Eye whirled around. "Shut up!" Chasing him to the boulder he whipped him a few times for good measure. Pimple cringed, thrusting his hands out protectively. "I'm sorry, Sor, I won't laugh anymore. I promise!"

Sag Eye staggered back to Kipp. His arm swung down again and again like a hammer. Twelve lashes. Grunt. Thirteen . . . The whipping suddenly stopped. Kipp heard a loud gasp. Out of the corner of his eye, he saw the man reel back and stumble onto his knees.

"My pills, boy!" Sag Eye gripped his chest with both hands, trying to breathe.

Pimple was still crouching by the boulder nursing his wounds. "Sor?" He wiped the snot from his face.

"They're in my coat pocket!" Sag Eye moaned. Going down on all fours, he rolled over on his back.

Kipp's knees were like putty. His back was on fire. He half-watched, half-heard the scene between his captors as Epopo circled the tree and went to work chewing the rope to free him.

"Hurry," Kipp pleaded. A few feet away he could see Kwaja rising and twirling slowly in the air toward Sag Eye. *Just the wind*, Kipp thought. But he knew it wasn't true.

Pimple found his master's coat by the bedroll, quickly searched one pocket, then jammed his hand into the other.

Strange noises were coming from Sag Eye's open mouth, something between a growl and a snore.

"Come on, Epopo," Kipp ordered under his breath. The lashes on his back throbbed along with his heartbeat. Time seemed to have slowed down or fled. It was as if Tiatuu's egg had never been speared, as if the endlessness surrounded them. The fire was the only bright thing in the dimness where Pimple knelt by his master.

Kipp's waist was finally free. He slumped down onto his trembling knees. The ground swayed beneath him as Epopo chewed behind his back to free his hands.

Sag Eye had gone silent. Pimple shoved the pill into his open mouth and poured whiskey in to wash it down. The whiskey dribbled down the man's cheeks. "Sor? You have to swallow, Sor," he pleaded.

Sag Eye didn't move. Behind Pimple's back the soul sack drifted toward them. The boy looked up and saw Kipp and Epopo at the base of the tree.

"Hey!" he shouted. He came to a threatening stand, saw Kwaja floating two feet from the ground, and leaped back. "What is that?"

Epopo finished freeing Kipp's hands. Kipp rubbed his raw wrists, not sure if he could stand. Above the sprawled body, he saw Sag Eye's soul rise gray as a breath on a cold day and disappear into the sack's black mouth.

"Get back!" Pimple screamed. He grabbed his master's whip and flicked it at the hovering sack.

Kwaja drifted to the tree and draped itself across Kipp's naked back.

"Stay back, demon!" Pimple cried. "I'm . . . I'm warning you!" He was trying to sound threatening, but his voice cracked with fear as he knelt and slit the coin bag from the dead man's belt.

"Listen," Kipp said. "I can explain. You don't understand. I—"

"I said to stay back!" Racing over to the bay, he slit the hobble cords on both horses, threw himself onto the bay, and rode into the dark, pulling Sag Eye's stallion behind.

The drumming hoofbeats lessened to silence. Kipp looked down at his swollen wrists and hands.

The soft touch of the cloth eased the sharp pains across his back. His eyes swam. He suddenly felt sick.

Epopo had freed him in time.

He could have stopped Kwaja.

He hadn't made a move.

CHAPTER TWENTY-NINE

ZALIKA WAS LIKELY taken to the jail in her hometown of Napulo and awaiting trial there. Kipp didn't know how he'd free her when he reached Napulo; still he would go. His skin was raw from Sag Eye's whipping more than a week ago and scabs snaked down his back. After burying Sag Eye in the camp, he'd ridden southward day and night, except for the times the sack awakened and he was forced to dismount and walk until Kwaja quieted down.

ChChka's saddle made soft leather sounds as they headed for the Escuyan village in the distance. To the left of the village, children splashed in a shallow river. The happy sound sent unsuspected pangs of jealousy through him. He'd played that freely a few times when Sor Joay had taken him and Royan fishing, and once more on the day he and

Zalika caught turtles in the Sway. He was another person then. It had been another life.

An elder emerged from a hut and was joined by a curious crowd of villagers. Kipp dismounted and stood between his horse and dog. Epopo's hackles rose.

"Sit," Kipp ordered. Epopo obeyed, his ears pressed back.

The elder eyed ChChka appreciatively, from her proud head to the distinctive shadow marking on her white neck down to her perfectly muscled legs. Kipp cleared his throat, shifting his weight. The old man's nose wrinkled slightly.

Kipp knew how offensive he smelled, how dirty he must look. The back of his shirt had been stained with blood from Sag Eye's whip before he'd soaked it in the stream yesterday. The only decent bit of clothing he had was the hat he'd taken from the ground by Sag Eye's bedroll.

Hands out, palms up, Kipp said, "Aum, Sor."

The elder noted that he held no weapons. "Aum, traveler."

Kipp removed his weather-stained boots and stepped back a few paces. The elder signaled to a tall young man with a bronze serpent coiled about his arm to remove the hunting knife from Kipp's right boot. They would keep it until the visitor departed.

"There is another hunting knife and a slingshot in my saddlebags," said Kipp, agreeing to speak man-to-man without the need of weapons.

The villagers watched a few paces behind the elder as the man dug out Kipp's slingshot and Sag Eye's knife. He did not find Sag Eye's whip. Kipp had buried it with him.

"I have come to sell some things to you, Sor, if it pleases you." Kipp rested his hand on ChChka's warm shoulder. "I have a fine blanket and three good metal cooking pans, Sor."

"You are called Kipp," said the elder.

"Sor?"

"Two days ago, a man with many dogs came to our village in search of a boy who rides a white horse with a mark upon her neck." He nodded at ChChka.

Kipp swayed on his feet. The Gwali had been here.

"I know this boy," said a voice from behind.

Kipp turned to see who had spoken for him. The bone thrower stooped in the bright sun with his sack of bones.

Kipp licked his cracked lips nervously as the bone thrower stepped up beside him. "I have some business with this boy, Sor Tetswii. I would like to speak with him."

The elder stood, silent, his orange robe blowing in the hot wind. "You may speak," he said at last. "We will inspect the goods he brought to sell."

"Taka, Sor." The thrower bowed reverently.

Kipp's ears rang. What was the thrower doing in this village? He pulled Pimple's abandoned cooking pots from the saddlebag and untied Sag Eye's colorful red-orange blanket with a fittarr snakeskin pattern the Escuyans would appreciate. The elder handed them off to a small group of men to inspect. A moment later Kipp heard a metallic banging noise from one of the huts. They were

220

already testing the quality of the pots.

"Come out of the hot sun," said the bone thrower.

By the river, Kipp watched the children splash, and he let ChChka drink. Then he climbed back up the bank and tethered her to a willow.

"What did you do with Cassia?" Kipp asked testily.

The old man pointed downstream to the village corral. Kipp hadn't noticed her when he'd ridden in, but he was relieved to spot his old red roan in among the others.

The bone thrower lowered himself down, grimacing as he sat. Some people chewed kittu seeds for pain. Kipp wondered if the thrower had any. He nudged Epopo off the rug. Epopo looked affronted, but a dog did not belong on a man's rug. He should know that.

The bone thrower took some dried fruit, a jug, and two cups from his basket. "I have been looking for you."

Kipp crossed his legs and adjusted his position uneasily. What did he mean by that? He rested his hand on his right thigh, covering the thicker place under the cloth where Kwaja hid. After Sag Eye's whipping, the sores on his back couldn't tolerate the rough hemp rope he used to bind Kwaja.

"Why have you been looking for me, Sor?"

"I owe you money for the fittarr bones."

"That's true." Kipp brightened. He was relieved to hear the thrower had been waiting to pay him for the fittarr. He ate some of the blackened fruit. It was sweet and tough as leather.

When the old man finished his cold tea, he turned his

cup over on the rug. Kipp hesitated a moment, took a last gulp, and turned his over also. The upside-down rims did not touch, but the sign of agreement was made. They would speak of things no one else was meant to hear. There was more to the overturned cups, an understanding that what was said between them would not be shared with anyone else once they left this place. Kipp wasn't sure he trusted the thrower that far. He would choose his words carefully.

The bone thrower tugged his fat earlobe. Sensual, girlish, disturbing. Kipp ignored his ears, looked at the red beads in his long braided beard.

"You need to be careful," the old man said.

"Why do you say that?"

He cackled. "It is not a good idea to come to a village with a bounty on your head."

Kipp jumped up.

"Do not go," said the old man. "I will not turn you in."

"Why should I believe that?"

The thrower indicated the cups. "It would not be good for you and so not good for me."

Despite his doubts, Kipp felt drawn in. He had turned his cup over, agreed to this meeting. "What do you mean?" He did not sit down yet. He could put his boot in the stirrup with haste if he needed to.

"You have something I want."

"I don't have any skeletons."

"I do not need any more of those." He was looking up

at Kipp, his large, knuckled hand shielding his eyes from the sunlight.

"Why should I give you something? You already owe me four coppers for the fittarr."

"That was not my doing. You would not take my payment."

He reached into his coin bag and tossed the coins in the air. Kipp caught three and missed the fourth. Epopo barked and sniffed the coin by his paw. Kipp jammed them all into his pocket. More money than he was likely to get for the blanket and cook pots.

The thrower smiled. There was something unsettling about the man. Being with him was like visiting the Sanuu Witch.

"We are even now," said Kipp.

"I told you you have something I want," said the thrower. "I also have something of value for you."

"You just want to trick me. That's how you make your living, isn't it?"

It was not right to speak to an old man with disrespect, even if he was a bone thrower. Kipp did not apologize. He did not leave, either. Part of him wanted to know what kind of exchange the thrower had in mind. "I don't want a bone toss."

"We already did a bone reading at the fair."

"What do you have to offer me then?" asked Kipp.

"News about Zalika Tunassi."

Kipp went down on his knees. "How did you find out I knew her? I never told you—"

The man rubbed the base of his spine and took a few

shallow breaths. "Not long now," he said, not to Kipp but to himself. "You called to Zalika at the fair before the man with the sagging eye pulled you on his rope."

Kipp nodded. He had screamed her name. He remembered that, and the bone thrower must have heard him. This thrower might have some Naqui powers (all throwers were said to have them) but mostly he used his power of observation. He looked. He listened. He paid more attention than most people.

"What do you know about her, Sor?"

The man's eyebrows shot up at the sudden respectful address. "You agree to an exchange then: the information you want for what I want?"

Kipp was about to say yes, of course, when ChChka stomped her hoof, raising a small brown puff of dust. He scanned the road beyond the village but he saw only a few women walking with baskets on their heads. No rider in sight, and no dogs.

"You do not want my horse, do you?" he asked.

"I already have Cassia to pull my wagon. Why would I want more than that?"

"Or my dog?"

"Not your dog. I only want your help."

"Yes, then, I agree."

The man folded his hands. "After you left, Mistress Zalika went before a tribunal in Goba City."

Kipp's heart raced. He'd thought she would be taken back

to Napulo and tried there. "Was she tried for murder?"

"No. Sor Litchen did not die from his wound. But he is a rich man, and an angry one. He said the arrow was no accident, that Zalika meant to kill him. She attacked him with a knife once before, you see."

"The man is a liar! He tried to force her to be his mistress. When she refused, he cut a long gash in her leg."

"You know a different story than the one we heard."

"How do you know so much?"

"It was all over the city. Everyone talked about it."

"Then tell me the rest," Kipp said.

"The tribunal did not have to discuss the case for long. There were many witnesses to the shooting."

"But the barking dog threw her off her aim. What about the dog?"

"It was decided the dog was of no consequence. Mistress Zalika was charged with attempted murder and sentenced to prison."

Kipp shivered. "It . . . it can't be. Where is she?" *Don't say OnnZurr.*

The old man's eyes were on him. "You know where."

"But no one ever gets out of OnnZurr!"

Kipp was on his feet again, pacing. He could not sit with his heart racing so fast.

"I have to free her."

The thrower shook his head. "That is not possible."

"I have done the impossible before," snapped Kipp.

225

"I know." He patted the rug for Kipp to sit. "That is why I want you to help me."

"I have to leave now. What you need me to do for you cannot take long, Sor."

"It will not."

Kipp took his place on the rug again, though he wanted to be in the saddle, riding for OnnZurr.

"You are the master of the sack," said the bone thrower.

"I am . . . not—" Kipp choked. "How do you—?"

"I saw what you did at the fair. You did not let Sor Litchen's soul enter Kwaja. It was because of you he did not die. Not because of the doctor."

Kipp felt queasy. He rocked back and forth, trying to silence the blood thundering in his ears.

"Do not worry. I have keen vision through my Naqui powers. I'm sure no one else saw the man's soul. They all thought you were having a fit, remember?"

Kipp nodded, still dumbstruck.

The old man waited a moment for him to recover.

"You . . . you want me to save someone's life?" Kipp whispered. "Don't worry. Your friend, whoever it is, is safe. I stole the Gwali's sack because I do not want—" He was going to say he did not want anyone to die, but that was not completely true. Sag Eye was dead. He had not acted fast enough to save him.

"There is no one I want you to save. Not in the way you think."

"What do you want then?"

"I am very old. I have been in a lot of pain for many years now."

Kipp leaned forward. He had seen the pain in the way the man stooped, in his swollen joints.

"I sold my wagon to another bone thrower and gave Cassia to the children of this village. I have only these possessions." He indicated the rug, bone sack, and basket. "I am ready to go, Kipp."

"Go where?" He saw the answer in the old man's eyes. "No."

"We made a bargain."

"I won't help you in that way, old man."

"You are the only one who can. This is my day to die. I have seen it."

Kipp had heard of holy men who predicted their death day. Taking their last Lostwalk to meet their end quietly.

"You did not see it, Sor. Only holy men can do that, and you are not a holy man."

The thrower smiled. "Why am I not?"

Kipp was feeling more and more confused. "You cannot be a holy man. You are a bone thrower."

He was met with twinkling eyes. "Oh, that. The bones are nothing. They are for show. I look. I listen. I am a man of prayer. I tell the truth I see in people's hearts. That is what a true thrower does. The bones themselves have no special powers."

227

Kipp said, "I knew that."

"Then we both know it." He touched the bottom of his overturned cup. "You were not angry with me at the fair because I read the bones. You were angry because I told the truth."

Kipp did not reply. They both knew it was so.

"You said I am the master of the sack. I am not. I only stole it."

"This thing cannot be mastered through power. It is of the spirit." The bone thrower moved his hand slowly through the shaded air. "It takes great power to divert a river, but a man can get in, swim with the current, and get out again."

Kipp snorted. "You say you tell the truth, but you speak in riddles, thrower."

The old man lowered his hand. He sat still, eyes closed, he was breathing softly, very softly. What was he doing now?

Kipp felt the cloth rubbing his leg where Kwaja was tied. He jumped up. "You will not die today." He untied ChChka. "I'm going now." He tugged his mare back into the sunlight. "I have the coins I need from the fittarr bones," he said over his shoulder. "Thank Sor Tetswii for me. Tell the elder this village can keep the things I brought to sell."

Kipp reclaimed his weapons by one of the grass huts and mounted ChChka. He had not set his cup right again to end the secret meeting, nor kept his promise. He didn't care. He would take nothing from the old man. The thrower could keep his basket, his bones, his body, his life.

CHAPTER THIRTY

CHCHKA RACED along the road, her hoofbeats against the hard-packed earth sounded the words *OnnZurr, OnnZurr, OnnZurr* in Kipp's ears. He would head back to Sor Twam. He knew the danger of going near Sor Tunassi's estate, but Sor Twam had once worked in OnnZurr as a sweeper—he might know how to get to Zalika. And then there was Jilly. He needed to see her again, needed to hug his little sister and make her understand why he'd had to go away so suddenly.

The late-afternoon sun spread rusty light over the dry land. His sweat-soaked shirt clung to the sores on his back. Spotting boulders on the hill ahead, he turned ChChka aside, headed for the granite outcrop, and dismounted in the shade.

On the road far behind them, horsemen traveled in small

groups alongside wagons. Kipp squinted into the distance, keeping his eye out for a rider on a black horse surrounded by dogs. He craned his neck the other way. No dogs in either direction. Not yet anyway.

He was drinking from his water pouch when he felt Kwaja move against his thigh. He'd felt a gentle stirring this morning in the village, but the pull hadn't yet been strong. The tug was stronger now. Kipp sighed. He'd wanted to rest awhile. It took so much energy to fight the sack. He drank more and walked a little in the direction of the pull. It was easier that way.

Epopo stayed at his side, one shadow following another beneath the boulders. In his mind, Kipp turned over a cup, went back to the old man on the rug. What he'd said about mastering the sack, could it be true?

ChChka nibbled dry grass nearby. Kipp called her with a click of his tongue.

"Come to me, girl," he whispered. She turned her head, her body ghostly white against the dark boulders, and trotted to his side. *This thing cannot be mastered through power,* the bone thrower had said. *It is of the spirit.* The thrower had moved his hand in the air like a fish. *It takes great power to divert a river, but a man can get in, swim with the current, and get out again.*

Kipp placed his hand over the mark on ChChka's neck. He'd been afraid to ride when Kwaja's will was strong. He knew he could not divert the soul sack from its course, but if he could train himself and ChChka to ride within the strong current as a swimmer floats downriver, if he could learn to fly ChChka into the mighty pull and out of it again before Kwaja took them too close to the one who was dying, he could steer into the power of Kwaja's flight and use the sack to take him where he needed to go.

It was a risk but he decided to mount her and try. In the saddle, he urged the white mare to a gentle canter. Epopo raced along the ground beside them. Kipp did not pick him up. He'd seen the Gwali's hounds pulled into flight. He would find out if his own dog would be drawn in.

Warm air streamed past as ChChka gained speed and ran up the hill. At the top she kept going, her hooves pedaling the air. Epopo barked as his paws left the ground, and barked again, this time with delight, as they flew above the boulders.

Jilly.

Kipp gripped his elbows to keep himself from leaping out of his hiding place in the bushes and taking her in his arms. Peering through the greenery behind Sor Tunassi's mansion, he watched her leave the back steps and skip barefoot through the clipped grass. Her bright skirt was torn about the hem. Her golden hair was tangled, her face and arms sunburned, but she wasn't quite as thin as she'd been before.

Jilly sang to herself as she marched toward the henhouse at the far end of the herb garden. Kipp would have stepped out then if the henhouse weren't so visible from the kitchen window. He felt happy just now, watching her, knowing she was all right; she was safe.

Flinging the gate open, Jilly stepped inside the hens' yard and began to toss the feed. The hens clucked. Kipp watched their bobbing heads as they pecked the ground. He bit his lip. He could not wait any longer.

"Psst!"

Jilly's curls bounced as she turned her head.

"Come over here."

Jilly crossed her arms and frowned in his direction.

"I know where your brother is." She didn't recognize his voice behind his whisper but he could not say who he was. They were too close to the back entrance, and her happy shout might give him away.

"Who are you?" She shielded her eyes, squinting into the bushes.

"If I show you who I am, you have to promise not to scream."

"No! If you are bad, I will scream and scream!"

"Promise not to scream if I am not bad, then?"

She sniffed, unsure.

He took off his boot and put it in the open.

"That's my brother's shoe," she said accusingly.

"Shhh. We don't want anyone to hear you in the house."

"Why not?"

Kipp gave up and stepped out long enough for her to view him before ducking back into the bush. Jilly flung the gate open and ran across the grass. She was laughing and crying. He knelt down so she could cry into his shoulder. "You have to keep quiet, Illy Jilly," he said gently, patting her back.

She pulled away and looked at him. "Where did you go? They said you hurt Mistress Zalika and stole a horse and I didn't believe them. But you left me alone and that was bad!"

"I can't tell you now. Look." He pointed at the chickens strutting out of the open gate. "Get them back into the pen, hurry! I'll wait here."

"I won't." She wiped her nose. "You will go away again."

"I promise I'll stay here and wait for you. Just hurry."

"Shoo! Get inside, you stupid chickens." She waved her hands at the fluttering hens. When that didn't work, she stepped through the gate and flung new feed on the ground. The hens hustled back, knocking into one another for the scattered seeds. Jilly flashed a victory smile at Kipp before shutting them all back inside. His heart nearly burst with love.

"I have missed you so much, Jilly." He slipped on his boot. "I came back to get you away from here and to ask Sor Twam to come with us, but he has gone."

"He and Sa Minn went home to their village after the harvest. Master Tunassi made me come work in the kitchen." Her face hardened.

"Has it been rough working here, Jilly? Tell me the truth." She nodded.

Kipp stood again. "I'm sorry. I'll tell you why I had to go, why I couldn't come back for you until now. First we have to leave."

"To where?"

"Sor Twam's village. I need to find him. Do you know the name of it?"

She frowned, thinking. "I want to bring Scritch."

He looked down at her. "Scritch?"

"My kitty."

"We can't go get him, we have to—" Jilly was pointing. He turned and saw a little black cat hunting through the bushes.

"I have a dog, Jilly, he won't—" Kipp gave up. She had already tiptoed over and lifted Scritch into her arms.

Kipp put a finger to his lips and motioned for her to come.

Epopo did not like Scritch, and the feeling was mutual. As soon as they reached the hidden spot along the Sway where the animals were waiting, Scritch hissed, puffed up twice his size, and jumped down to swipe Epopo's nose. Epopo yelped, sending the cat skittering up a tree.

"Sit, Epopo. Now!" Kipp knelt to talk some sense into Jilly. "We should leave Scritch here."

Her blue eyes narrowed. "No. You do not leave people like that."

Not a person, a small black cat, but he wouldn't argue with her. "He is a very smart cat, isn't he?"

She brightened. "Yes."

"I am sure he can find his way home."

"No."

In the end he climbed the tree and slipped an angry Scritch into Jilly's bag of chicken feed, where he growled and hissed as Kipp made his way back down the trunk.

"I'll take him." Jilly held out her hands for the bag.

Kipp slipped off the strap. He'd tied the top to keep the cat inside before climbing down. "Okay, but we'd better keep him in the bag while we ride."

She nodded.

"Why did you name him Scritch?" he asked.

She pointed to the red marks on her arm. "He does this sometimes, but he doesn't mean to. A scritch is different than a scratch. It is an accident."

They had the day before them but could not risk riding on the open road. Kipp figured the landlord had guessed he would come back at some point to rescue Jilly. He'd set his trap carefully, bringing Jilly to his house, and waiting for Kipp to make the next move. It wouldn't be long before the kitchen staff discovered she was missing. Kipp was glad he'd explored some of the unused trails on the far side of the Sway with Zalika.

After a valiant battle with the inside of the bag, the cat gave up and quieted down.

High in the saddle, Jilly's blonde head bobbed just under Kipp's chin. She talked to herself, to Kipp, to Scritch. She spoke in little bright bursts like pearls on a string, rambling on about all the food in Sor Tunassi's kitchen, about the hot spice powder they put on her tongue to keep her from talking so much. She went on about the times she brought toast and kora up to Mistress Zalika when she was getting better from her fall.

"Everyone said you stole a horse or two horses. Cook said that you hurt Zalika and left her on the road to die. I did not believe them, but then you said you would never leave me, and you did, so I was mad at you and Zalika was mad at you, too, and—"

"Did she think I left her there to die?"

"That is what everyone was saying and—"

"Did Zalika say that to you?"

She swayed a little in the saddle and leaned the back of her head against his chest. "I don't remember. It was too long ago."

"Only a few months ago."

"Too long. I'm only seven." She let out a sigh.

Kipp knew she said "only seven" when it suited her. He'd heard her rail many times about how little attention people gave her because she was "only seven, as if a seven-year-old wasn't a real person!"

Kipp said, "Do you know where Zalika is now?"

"Cook said she went to OnnZurr."

"Do you know what that is?" he asked.

"A bad place. A prison."

"I want to rescue her, Jilly. Do you want to help me do that?"

"Yes."

"Sor Twam knows about OnnZurr. He used to be a sweeper there when he was a boy. Remember when he told us that?"

She nodded. "He swept the floors there."

"We need his help. You said he went back to his own village. Can you tell me the name of the place where Sor Twam went?"

"It was a long time ago," she said. He could not see her face, but he knew she was frowning.

"It's important, Jilly. Try to remember."

They stopped to rest at midday along a bend in the river. Jilly lifted her skirt and waded ankle-deep into the shallows. "Titaun Ezze."

Kipp translated. "Dragon's eye."

"That's the name of Sor Twam's village," she said with a nod. He wanted to hug her but she was standing apart from him, her feet in the water, her eyes looking up at the blue, blue sky.

CHAPTER THIRTY-ONE

W HAT'S THE MATTER with your leg?" Jilly
asked, peering down at Kipp from the saddle.
Kwaja was awake, and he'd hopped down to keep ChChka
from flying.

"Nothing, Jilly."

"Something is the matter with you," she insisted. "You
are walking funny."

They were deep in the sweltering Farlands, far from shade,
or rest, or water. Titaun Ezze was more than three hundred
miles away and it was slow going with his little sister. Kipp
had practiced flying with Kwaja's pull a few times on his way
to Sor Tunassi's estate. He'd slowly learned to interpret the
strength of the tug against his skin, to read the signals both
subtle and strong. He'd taught ChChka to race into the power,
fly with it, then head back down to the ground again. Landing

before the sack reached its destination was the hardest part. ChChka had to free herself from Kwaja's current on Kipp's command when the sack's power still urged her on. He knew it took courage and skill to go against Kwaja, to obey one master above another. But again and again she had chosen him.

Jilly frowned down at her older brother. "Get back in the saddle with me, Kipp."

"Not right now."

"Why not?"

Leading ChChka, he strained against Kwaja's pull, putting one foot in front of the other. Epopo panted at his side, his tail dragging in the sweltering heat. They would get there so much faster if they flew, but how could he explain the power to Jilly without bringing up the Gwali?

"Scritch won't scratch you," Jilly promised, still trying to coax him up. "He's in his feedbag."

"Do you know about Naqui powers, Jilly?"

"They are powerful powers," she said firmly.

"Yes, they are. If I told you I had Naqui powers, would that surprise you?"

"You do?"

He nodded.

"Is that what's making you walk funny?"

"In a way."

Jilly sighed and looked unimpressed.

"If I got into the saddle right now, something magic would happen."

Her eyebrows shot up. "What kind of magic?"

"ChChka would fly."

Jilly squealed with delight. "Get on now. I want to fly."

"Aren't you afraid?"

"I want to fly," she said again.

"You have to promise to keep this a secret."

"I will. I promise."

Kipp leaped on. "Hold on tight!" he called, and they took to the air.

"Oh!" she cried with glee. Wind whooshed past them. "What about Epopo?"

"Watch, Jilly. He'll come, too."

A moment later Epopo was soaring in the air beside them, his black-and-white fur ruffling in the breeze.

They flew over hills where the rocks were layered in rings like ripples across water, as if Ahyuu had stirred them with a finger. His sister laughed. Cool air blew back her curls and washed up Kipp's face. He felt like he was flying inside Jilly's laughter.

On the way to Titaun Ezze, they flew when Kwaja wakened, and rode on land when it was quiet. Flight quickened their journey and less than a week after leaving the estate, they came to a small pool in the dunes and dismounted in the reeds. Stars hung bright over Titaun Ezze. They had missed the evening meal, but Sa Minn invited them to Sor Twam's hut, where they were given steaming bowls of millet and spiced meat.

Sor Twam flicked the light jar on the straw mat between them. Three young cheewii lizards awakened, their scales shining as they wriggled in and out. Now they could see each other's faces while the guests ate.

Jilly fell asleep soon after the meal. Kipp covered his little sister with a blanket, and Scritch curled up by her shoulder.

"Why have you come to Titaun Ezze?" asked Sor Twam.

"To see you and Sa Minn, Sor." That was true, but there was more, and Sor Twam knew it.

A dirty thread hung from Kipp's sleeve. He wrapped it around his finger. Sor Twam and Sa Minn had helped him care for Jilly when they were pickers. He owed them much.

"Sor," Kipp said respectfully, "Sa. I had to take Jilly away from the landlord's house. She is only seven. She was not meant to be a slave."

Sa Minn's eyes narrowed. "You stole her?"

"You cannot steal what is already yours," said Sor Twam.

Kipp nodded gratefully. "Jilly is the only family I have left. I could not leave her there alone."

Sor Twam adjusted his wool cape. The night was cold. "Where will you go, boy?"

"I don't know, Sor. You two are our only friends."

Sa Minn cleared her throat. Sor Twam kept his eyes on Kipp. "There is more you have to tell us," he said.

Kipp adjusted his position on the mat. The cheewii lizards in the jar were already growing wings. Sor Twam would have to let them go soon and search for younger, wingless males.

"Sor. I have come to rescue Zalika from OnnZurr."

Sa Minn shook her head. "We heard she was taken there and why. But it is impossible. No one has ever escaped from OnnZurr."

Sor Twam did not speak, waiting to hear the rest.

"You told us you went inside as a sweeper when you were a boy, Sor."

"Many years ago, Kipp."

"Could you do that again?"

"They would not let an old man inside. They want women to sweep, and young people with strong backs to empty the sewage buckets." He fingered the beads on his braid. "Your pale skin might help you with this."

"How?"

The cheewii jar spread yellow light across the old man's face, showing his troubled eyes. "The OnnZurr guards might take pleasure mistreating an immigrant, especially a poor one from the northern lands. You know how some people are."

Kipp did not answer, but he'd been called a pale plenty of times.

"You might go as one of the beggars who sweep the cells of OnnZurr to earn money for their day's bread."

"I can go as a beggar, Sor." Kipp would do what he had to do to get inside.

"So you think you will go into the prison and sweep the girl out?" Sa Minn said. Kipp blushed. He had forgotten what a sharp tongue the old woman had.

Sor Twam raised his hand. "Let the boy finish, Sa."

Kipp thought of what he'd told Sa Minn long ago, that he'd seen the Gwali take his family on the night their farm burned down. He'd told her that the night he'd stayed awake to watch over Jilly. She'd given him a bloodstone then, but she had been afraid. Sa Minn had warned him not to talk about the Gwali, that to speak his name was to call him.

"I know I cannot sweep Zalika out, Sa. But I have Naqui powers. There is another way."

"What way?"

Kipp rubbed his thigh where Kwaja hid. "I cannot say."

There was a long silence. He was afraid to tell them where he'd been, what he'd done. Sor Twam jiggled the jar. A lizard raised his head and flicked his tongue. Another beat his tail against the jar before curling up again. The disturbance made them glow brighter. "You ask for our help, but you hold things back from us."

Kipp looked down. He could not say more.

"Where did you get your Naqui powers?" Sor Twam asked.

"Sor Joay taught me."

"You cannot teach a man Naqui powers. The powers emerge after the Lostwalk at age fourteen. Some Zolyans have them, but it is mostly Escuyans who carry Naqui powers because we follow the old ways, and the Farlands are in our blood."

Kipp fingered the edge of his empty bowl. He hadn't been on a Lostwalk when he was fourteen, but he'd found the sacred dragon cave soon after he'd earned his first braid-bead. That day Sor Joay had said, *You might have this gift. I think the cave would not have opened its mouth to you if you were not meant to come inside.* Surely finding the sacred cave meant something? But his presence in the cave went against custom. Most people who followed the old ways would not welcome the idea; he'd given his word not to speak of it.

The straw hut felt cold. The jar between them gave off light but no heat. *I only need to get inside OnnZurr,* Kipp thought. *I can do the rest.* "Sor," he said. "I need your help. I do not know what you heard about the incident, but Zalika did not mean to shoot Sor Litchen. She was sentenced unjustly. She should not spend the rest of her life imprisoned in OnnZurr."

"How do you know she did not mean to shoot him?" asked Sa Minn.

"I was there, Sa. I saw it happen. A dog barked when she released the bowstring and threw her off target. She needs our help," he said. "My help," he corrected.

Sor Twam stood suddenly and went outside. Kipp watched the glowing cheewiis until his eyes stung. At last Sa Minn waved her hand toward the doorway. "Go out to him."

Outside the stars were bright orbs, but the half-moon shone dull as a moth's wing. Beyond the millet field, he found Sor Twam swinging his scythe, cutting the long, dry grass.

Kipp stood behind him, listened to the old man grunting with effort as he swung.

"May I help you with that?"

Sor Twam turned and handed him the scythe. "Cut the stalks low. We will need enough hay to make two sturdy brooms."

CHAPTER THIRTY-TWO

THE SUN WOULD be up in three hours. Kipp tucked the tail end of the cotton cloth into the folds of his turban as he followed Sor Twam through the darkness to the millet field. Sa Minn met them there, wearing a plain brown wrap skirt and dirty headscarf.

Sor Twam passed out the new brooms then drew the scarf across Sa Minn's face, covering her nose and mouth.

"You will need to wear your scarf like this when you sweep," he said in a whisper.

"I know what to do," she argued.

"Your skirt is too clean," he said.

These two argue like an old husband and wife, Kipp thought, though he knew they were just friends. Still, he was grateful to Sa Minn, who bent down to rub some soil into her skirt.

Sor Twam appraised Kipp. His clothing was certainly disreputable enough after months of travel; still the old man found something to criticize. "You will not be taken in wearing those boots," he said.

Kipp removed them and stood barefoot on the dusty earth.

Stars hung ripe above, but the moon was already low on the horizon. The acacia tree where Epopo was tied was a thick black shape in the distance. A small shape left the tree and bounced toward them. The dog had somehow gotten loose. Trotting past the huts, he stopped to sniff Kipp's abandoned boots.

Sor Twam crossed his arms. He'd spent the night helping Kipp and Sa Minn make their brooms and warning them of the perils they would face. "When they think to hire you, you must keep your eyes cast down," he said now. "Do not look into the faces of the prison guards. If they speak to you, do as they say and no more."

Kipp nodded and went down on one knee. "You have to stay here, Epopo." Epopo wagged his tail energetically. "I think you will have to tie him up, Sor."

The warm wind blew dust swirls about the huts. Sor Twam turned and led Epopo back to the tree. It would only be a few hours before Jilly would awaken, hungry for breakfast.

The bristly broom erased Kipp's footprints as he dragged it along the landscape. There were many rules to follow. Sor Twam said some halls must be avoided if a sweeper did not wish to be attacked. If a sweeper stirred up too much dust with his broom the prison guards would whip his ankles. If he spilled a scour bucket in the yard, he would be tied to a pole and given ten lashes. Kipp remembered the sting of Sag Eye's whip. He did not want to feel that kind of pain ever again.

OnnZurr was a two-hour journey on foot. They'd walked for more than an hour when the sun broke across the far horizon, spreading a soft red glow over the desert. *Night dies. Day is born. Blood light flows over the sand.* The words of the old Escuyan song filled Kipp's thoughts as they walked. There were more words to the song. Day also died so night could be born, but Kipp was too worried about what this day would bring to think about the night.

The silence of the desert and the morning heat greeted him like an old friend. He smelled the spicy kwik bushes and caught the clicking of the insects hidden in the tiffa grass as they started up the steep hill. He was three hundred miles from his family's farm, but the sand, kwik bushes, and the red rock pillars matched the places he'd traveled with Sor Joay as a boy. He'd seen all the varied landscapes of Zolya while he was on the run; still the beauty of the wild Farlands had a power over him. He let the pleasure of the familiar landscape fill him even as he dreaded what lay ahead.

Just after dawn they reached the last dune and blinked down at OnnZurr. The enormous sandstone structure had been built in this isolated place in ancient times. Kipp gave a low whistle as he took in its high thick walls and the four turreted guard towers, one at each corner, made of the same sandstone.

A figure leaned his head out of a tower peering down at the crowd of sweepers gathering by the front gate. They were only just in time.

Sa Minn asked, "Are you ready, Kipp?"

Hot wind blew sand across his bare feet and shins as they hurried down the hill. Kipp counted more than thirty sweepers at the gate. Sor Twam said only ten or fifteen would be let in each day. He pushed his way to the front with Sa Minn. Their garments were dirty, like the rest of the sweepers, but their grass brooms were new. Sor Twam had instructed them to hold their new brooms in the air so the guards might notice them.

Two of the armed men by the gate drew closer to the crowd. The taller one hawked and spat as he scanned the would-be sweepers. Kipp tried to keep his limbs from trembling from fear of what might happen if he were let in to find Zalika. And worse, fear of disappointment if he were rejected.

He eyed the two men from under his brows. Both guards held their whips at the ready. The tiny iron balls at the end of the whipcords clanked as they paced. Kipp felt the scars on his back tighten with the sound.

"Step out!" ordered a guard, pointing at a short woman with blistered feet.

"You!" called the second guard. "And you."

The selection had begun. Kipp and Sa Minn held their brooms up higher, waving them like flags. Sweat dripped down Kipp's neck. He wanted to run, to leave the great stone prison behind and lose himself in the desert. But he was here for Zalika. He had one day to warn her, and the next to rescue her if this was going to work.

"You. And you!" The broad-nosed guard who singled them out was already waving his arms and herding the sweepers toward the tall iron gate. Sa Minn gave Kipp a gentle shove, and they joined the line. Someone in the crowd behind him moaned. The women and children must have walked far to earn a sweeper's wage to buy a bit of food. They would have to return and beg in the closest town or go hungry today.

Kipp entered a half-lit hall. His crew was told to sweep the women's cell block first. The hall reeked like an open sewer. Breathing through his mouth, he passed cell after cell behind Sa Minn, looking for Zalika.

The torches on the walls kept the small cells at his left in shadow. There were two women to a cell. A few women looked his way as he passed, their faces ghostlike in the half dark.

The guard pointed to the sluice buckets they would use to empty the prisoners' waste after the women were taken outside. Kipp had reached the end of the corridor and still hadn't seen Zalika. Was she in another cell block or had he passed her by in the shadows?

Sa Minn went to work down the hall. Kipp jammed his broom in the corner.

"Sweep downward," Sor Twam had said. "Long strokes

to gather the dust into piles. Swing your arms too much, and the dust will fly up and you will be whipped."

Kipp swept his first pile into his gathering bag. If Zalika was in another block, how could he find her and speak to her? Loud clanking sounds echoed down the corridor as the guards opened the barred cells to let the women out. He would have to try to see her when he passed through the courtyard to empty his sluice bucket.

The prisoners lined up, shivering. Kipp dragged his broom along the base of the wall. Was Zalika here in the line? He caught Sa Minn's eye, and she shook her head.

Over the next half hour they worked to sweep all the floors in the empty cells. Each cell had a bucket full of waste and two rough burlap blankets for beds. Kipp pulled the end of his turban cloth over his nose to keep from retching as he emptied the buckets into his larger one. His eyes watered with angry tears. The women were kept like caged animals. What had they done to be treated like this?

Under the guards' watchful eyes they carried their full buckets back out into the courtyard. It had been too dark to see the women clearly in the cell block. Now it was too bright. Kipp squinted as he hauled his bucket out the heavily guarded gate to the cesspit. Back in the courtyard, his eyes slowly adjusted to the light. The heated air moved in gentle waves. Forms began to soak in liquid color where the women walked around the perimeter of the courtyard.

He scanned the prisoners. They wore long kirifa dresses

and headscarves, but the cloth was not the thin silks or the colorfully patterned cotton most Zolyan women wore. These kirifas were pale yellow, stained, and torn. He glanced down and followed the trail of the broom with his eyes. The women looked dirty and very thin.

A line of prisoners advanced and passed by on blistered feet.

Sa Minn stepped closer. "Come, Obi." Her voice was quiet as she spoke the name they'd chosen to signal that she'd found Zalika. At the sound of the horse's name, a prisoner's head whipped round. Brown eyes stared intensely above a dirty veil.

Zalika. Kipp mouthed her name silently. He did not dare speak it aloud, but she saw him and her eyes widened with recognition.

"You! Sweep that end of the courtyard!" A whip flicked at his feet. The metal balls slashed Kipp's ankles. He leaped to the side and began to sweep near Sa Minn.

Small streams of blood trickled across Kipp's feet as he worked the bush broom. He licked the salty sweat from his upper lip. The circle moved and Zalika stepped closer. "What are you doing here?" she whispered as she marched by. No time to answer or speak of his plan.

She circled round again with the others. At her second pass, Kipp whispered, "Sa Minn and I are here to rescue you." He indicated Sa Minn with a tilt of his head. "Tomorrow I will—" But he could not say more. In a swirl of filthy scarves and rags, Zalika was gone again.

Kipp swept round the stone benches. *Deysoukus!* Devil. How could he talk to Zalika bit by bit in front of all these prison guards? Down the line a guard shouted, "Move along!" He flicked his whip at a bent old woman. Kipp winced and dug his fingers into the broom handle. He was here to rescue Zalika, but these other women should not be suffering. He wanted to free them all.

Someone left her place in the line to help the old woman. She walked a little faster now, supported by her companion.

"You!" shouted a guard. The whip lashed his back before he could swing round. Kipp clenched his teeth as the whip tore his cloth shirt and lashed his tender skin.

"Take your broom and bucket down the hall!" The guard pointed to an entrance at his left. *Not now. I haven't told Zalika the plan. I can't leave the courtyard now.*

Kipp's temples throbbed beneath his turban. There was nothing he could do but grab the bucket and head for the stone archway. From the shadowy entrance he caught one last look at Zalika in the long, uneven line.

Swinging round, he fumbled his way down the torch-lit hall, suddenly blind as a desert mole in the catacombs. He flew from cell to cell desperate to finish the work and get back outside before it was too late. *Sa Minn is still in the courtyard,* he told himself as he emptied another chamber pot. *She might get a chance to speak to Zalika.* His bucket was nearly full when he heard a woman scream.

Kipp felt Kwaja give a violent tug. Someone was about to die. Outside the prison guards were shouting. Was Zalika all right? Abandoning his broom and bucket in the corner, he raced down the hall. Prisoners swarmed in through the archway. The crowd threw him against the wall. He took a breath and elbowed his way through the mob.

Kipp covered his eyes in the blazing courtyard, saw the guard standing over the body on the ground. His heart raced.

"You! Take this filth back to her cell!"

Kipp hurried over, obeying the pull from the hidden sack tied to his leg as much as the shouting guard. Squatting down, he lifted the crumpled body, was relieved to see it was not Zalika but the old woman who'd been whipped earlier. She moaned. At least she was alive. Kipp carried her through the archway back into the noisy hall where the guards were shouting orders, slamming doors, locking prisoners in. Many were weeping. What had happened in the courtyard?

"Put her down over there!"

Kipp carried the woman to her cell and laid her on the burlap blanket. She was breathing unsteadily, but the soul sack had quieted down. She was out of danger now. Her younger cell mate fell on her knees beside her.

"Sa Trivvi?" she said, her voice choked with fear.

"She will live," Kipp said. He could say this. Kwaja was completely still. "She will need water," he added.

"The guards bring the male prisoners to the yard now, but when we get our water, she can have my share, too."

Kipp studied the girl's narrow face. Her lips were swollen. The upper lip had a large red sore. She did not look strong enough to give away all her water.

"That is good of you," he whispered. "Save a little for yourself."

The girl felt the old woman's forehead with the back of her hand.

"Obi?"

Kipp turned and saw Zalika peering at him through the bars only two cells down. They'd all swarmed in at once and he'd passed her in his hurry to get outside. Leaving Sa Trivvi in her cell mate's care, he closed the cell door and headed for Zalika. There wasn't much time.

A guard hustled down the hall with his keys. "Where are you going, sweep?"

"Sor, to get my broom and bucket, Sor."

He slowly passed Zalika's cell. "Tomorrow," he whispered. "Sa Minn will tell you what to do. Be ready."

"Be ready for what? I—"

The guard was too close, and Kipp had no time to give an answer. He ran down the hall and grabbed his full bucket. At the sickening smell of human waste, guards frowned and drew quickly aside to let him pass.

Tomorrow, he thought, *Ahyuu, let it be tomorrow.*

CHAPTER THIRTY-THREE

JILLY WAS STILL awake when he entered the tent after taking a late meal with Sor Twam and Sa Minn outside by the fire. Sa Minn gave him sweal oil to ease the sting from the guard's whip, but he would wait to use it. His little sister should not see the fresh cuts on his ankles and back.

"Sor Twam said you went to help Zalika today," said Jilly. "Did you help her?"

"Yes," he said. "But I will have to go back and help her again tomorrow. Go to sleep now."

"Tell me a story," she whispered. Scritch was a round black ball curled on her belly.

Kipp lay on his bedroll and rested his head on his elbow. "I will tell you about a brother who saved his little sister from an evil landlord."

She giggled. "I know that story."

"You know it because it is yours."

She put out her hand, and he took it in his own. It was small and warm.

"There was once a brave little girl—"

"Don't call her little."

"There was once a very brave girl who was enslaved by a cruel landlord—"

"And her cat was named Scritch."

He smiled. "Quiet now," he whispered, "or I won't tell it."

At dawn Kipp lay belly-down on the sand dune and peered over the ridge, watching Sa Minn pass through the prison gate with her broom.

Now he would wait. There was no tree here to tie ChChka to. He'd tethered her to his ankle to keep her from wandering to the top of the dune where she might be spotted by tower guards. The mare's shadow cooled his back and darkened the sand by his arm. He scooted down and untied the knot so he could walk her about. Clouds passed overhead and eased the brightness of the morning sun. He felt it was a good sign, one to balance out the dead buck they'd passed on the way here.

Seven screeching vultures had surrounded the carcass. Kipp knew it to be a warning sign. Sa Minn noticed the sign, too, and she'd tightened her grip around the broom handle. She did not speak.

Beneath the dune, Kipp and ChChka paced, stood still, paced again. "You are my ChChka," he said. "My white lightning."

Kipp traced the rope lines wrapped about the sack beneath his right pant leg. Kwaja was completely still. He turned ChChka about another time. The prisoners would be marched outside again today when the sweepers cleaned their cells. He needed Kwaja to awaken. Without the sack's power they couldn't fly over the wall.

"Don't worry, ChChka," he said.

He thought of the vultures again as he walked, his muscles drawn tight as a slingshot. Half an hour passed. His hope of the day's rescue had begun to sink very low when he thought he felt the sack move. Kipp stopped, held his leg very still, waited. Yes, there it was, the unmistakable feel of Kwaja awakening to a call. The women were in the courtyard. He could not wait any longer.

"Now we fly over the wall for Zalika." He kissed ChChka for good luck the way he'd seen Zalika kiss Obi so long ago, very gently on the nose, then gathered a handful of sand and rode her along the base of the dune until ChChka's long legs left the ground and pedaled the morning air.

"You are mighty, ChChka," Kipp called.

Invisible, they rose over the stark desert; only the dark shadow racing across the sand rumored their existence. Cool wind washed over him. He thought of Zalika's dusty face and questioning eyes the day before. She would know what to do when Sa Minn delivered her message.

Be outside, he told her in his mind. *Be ready.*

OnnZurr seemed to grow larger as ChChka sped toward

it, a solid red wound on the landscape. Its high old walls dwarfed the newer iron gates. It still looked more like a tomb than a prison.

ChChka soared above the outlying cesspit where two sweepers emptied their buckets under a watchful guard. Kipp tensed. He had to be ready to grab Zalika fast. Before they reached the first tower, he urged ChChka to fly a little lower. The air around them changed; Kipp smelled unwashed bodies and sensed the despair that blew up from the prison. He imagined the prisoners' breath escaping in a mass, stirring a hot wind of prayers, of yearning and silent angry screams. Was Kwaja giving him this power or was he only imagining it?

Passing the high wall, he tugged the reins to the left and made ChChka wheel over the courtyard. Far below, women prisoners walked in a circle. He looked around, did not see Sa Minn. She was supposed to tell Zalika to let her headscarf fall across her neck. Two women were bareheaded below. Which one was Zalika? Kipp's heart pounded. He had to bring ChChka farther down.

He and ChChka were invisible, but they cast a shadow. Sa Minn had told Zalika to watch the ground for a horse-shaped shadow this morning. A guard had already noticed the dark shape moving at his feet and looked up, confused, until he spotted a few roving clouds overhead.

ChChka skimmed down. *When you see a strange shadow. When the wind blows sand overhead, put your hands up as if you need to stretch.* That was the rest of Sa Minn's message to Zalika. He spotted Sa Minn exiting a tunnel below with two sewage buckets. Kipp prayed she'd had the chance to speak to Zalika. ChChka flew in dangerously low, six or seven feet above the ground. Her hooves swept over the women's heads as Kipp released his handful of sand.

Halfway around the circle, a prisoner lifted her hands up as if to stretch out her back. Kipp saw her and swept closer in. *Take her.* Before ChChka passed the girl, he caught her arms and yanked with all his might. Zalika's weight nearly pulled him off the saddle. He strained to keep hold of her.

"Kipp?"

"Don't make a sound," he whispered. "No one else can see us in the air."

ChChka was heading down to land in the prison yard. He'd trained her to fly low, not to touch the ground without his signal, but the unexpected weight seemed to confuse her. Detch! He should have trained her to respond to his heels or his knees, should have known his hands would be busy trying to help Zalika up into the saddle.

A prisoner on their left screamed, "Deysoukus!" and pointed wild-eyed at the strange moving shadow. ChChka was only six feet up, weighted down with two riders when the guard rushed over, flailing his whip at the screaming prisoner. Dozens of tiny iron balls stung Kipp's arms and Zalika's back.

Zalika bit down a scream. ChChka startled and kicked

the guard's head as she tried to get away. The man groaned and slumped to the ground. More guards ran over. ChChka suddenly sped upward to flee the knot of dust and noise below.

As Kipp gave a final heave, Zalika put her leg over the saddle and gripped the horn. Reeling under the new weight, ChChka swerved away from the guard tower, barely skidding over the stone wall.

In the next moment, Kipp heard a whistling in the air. The warm desert breeze swept Zalika's yellow scarf against his cheek. The shouts from below faded. The prison courtyard shrank as they soared over the dunes.

CHAPTER THIRTY-FOUR

SPARKS FLEW ABOVE the central village fire where three women danced the story of Tiatuu's Egg. It was one of his favorite tales, but Kipp had never seen the dance. Zalika offered him a gourd. He sipped the sticky mebe juice and licked his lower lip. On his right, Sor Twam sat very stiff and erect. Kipp was eighteen tonight and had a right to celebrate Zalika's rescue; still, if he swallowed much more mebe, he'd be drunk. It would not be good manners for a guest to drink himself into a stupor. He passed the gourd along.

Just down the circle, Jilly sat in Sa Minn's lap. She'd been very excited to see Zalika today and had wanted to hear all about the escape. Kipp and Zalika had walked with Jilly by the village water hole to tell her everything in private. Except for Sor Twam and Sa Minn, the villagers were not to know who Zalika was or where she'd come from.

"We are old friends of Sa Minn and Sor Twam," Kipp had said. "We met when we all picked kora together. That is what you are to say. Can you remember that, Jilly?"

His little sister's eyes drooped now and she leaned against Sa Minn's chest. The woman's head swayed in rhythm to the music. *She must be very tired,* Kipp thought. He was sorry she'd had to stay on and finish out her workday at OnnZurr, but there was no other way to do it. She had to play out her part like an ordinary sweeper. When Sa Minn arrived back at Titaun Ezze, she'd built a fire, burned her broom, and clicked her tongue in disgust. "OnnZurr is a terrible place," she'd said. "I will never go there again."

"Taka, Sa, for everything you did to help Zalika." Kipp had given her a water bowl to wash the prison dust from her face and hands.

"You were very brave, Sa Minn," Zalika added. The Sa had dried her hands and nodded in agreement. "You," she said, "will need a fresh kirifa to wear." And she'd taken Zalika into her hut.

Drummers kept a steady beat. In the middle of the circle the dancer with the dragon mask gave Tiatuu a beautiful glowing egg.

When the dragon gave Tiatuu a sacred egg as a wedding gift, an egg with a crystal shell and a shining golden orb inside, Tiatuu treasured it above all her possessions.

The dancers used a small light jar with a glowing cheewii lizard inside for the "egg" in the dance. Musicians played gourd flutes, drums, and skree pipes. No one had to tell the story. They all knew it very well. Now the dragon was dancing in a circle around Tiatuu, warning her not to break the precious egg.

Kipp's belly was full. His head reeled. Zalika and Jilly were safe for now. He'd carried his worry for them both the whole time he'd carried Kwaja. Zalika was at his side now. She was thinner from her time at OnnZurr, but her eyes sparkled with the firelight. It was not just the mebe that made him feel this good. He was nearly bursting with pride over what he'd done.

He spoke into Zalika's ear. "Did you see the look on that guard's face after you disappeared?"

Zalika nodded, her head bobbing in rhythm with the drums. "I felt sorry for the prisoner who screamed."

"The guard shouldn't have whipped her," he said.

"They whip anyone who makes too much noise or steps out of the walking circle."

Kipp eyed the crowd watching the dance. The music veiled their private conversation as long as they spoke into each other's ears.

"I have to change my name," Zalika said. "Too many people have heard about the girl who was sent to OnnZurr for shooting a rich man." She tapped her knee in rhythm with the drums.

Kipp still did not know if she'd shot Sor Litchen on purpose. He'd told Sor Twam how the dog's sudden bark had thrown off her aim and emphasized that the shooting was an accident. In the light of the village fire, he eyed the outline of her face, her proud nose and delicate chin curving back to her long slender neck. At the archery competition he'd heard Sor Litchen call her a slut in front of everyone moments before she'd pulled back her bowstring. Was that why she'd done it? Did she want to hurt the man who'd made the deep and lasting scar down the inside of her leg? Or had she meant to hit the target all along, and the barking dog truly was to blame?

Zalika whispered, "What if I changed my name to Omaja? Do you like that name?"

He shook his head. Why would she choose the name given to the Daughter of Time? Maybe the dance gave her the idea. "It's not right for you."

"Why not?" Zalika toyed with the ankle bracelets Sa Minn had given her. She'd discarded her filthy yellow kirifa dress for a colorful orange-and-blue-lined skirt and top. *Outsiders might mistake her for a villager,* Kipp thought, *but the people here know she's not one of them.* He wrapped his arms about his knees and frowned. He'd thought only of rescuing Zalika from OnnZurr. But he hadn't had time to consider what to do next.

He wanted to be with Jilly and Zalika, not live constantly on the run, but he knew he couldn't do that as long as he had Kwaja. The Gwali and his hounds were on his trail and would find him sooner or later. They always did.

Watching the dancers twirling and swaying, Kipp allowed himself to think. It might be the mebe juice freeing his mind, or it might be the beauty of the dance, but he let himself consider the feeling that had been growing over the last few months. He'd hated being followed, always hunted down, but part of him liked living in the wild Farlands with his animals.

Sor Joay had taken him to the Farlands many times when he was young to hunt for food, for the table at home was often spare. He'd loved the rough journeys and was always sad when they had to return home. Like the Escuyan nomads, he longed for wide-open space.

Sor Joay said it was a man's right to live within the wind.

In his heart, Kipp had always wanted to live that way, to go from one place to another, to capture and raise wild horses as Sor Joay had taught him to do. He couldn't see how he could possibly do it with Zalika and Jilly to care for. He was not Escuyan and neither were they.

The gourd was passed his way. He took another gulp of mebe juice. "You are frowning," said Zalika. "What is the matter?"

Kipp shook his head and kept his eyes on the dancers. The flute song had changed. The story was unfolding.

Tiatuu was always and forever gazing at the golden yolk of the egg on which a tiny emerald dragon fed, so her husband became jealous of the pleasure it gave her. He fashioned a sharp spear and pierced the crystal shell.

The drummers made the sound of thunder as the "egg" was speared. And here the dance became more beautiful, for the cheewii in the jar they were using to represent the egg was a mature male with wings. When the jar was broken, he flew upward in the night, shining like a little yellow sun. His flight told the next part of the tale, how the golden yolk became the sun—and the first day was born.

The villagers sighed with pleasure at the tiny lizard's flight. The drums pattered down to silence. There was no music as the creature flitted higher and higher above the crowd.

The golden yolk rose as the sun. The first day was the end of the endlessness. Night followed day. In this way Time began.

The dancers escorted a little girl into the center. *Tiatuu's daughter, Omaja, was born soon after the crystal egg was broken. The girl was also called the Daughter of Time.*

Kipp had been thinking of each part of the story as he watched the people's graceful movements. The child dancing the part of Omaja carried a hand loom. She pretended to weave, then pulled a small colorful bag from her loom. A male dancer spun out from the crowd and pranced around the circle as if he were on horseback.

Zalika nudged Kipp. He smiled, too. The prancing man looked ridiculous, like a child pretending to ride a stick horse. Two other men danced out wearing hunters' armbands. One carried a small torch, the other a spear—the same spear used to pierce the egg.

The women had left the circle; only the little girl and the three men danced beyond the fire. Kipp wondered why the hunters and the horseman had come into the dance. He thought the story ended with the birth of the Daughter of Time.

"What are they doing?" he asked Sor Twam. The elder put a finger to his lips and pointed back to the three. He refused to speak while the dancers performed.

The music changed. It was very loud now. Kipp thought the musicians must be drunk on mebe juice. The gourd flutes and the stringed instruments were completely out of tune. The drummers pounded harder. Kipp wanted to plug his ears but it would not be polite. A good guest would pretend not to notice the trouble. Some of the villagers in the audience began to howl like dogs. The sound might frighten Jilly. Kipp looked along the circle and was relieved to see his sister fast asleep in Sa Minn's lap.

He returned to the dancers again. What he saw next sent a sour taste to his mouth. One of the hunters did a dance of murder, pretending to spear his companion in the heart. More villagers howled as the wounded man fell.

The horseman pranced closer and took the sack woven by Omaja, the Daughter of Time. The girl playing Omaja twirled over and seized the dead man's torch. The howling stopped, but the drums were deafening as she blew out the flame and plunged the smoking end into the sack.

Kipp swallowed. His pulse raced. The horseman was the

Gwali. He leaped up, sure he was going to be sick, and stumbled away from the circle.

"Kipp?" Zalika called behind him. "Wait."

Kipp didn't slow down. He fled the village fire, the ground swaying under him as he ran.

CHAPTER THIRTY-FIVE

ZALIKA WAS WAITING for him under the trees. He'd left the village dance to be alone. Couldn't a man go off to retch in private?

"Feeling better now?" she asked.

Kipp didn't answer. He watched her pluck a crescent-shaped eucalyptus leaf and run her finger along the curved edge. She crushed it to release its pungent fragrance and looked up. "You drank too much mebe."

Was she sniffing the leaf because his breath stank? He stepped back a little. "It wasn't the mebe, Zalika. I am eighteen now. I can drink as much as I want." Scenes from the dance came back to him: the Daughter of Time blowing out the dead man's torch, stuffing it into the sack. He knew the torch represented the dead man's soul, that the sack was Kwaja.

"What upset you, then?"

"I didn't like the murder," he admitted.

"It was only a dance."

"It was more than that, Zalika. Don't you see the horseman was supposed to be the Gwali?"

Zalika shrugged. The small motion infuriated him. Everything he'd done for her became a sham, something she could simply shrug off. Didn't she care that he'd saved her life not once but twice, or that he'd used his power to free her from OnnZurr?

"How did you think I got you over the wall today?" he snapped.

"You're drunk, Kipp. You're not making sense. I thought we were talking about the dance."

Kipp turned and climbed the hill. Zalika caught up with him, took his shoulders, and spun him back around. He pressed down another wave of nausea and peered at her defiant face. She'd fight if that was what he wanted to do. She was not the sort to shy away.

"I'm not drunk. I rescued you. We flew over the wall. How do you think I did that?"

"You said you had Naqui powers, remember?"

Kipp sat and plucked a foxtail from the grass. She was right. That was all he'd told her. He had not mentioned Kwaja or the Gwali to anyone today. He'd kept Kwaja's presence a secret from Sor Twam and Sa Minn, from Jilly and Zalika, and said only that he had Naqui powers. It was the truth, just not the whole truth. He had certainly not wanted to say more when he had soared over the prison wall with Zalika, tasting the sweet wind and the blue freedom of the sky.

On the moonlit hill above the dance, Zalika took a seat on the grass beside him. "Yesterday was the first time I'd seen you since I fell off Obi and you left me on the road. It was a shock seeing your face, hearing your voice there in OnnZurr." She, too, picked a foxtail. "I was furious with you for leaving me. I thought I would never forgive you. But after the first few weeks, I came to understand that you did what you had to do. I didn't blame you so much."

"Understand what?" *What did she think he'd done?*

"Well, if you had stayed on my father's land, you would have been whipped for taking me out riding. But after I fell, your punishment would have been much worse. Father would have had you arrested and taken to jail for my injury, and for stealing his horse."

"My horse. Cassia is . . . was mine."

"That would not matter to my father."

"Zalika—"

She put up her hand. "Let me finish. I thought about this for a long time. It wasn't entirely your fault. I asked you to teach me how to ride as a man rides. I was the one who decided to make Obi jump. And I know you took a risk after I fell. You rode back to the stable to tell Sor Jaffon that I was hurt and told him where I was. That was all you could do for me that night. After that, you had to get away. I wasn't so angry with you once I understood." She paused and looked at him a moment. "I would have done the same thing if I were you."

Kipp's insides were all in a knot. On the one hand Zalika thought he'd deserted her to save his own skin. On the other hand, she was able to forgive him for acting so selfishly. How could she forgive him when he could never have forgiven himself if he'd acted in such a cowardly way? She said she would have fled herself if she'd been in his position. Would she really have left him to die on the road? He couldn't believe that.

"Say something," she insisted. "I thought you would be glad to hear that I understood what you did, and why you had to go."

"It . . . wasn't that way, Zalika." He hardly knew where to begin. He sucked the moist end of his foxtail and gazed down the hill. Someone in the village played a lone skree pipe, but the drumming had stopped. The dance was ending, and Sor Twam might come looking for him soon. He didn't have much time.

"Remember the story I told you about the fire on my father's farm? I told it just a little while before you fell off Obi."

Zalika watched the trail of smoke rising over the huts toward the starry sky. "You saw the Gwali come with his hounds."

He nodded. She touched the scar on his neck with her

forefinger. It told him she remembered it all, even the part about giving his blood and braid to the Sanuu Witch in exchange for the potion.

"Did you believe me, Zalika?"

"I half-believed it. It was a strange tale. Some people think the Gwali is real. Others say it's an old ghost story and that's all."

"And now?"

She raised her brows and tapped her chin with her foxtail. "You helped me escape from OnnZurr on a flying horse today. That flight was like the dream I had the night I fell and hit my head. I dreamed then I was soaring through the night sky all the way to the golden edge of day. I was completely happy, flying into that light." She twirled the foxtail. "That was just a dream. But today was real. After our flight on ChChka's back, I think I can believe anything." Zalika took a breath and let out a long sigh.

Her sigh seemed to surround the two of them. Kipp imagined it spreading out, sending waves across the rustling grass. The hill they shared was a larger wave in a sea of grain.

"Why did you ask me about the Gwali?" she said.

"It has to do with what happened after you were injured." He told Zalika about stealing the Gwali's horse and sack to save her life. He spoke of all that happened as if in one long breath, even the thing he was most ashamed of, Sag Eye's death.

"I might have caught Kwaja and stopped it from taking

Sag Eye's soul." His stomach clenched remembering the man's cry for help.

"Sag Eye deserved to die," Zalika said.

Kipp thought of Pimple's slow response. Sag Eye had whipped the boy that night, so he'd crouched protectively beside the boulder, assessing the danger of the situation before going after his master's pills.

Still, Kipp had watched the sack floating closer to the dying man, and Epopo had freed his hands by the time Kwaja opened its mouth.

Crickets sang in the grass as if the stars were speaking.

"You are too hard on yourself, Kipp. You can't save everyone." Zalika reached over to run her fingers through his hair. Her touch sent a shiver down his neck. She pulled his hair toward her and plaited it. It had grown long enough to hold a man's braid for a while if it were braided tightly enough. Zalika tied it at the end with a small leather strap she'd worn about her wrist. This was a very personal act, her way of thanking him for all he'd done. He turned and touched the small scar on her cheek.

"You forgive so easily, Zalika." He kissed her chin and forehead before putting his lips against her mouth. She wrapped her arms around him and returned his kiss. The rich smell of the earth at night, of the crushed grass under their bodies, filled him. The tighter she held him, the freer he felt.

CHAPTER THIRTY-SIX

THEY KISSED a long while.

"You think I forgive easily?" She tapped the tip of his nose. "You're wrong about that. Sometimes I like to take revenge." She drew him closer and kissed him harder, revenge for his earlier kiss. Here on the hill outside the village, the only sounds were the crickets, his own heartbeat in his ears, the faraway pipe, the quick, warm breath coming through her nose as she kissed him.

"I like the way you get revenge," he said with a quick smile.

"Not everyone does."

The words rankled. Had she kissed others the way she kissed him? "What do you mean?"

"I was put in jail for taking revenge."

Kipp sat up and brushed off his clothes. "But that was an accident."

"How do you know?"

"I told you I was there and I saw what happened."

"I know, but you told me you climbed a tree to watch the competition from a distance. Did you hear what Sor Litchen called me?"

"Yes."

Kipp felt his shoulders tightening. What was she telling him?

"You heard it. It seemed like everyone there heard it when he called me a—" She stopped herself, refusing to say the word. "When he called me that, everything he'd done to me came back, Kipp. The scar down my leg started to scream. I wanted to hurt him. Do you understand?"

It was his turn to understand and to forgive her. "But you didn't mean to shoot him, Zalika."

"I did mean to, Kipp."

"To kill him?"

"I don't think so." She heaved a sigh. "I don't know."

Kipp tore out a thick handful of grass, a clump of earth clinging to its roots. Even this grass clung to life, held on to the thing that fed it.

Zalika gazed at the grass rooftops below. "I hate him for ruining me."

"He didn't ruin you. You did not become his mistress. You can still be pledged."

"To whom? Everyone in Zolya would know his version of the story by now. What man would pledge with me?"

Kipp dropped the grass clump. "Give me time, Zalika."

It was not what he'd wanted to say, but Zalika kept changing, shifting. He loved her, but she'd shot a man, maybe even meant to kill him, and here he'd spent the last few months fighting death. This new truth made his head pound. This beautiful, strong girl was so completely different from him. She was so resolute, so free from shame over what she'd done. He had to think.

"Your valor would have earned you the white braid-bead a man needs to win a wife if you could speak to anyone about what you've done the past few months," she said. She was not looking at him now. "But we would always be outsiders if we pledged. We both know that."

Kipp put his arm around her and held her close enough to smell her hair and skin. He could not think of a place where he and Zalika and Jilly might be accepted. Much as he liked the Escuyan people, he was sure they would not want them to build a hut here or in any other village. They might farm a piece of land even more isolated than the one Kipp's father had worked, but his father's dream had failed and Kipp couldn't repeat the past.

He was too confused to talk about their future any longer. "You know I'll have to leave again soon. I still have to find a way to get rid of the Gwali's sack."

"Can't you just bury it again?"

"His hounds would find it. Kwaja draws the Gwali to it somehow; at least I think it does." He thought of burying

Kwaja under the acacias, of the towns and villages he'd passed through only to hear the Gwali had just been there looking for him. "I have managed to get away so far, but they always find me sooner or later no matter how far I fly or ride."

"What will you do then?"

He shook his head. He didn't know, but he could not stay. They held each other a long while in silence. Then Zalika said, "I want you to take me with you."

He could not respond to this. His throat felt hollow.

Sa Minn was walking up the hill toward them. "It is late, Zalika," she said irritably. "Come with me to the hut."

Zalika did not argue with her. She followed the old woman through the blowing grass, her long scarf fluttering behind her in the moonlight. A little while later, Sor Twam climbed the hill and settled beside Kipp. He sighed as he placed his light jar on the ground between them. The cheewiis inside glowed softly in their sleep.

"When you left the dance with Zalika, it did not look honorable."

"I'm sorry, Sor. I didn't ask her to come. I meant to get away alone because I felt sick."

"Too much mebe juice," Sor Twam said. He cleared his throat and turned the light jar. "You did not join with her tonight, did you, Kipp?"

"I would not do that to a girl when we are not pledged, Sor."

The old man nodded. "That is good."

"I wanted to."

They both laughed. Sor Twam was old, but he was a man. He understood.

"What will you do now?"

"I will have to leave again soon."

"What about Zalika and your sister?"

"I cannot take them, Sor."

"What is so important that you would leave these two girls who now depend on you? A man does not do this. A man does what he must to protect the ones he loves."

He said this in a challenging voice; his eyes focused on Kipp's new braid.

"It's for their protection I have to go. Will you look after them for me, Sor?"

It was a lot to ask his friend. Kipp knew it. But he had nowhere else to turn, no one else he trusted.

"I cannot look after them for you."

Kipp felt hurt. "Why, Sor?"

"I'm leaving the village soon to take my last Lostwalk. I will go in search of the titauns."

Kipp drew his knees closer to his chest. The Sor's words troubled him. What did he mean by his last Lostwalk? Where would he walk in search of dragons?

The old man unscrewed the lid on his light jar. "Wake up," he said, nudging one of the lizards with his finger. The cheewii lifted his head. Gently tipping the jar on its side, he let the lizards out. The cheewiis' dull, sleepy color changed to a bold yellow-green as soon as they stepped into the grass. Kipp watched them opening their wings.

"Go now and find your grandfathers," Sor Twam said. "Tell the titauns I am coming."

The cheewiis walked in a tight circle head to tail, moving their bright wings up and down to gather strength. Then they took to the sky, rising like twinkling stars in the direction of the heavens.

Kipp was sound asleep in the hut when the howls awakened him—a wild baying that made him jump from his bedroll. Shivering, he crept to the door flap and peered outside. The stars hid behind heavy clouds. He could not tell how late it was or when the dawn would come, but he recognized the chilling call of the Gwali's dogs somewhere in the distance, and knew he had to run.

Sor Twam snored in the corner. Kipp looked around, his eyes adjusting to the dark. Down on his knees, he pushed Jilly's blonde hair away from her cheek. She was breathing softly, her hand resting on Scritch's back. He had to leave her behind again. He was always promising to stay, always leaving. She was too young to understand; still, he knew how much it hurt her.

He dressed, grabbed his bedroll, and slipped outside. Epopo followed him to the village corral. Once he was in the saddle, he ran his hand along his leg. Kwaja lay perfectly still. There would be no pulling into flight this time. Detch! Just when he really needed to fly!

Dust whirled behind them as they fled the village. Zalika had wanted to come, but he wouldn't think of putting her in such danger. Sor Twam had said, *A man does what he must to protect the ones he loves.* It was right to finish what he had started when he'd stolen Kwaja, and right to do it alone.

A stark wind blew against his back as ChChka raced beyond the trees. Titaun Ezze was a warm and comforting place. It was also confining. Alone with his animals again, he came into himself. His senses sharpened. Alert. On the move. He felt like a young male cheewii lizard abandoning its jar.

CHAPTER THIRTY-SEVEN

K IPP CINCHED IN his belt another notch. A week had passed since he'd outrun the Gwali and his pack. They'd spotted him only a mile away from Titaun Ezze and chased him till dawn when Kwaja mercifully awakened and flew ChChka over the dunes. Out in the Farlands again, living on the run, he'd carved a new slingshot, killed a mongoose one night, a quail three days later; still, his stomach churned with hunger the next day when he passed a lion's kill.

Screeching vultures were hopping up and down around the antelope's half-eaten carcass. Kipp quickly dismounted and raced up, shouting and waving his arms. The vultures flew upward, their wings flapping like dry leather. As he approached the antelope, they took turns diving at his head to drive him away. Kipp swatted the air and fell on his knees, hungry enough to eat the raw meat.

Epopo was already gnawing a leg. Kipp lowered his head, saw the state of the kill, and covered his nose. The meat was rotting in places and already crawling with maggots. He knew if he ate any, he would be sick.

"Let go, Epopo!" He pushed his dog away. Epopo growled and curled his lip. Their eyes met. Epopo had never growled like that before, but Kipp understood the hunger that made him do it. He stood and slapped his leg. "Come, boy," he ordered, "Now!" He didn't need a sick dog on his hands.

Epopo gave in and followed him back to ChChka. The vultures landed, their dark wings covering the body like a rippling, moth-eaten blanket.

Later that day Kipp found a few silouk, quickly dug them up, and ate the thick roots raw. He caught and cooked some locusts and shared some with Epopo, though there were not enough for either of them. He drank water to fill his belly. Two nights later, as he cleared the debris to make camp in a rock-strewn gully, he spotted a thin line of smoke rising over a distant glade and caught the rich scent of spiced meat cooking over an open fire. Kipp jumped back into the saddle.

"Remember the story of Prince Epopo?"

Epopo looked up as if to acknowledge the question.

"You should not give up your kingdom for a meal," Kipp said. He was telling himself this, not his horse or his dog, saying the words aloud so he would remember to approach a stranger out here in the Farlands with caution. But the words were sounds and air. They would not fill his belly, and at this moment, he felt as if he would all too easily give up a kingdom for a meal. He was ashamed, but it was the truth.

Kipp drew the knife from his boot as they topped the highest hill. The trees provided some covering to peer down without being seen, but they also obscured half of the cook fire. No one was talking. Either these men were silent, or there was but one man below. Kipp checked the woods, and listened for any sounds the Gwali's hounds might make. A figure in Escuyan clothing came into view. A lone hunter? He stood with his back to the hill, his short, bent stature telling Kipp all he needed to know. He was not the Death Catcher.

Relieved but still cautious, Kipp proceeded down on ChChka. Her hooves made crackling sounds on the forest floor. He should probably dismount, leave her here, and creep soundlessly the rest of the way to the camp, but he might have to make a quick getaway. He stayed in the saddle.

When they were less than ten yards away, Kipp peered between the tree trunks and saw the fire was now abandoned. He whipped his head about, searching for the place where a man or men must be hiding.

"I mean no harm," he said. A good thing to say if these were peaceful men. A stupid thing to say if they were thieves.

The old man stepped out from behind a tree.

Kipp rode up a little closer, dismounted, and raced over to him.

"Sor Twam," he said. His heart was ahead of his mouth. He could not believe his friend was here. Kipp laughed so hard it forced out tears, then to his great embarrassment, a sob wrenched free, like a rock coming off a mountain. He put his hands on his knees and bent over, laughing, crying, trying to control the wild sounds leaping from his mouth. Out of the corner of his eye he saw ChChka backing away from him, Epopo's ears twitching with concern.

"It's all right," he said, taking several breaths. "I'll be all right, just give me a moment." His knees felt weak. He half sat, half fell onto the log, and adjusted his hat. He wished he could pull the brim down and cover his wet face. He wiped his nose and eyes as Sor Twam took his seat across from him.

"Sorry, Sor. I am . . ." He couldn't explain his outburst. He didn't understand it himself. "I was surprised to see you here," he said at last. That accounted for part of it, anyway.

Sor Twam had not yet said a word. He poked the meat with a stick. It was some kind of wild bird, but Kipp could not see the color of the feathers piled up nearby where the old man had plucked it. Sor Twam took the meat from the flames, cut it up, and offered some to Kipp.

"Taka, Sor."

The old man did not nod back or say, "Ee-tak."

Kipp inhaled the meat. Sor Twam passed him another piece. This time he shared some with Epopo. Unlike Kipp and his dog, the elder ate slowly and seemed to be in no hurry. The hot spices in the meat stung Kipp's mouth, and he paused to lick his lips. The sting was like Zalika's angry kiss before her mood changed and became playful.

He eyed Sor Twam. He was growing more and more uncomfortable with the man's silence. "I'm grateful to you for the meal, Sor. I can't tell you how hungry I've been."

Still silent, Sor Twam turned his drumstick to chew the other side.

Kipp adjusted his position on the log. "You are angry with me for leaving so suddenly," he said. "I couldn't stay to say good-bye to Zalika and Jilly or make arrangements for them. I had to leave that night. I hope you can forgive me, Sor."

No nod of acknowledgement, only a blank stare. Kipp shifted on the log uneasily. "I hope Sa Minn was able to take care of Jilly and help Zalika after I left, Sor. I hope they did not cause the village any trouble."

Kipp was desperate for some reassurance now. "Sor, why won't you speak?"

The old man pointed overhead. Kipp looked up. Did he mean the branches? No, he was pointing at the stars.

"Sor, I don't understand."

Sor Twam lowered his hand and waited as if to say he would explain no more than that. Kipp closed his eyes a moment, remembering the last time he'd spoken with his friend. He thought of the words he'd said as they watched the cheewiis fly into the sky. *Go now and find your grandfathers. Tell the titauns I am coming.*

Kipp stood up to go. "I have disturbed your Lostwalk. I am sorry, Sor." He did not want to leave, but he was trespassing on a sacred rite and had broken the man's solitude. The steps back to his white mare were few. They were not easy.

Sor, he thought, *let me stay with you tonight. I will leave tomorrow, I promise.* He cared too much for his friend's journey to say the words aloud.

"Kipp?" He was not imagining it. Sor Twam had said his name. Kipp turned. "You have been on your own Lostwalk, I think."

Kipp had not thought of it that way. "Yes, Sor," he said. He rubbed ChChka's neck, waiting.

"A Lostwalk is taken alone."

"I know that, Sor."

"When my fire called you here, my silence was broken."

"I am sorry for that. I did not think—"

"Sit." Sor Twam motioned for him to take the spot he'd abandoned. He stroked his stubbled face. Escuyans did not shave when they were on a journey. "I will make us some hot kora."

"I would like that," Kipp said gratefully. "I will leave after that, if you wish."

Sor Twam swiped his hand in the air. "Sometimes the fire spirit, Techee, serves us. She cooks a meal. She brings a friend. Let's wait to hear what she has to say."

Kipp looked into the flames, wondering if this was so.

Techee had taken so much from him. Right now she was giving him warmth, she was boiling water for the kora.

The golden flames were so hot they tightened the skin on his face, so bright they stung his eyes. He thought of the torch the Daughter of Time blew out at the end of the dance. In that enactment, Techee's flame was supposed to represent a man's soul.

"Remember the dance that was given the night I left the village?"

Sor Twam nodded as he took out a cup. Kipp talked about the disturbing part at the end of the dance as his friend made the kora.

"Why did this bother you?" Sor Twam asked as he passed him a cup.

Kipp pursed his lips and blew a narrow stream of breath to cool the steaming drink. "I had never heard that part of the story. I only remembered the part about the birth of the Daughter of Time."

"That is only half an ending. When time began, death followed."

"Why, Sor?"

"Things that have a beginning will have an end."

"The mountains had a beginning, the rocks and the rivers. They do not die."

"They change very slowly. The mountain loses rocks, the rocks go to sand, the rivers dry up when the snow and rain does not feed them."

"But they do not die," Kipp insisted. "Why do we have to?"

"Death is one of the changes. You can think of it that way. When the Daughter of Time wove the soul sack, Kwaja, on her loom, she—"

"Sor?" Kipp trembled violently. Kora lapped over the side of his cup, burning his fingers. "Is that who made the sack?" He'd seen that part of the dance, the girl twirling in with her hand loom, freeing the bag before she gave it to the rider. His eyes had taken it in. His mind had shut against it. He only remembered the part that came later, one hunter killing the other, the man's soul, an extinguished torch, stuffed into the sack.

"It is an old story," said Sor Twam. "Drink your kora before it turns cold."

Kipp could not drink. His head brimmed with new thoughts. He had not been able to burn Kwaja, knife it, unravel it, or bury it. He could not destroy a thing the gods had made.

He put the cup down and placed his hand on his pant leg where Kwaja hid. "There is something I must tell you."

The fire had eaten two more logs before Kipp's story was done. Smoke rose like many ghosts. Kipp's throat was raw from the telling, but he was not ashamed. He'd done his best to close the sack and save the ones he loved from the Gwali.

It would be morning soon. Sor Twam stirred the coals with a long stick; orange eyes peered out of the ashes.

"This sack you have," he said at last. "You cannot destroy it."

"Sor, I will not let the Gwali take it back."

"You are determined?"

Kipp nodded.

Sor Twam put down his stick. The end was smoking like a dampened torch. "The Daughter of Time wove Kwaja," he said. "She is the only one who can destroy it."

CHAPTER THIRTY-EIGHT

K IPP LED CHCHKA over another dune. Sor Twam looked down from the saddle.

"When my father took me to the dragon cave, he said the painting on the wall is also a map."

Kipp held the reins and stepped into his shadow. It was Sor Twam's turn to ride the mare. They'd traveled together nine days and nights heading for the Pinnacle Mountains. He tried to recall the details of the dragon paintings he'd seen in the sacred cave when he was fourteen.

"Where is the map hidden, Sor? I do not remember seeing one." Sor Twam now knew how Kipp had entered the cave to bring Sor Joay out of the driving rain when the old man was burning up with fever.

"It is not hidden," he answered. "The titauns shape the map."

Three nights later, torches in hand, Kipp explored the cave walls with Sor Twam.

He choked on the torch smoke curling up from the flame. He'd lowered it to see the bottom half of the painting. There were many ancient paintings in the underground caves, but this was the largest one, the only one with dragons. He shivered as his eyes passed over the people. They were running in a large group below the dragons the way the antelopes had run below him when he'd flown over the Farlands on ChChka.

Were the dragons the hunters and the humans the prey? "Why are they running, Sor? Do you think they are afraid?"

"Look." Sor Twam pointed at their empty hands. "They have no weapons. They would carry spears or be in hiding from the titauns if they feared an attack."

"Unless the titauns surprised them," said Kipp. "They might have hidden here in the cave and made these paintings to tell their story."

Sor Twam nodded. "That is one way to see it."

Kipp stepped along the wall and raised his torch higher. The cave was very cold. He'd welcomed the chill after so many long days under the scorching sun; now he wished he'd put on his coat.

This part of the wall was more than thirty feet long and twelve feet high. It was the largest painting. Kipp studied the green-and-silver dragons. Their bodies were the color of wet kora leaves after a good storm, their wings the clear bright color of a mountain river.

From one end of the wall to the other, the dragons seemed to fly in a great circle. How could a circle be a map? He walked to the middle of the wall. Moving his torch left and right, he saw the silver oval painted high above. Next to it another oval, split in half, was tipped to one side.

When he'd looked up at it years ago, he knew those shapes to be phases of the moon. But the full one was not quite round. Had the painter become lazy or . . . An idea flitted through his mind.

"Sor?" His hand shook as he pointed. "Is that Tiatuu's egg?"

Sor Twam studied it a moment. The whole egg, the broken shell next to it. Then he spoke a line from the old tale: "The dragon told Tiatuu the egg would always and forever glow for her, and she must never break it."

Kipp said, "But her jealous husband speared the egg, and in that moment, time began."

He pointed to the broken egg. "Here is where the map begins, I think, Sor."

A map that began high up in the middle of the painting. How was he to read it? What did it mean? A far-off mountain range was lightly painted in the background below the celestial egg. Sor Twam raised his arm and traced the mountains with his finger. His hand grew still, hovering in the air so it cast a shadow across the painting. "And this is TeySaaNey, the singing towers at the edge of the world."

Kipp looked closer and shook his head. "It can't be, Sor.

I know that shape. That mountain shelf is Titaun Koy, the dragon's jaw. It is only two miles from the place I used to live."

"Why would it be painted here, three high towers"—Sor Twam pointed to each tower—"standing so and so and so, just below the dragon's egg shell in the sky, if it were not TeySaaNey?"

"They are not towers. We call them Titaun's teeth. I have been there, Sor. It is not the edge of the world."

The old man turned. "How do you know this?"

"I know, Sor!" His words echoed around them as if many ghosts were shouting.

When the cave grew quiet again, Sor Twam said, "Look at the painting, Kipp. Tell me what you see."

Kipp shivered. Sor Joay used to ask him this very question. He'd said these words here in this cave when Kipp was fourteen.

He studied the wall again, starting at the place where the broken dragon's egg hung high above, then sweeping his eyes across the dragons flying in a great circle.

The dragons' colors were bright as they swung down over the people's heads, but as they turned left again over the mountains, heading back to Tiatuu's egg, the pigments dimmed, as if that part were much older and had worn away. But what if the lighter, less distinguishable dragons were painted that way from the start? What if the painter meant to show the dragons disappearing as they flew out-

never still in the highlands; it washed restlessly over the earth. It stung the ears and chapped the face in winter. It blew hot breaths across your back in summer. It whistled playfully at night, or moaned like an old man begging at the door.

Sor Twam asked, "Which tower is past? Which one is present? Which one is future?" Here was the riddle they must solve if they were to find the dragons.

"It is like asking where this song begins," said Kipp.

"It is the same question."

Sor Twam went to the right-hand tower and walked about the base, Kipp following behind. Both ran their hands along the rough surface as if seeking out a door. The old man stooped, leaning now and then on the spire like a giant's staff. Epopo began racing in a wider circle around them. Cold gusts slapped Kipp's face, then shifted and pushed against his back.

"I have come here before." Kipp shouted over the wind to be heard. "I've never seen any dragons here."

The old man went to the next and tallest tower, rising fifty feet or more. He had not heard Kipp, or else he was ignoring him. Putting his hand out, he felt along the sides as he half-walked, half-stumbled around the base.

"Sor, you should rest."

Sor Twam turned, shouting back, "Go rest if you want to, Kipp. I have come to see titauns before I die."

"You won't die, Sor. I won't let you."

Kipp tried to take his arm. Sor Twam pulled away. In the ghostly moonlight, his skin seemed parchment-thin across his bones. Kipp saw the shape of his skull beneath; saw the crazy, haunted look in his eyes. *His face hasn't changed,* Kipp thought, *it's a trick of the moonlight.* Still he feared for him as he continued to walk around the stone spire, feeling the rough surface like a blind man.

When Sor Twam's dark fingers disappeared into a crevice, the old man felt upward and found another hole. Placing his foot in the lowest groove, he reached for the handhold above.

"Sor? What are you doing?" Kipp watched in awe as Sor Twam began to scale the lower section of the tower like a spider crawling up a wall.

"Come down," Kipp called. "It's not safe up there. You will fall!"

Again the man played deaf. Racing back to ChChka, Kipp drew the rope from the saddlebag, tied it about his waist, and left the rest coiled over his shoulder. He found the handholds and carefully began his ascent. After a few minutes, he stopped to look down and was overcome with dizziness.

Ahyuu, help us. I don't want him to fall. I don't want to fall.

A wicked wind was rising. It swept in from all directions, pounding the mountain like a drum. Gusts whipped past Kipp as he clung fiercely to another handhold and pulled himself up. The dark sky above filled with swirling flashes as if Ahyuu were stirring the stars in the great bowl of the night.

The sparkling lights wheeled high above. He'd heard the cheewii lizards swarmed very high in the sky when they did their mating dance. When the females flew in close enough, the two cheewiis would join together, coupling in the sky. He'd seen the winged males before but never in such numbers.

Kipp found another foothold, clenched his teeth, and pulled himself up. The cheewiis circled lower. They looked so much bigger than their younger wingless brothers captured in the jars. Kipp did not know they grew that large.

The song of the singing towers was in the scouring wind. His ears were full of sound, his eyes full of dark and spinning light. It was madness to climb so high. The old man had lost his mind. He wanted to die. He was like the bone thrower, bringing Kipp along to open the sack for him when he was ready. Was that why Sor Twam had come here? Was that what they were doing?

Kipp took a breath and strained for another pull. *The bone thrower lived. He did not get his wish.* Kipp's fingers ached from clinging to the handholds. *Sor Twam would not get his wish, either. Kipp would not open Kwaja for him.* The sack rubbed against his leg as he climbed. He'd tied the knots himself to keep it bound.

Kipp's muscles trembled with exertion. He wondered at the old man's strength.

As he closed in on the top, Sor Twam stopped moving

and clung to the tower. Maybe he was coming to his senses at last. Kipp pulled himself closer. If he climbed high enough to pass the rope, the old man might be able to loop it over the top of the stone pinnacle so they could climb safely down.

"Sor?" Kipp called. They would have to work together; even trying to pass the rope would be a feat. He would have to cling to the crevice with one hand to do it, and that alone could make him fall.

The old man did not respond. His head was up as he watched the circling cheewiis. "Ah . . . Ah . . ."

Kipp clung tighter and gazed up. Two eyes see what they want to see, but to follow another's eyes is to look through them and find what they are seeing. That was how he saw. The winged ones were not cheewiis; they were dragons.

CHAPTER FORTY

T HE WHEELING BODIES shone greenish-white
with the same luminescence as the cheewiis, but as
they flew lower down, Kipp saw their true size and felt their
great silver wings churning with the power of waterfalls.

Sor Twam groaned with pleasure or fear or both. Kipp
couldn't make a sound. His eyes could not take in what he
saw. He felt the titauns with his whole body, with his prick-
ling skin, his open mouth, his racing blood and heart. The
titauns were living earth, living water, living light, and the
cave paintings did not speak the truth of them. He knew
now that the wind he'd felt from all directions had come
from the dragons' enormous flapping wings.

The gale strengthened as the dragons flew closer. Kipp's dark
coat fluttered behind him. His body went rigid fighting the
gusts. His muscles strained and trembled as he tried to hold on.

There was a terrified shout overhead as Sor Twam lost the fight and was swept away.

"Sor!" Kipp screamed.

Arms waving, the old man swirled like a leaf and smashed into a dragon's golden chest. Kipp gripped the crevices and tried to press his body against the tower. A moment later, another powerful gust blew him off TeySaaNey. He choked on a scream and the wind was knocked out of him as he was blown against a dragon. The creature clutched him to its chest.

He shut his eyes against the glaring light, then opened them again, sucking in a breath as the titaun ascended with the others. The night air was freezing. But the golden scales were warm against his back. He looked left and right, caught sight of Sor Twam with another dragon, and lost him the next moment as the flock spiraled upward.

Why had they ripped them from the tower? Far below, Titaun Koy looked as small as an anthill, the stone pinnacles shorter than his little finger. The Twilgar mountain ranges shrank below as the dragons winged higher into the night, into the moon, their circling bodies mirror-bright. One arm free, Kipp shaded his eyes against the brightness.

If the great mountains were small, he felt himself to be even smaller, like a tiny moth pressed against a glassy lamp. Moths reached the place they yearned to go, only to be destroyed. He was afraid for Sor Twam, disgusted at himself for thinking he could meet and understand dragons. Compared to these beings moving inside and outside of time at will, he was a mere insect. He did not know why the dragon still clutched him to its chest unless it was to take him somewhere and toy with him the way he and Royan used to toy with moths.

The fierce storm sent an icy wind through him. Only the hot scales at his back and the arm pressed against his stomach and chest kept him from freezing. The dragons flew faster in a great silver ring, their speed joining them head to tail. Kipp couldn't tell where one ended and another began as the bright crown rose heavenward. They sped faster and faster until he screamed, fearing he would be torn apart.

Then suddenly, everything stopped: the terrible spinning, the ripping wind. Across the great circle, he saw Sor Twam's dragon still holding the old man. The distance and brightness of the dragon's scales made it impossible to read the expression on his face. Was he elated or terrified or both? Was this what he'd gone on his Lostwalk to find?

They had come to a dark and starless place. The dragons folded their wings and hung tail-down in the abyss of night. All was black but for the creatures' luminescence. Where was this empty place? How could they hang here and not fall?

Kipp looked down. Far beneath the titauns, the world turned light to dark to light, blinking like a great eye as it sped from day to night in quick succession. Kipp trembled.

He was seeing things as Ahyuu might see them, the world small as a nutshell, each day a flicker.

Slowly, very slowly, the dragons began to turn the way a leaf wavers at the end of a spider's web in a quiet breeze. But there was nothing to hang from in this dark space, and no breeze to make them spin.

They turned softly like the flowers and insects suspended in the witch's jars. The roaring wind had swept away all sound. It was so silent in this dark, Kipp could not even hear his own breathing.

TeySaaNey, past, present, future—this was not how he'd imagined moving in and out of time. The titauns were not moving at all, they were waiting. The world spun in time below and they were suspended above it.

He was just beginning to take this in when the air around him began to stir. Wings unfolded gradually to flight and the dragons spiraled down. Through the mist, Kipp saw a great mountain range from above. He thought it was the Twilgar range until he saw they were flying over a vast open sea. His heart beat wildly. Where were they taking him? He had to call out, ask to be flown to the Daughter of Time. He was too much in awe to speak, too afraid not to.

"Sor Dragon?" He should use the formal Escuyan name. "Sor Titaun? Will you take me to the Daughter of Time?"

Wings pumped above, waves appeared below. The Daughter of Time had a name. He cleared his throat and tried again. "Sor Titaun? I have a gift for Omaja. Would you please bring me to the place where Omaja dwells?" He was mortal, asking to go to a place of the gods. Would the titauns take him?

They were speeding lower now over the sea. He couldn't see Sor Twam's titaun or the rest of the dragons to his left or right. They must be flying above him. The light moving across the face of the ocean could be coming from the other titauns above, or it could be sunlight. The dragon set Kipp down in a lone black boat. Two oars and no sails.

"Where am I, Sor Titaun? Where is this place?"

The creature dropped a small stone at Kipp's feet and left him with a single slap of wings. It rose into the clouds and seemed to become a part of the morning sky. Kipp picked up the gray-green stone and turned it in his hand. It was a bead, he realized, a moss agate with a small hole through the middle. Where had the titaun gotten the bead, and why had he dropped it at his feet?

Kipp looked up and saw only white clouds drifting over the water. *They are always here*, Kipp thought, *always watching, only we cannot see them.* There was no other boat floating nearby. Had Sor Twam's dragon left him on another vessel or flown him to the mountainous land, still veiled in mist ahead? Pulling the tinderbox from his pocket, Kipp placed the dragon's bead inside for safekeeping, took up the oars, and began to row.

The sea was bright turquoise and so clear that when he

reached the reef he could see giant sea turtles and small bright sunfish swimming under the surface. A river at the base of the mountain fed into the ocean. He rowed around the wet boulders, then put the oars down to disembark outside a cave. Before he could stand, a wave came behind him and washed his boat into the rocky opening.

The shining water at the entrance was reflected in dancing patterns on the walls, and the holes in the ceiling let more light through. Beams fell against the surface of the water and lit the riverbed below.

Oars in hand, he rowed again, but the craft only turned in place as he tugged the water. His right boot lost its footing. His leg straightened. Kwaja was awake, pulling him and his small boat deeper into the passage. Turtles swam below the craft in the direction of the pull.

Kipp didn't put up a fight. Some change had come into him. He felt closer to his goal and all the stronger for it. "Is your mistress near, Kwaja? Are you taking me to her?" He did not say his next thought aloud: *Will she agree to destroy the sack?*

The light faded as they drifted farther in. The dark was nearly complete when the boat knocked against a rocky shelf. Kipp drew out Sor Joay's tinderbox and struck a flint. The brief sparks showed him a stone stairwell. There was no tinder, not even a stick to burn. He would have to climb it in the dark.

A small hook jutting from the bottom step gave him a

place to tie up his boat. Feeling his way along, he ascended slowly. He felt slime and moss along the walls, and some on the stairs. Slipping twice, he scraped his hands trying to catch himself. The rowboat still knocked against the bottom stair far below. The sound was comforting. He could race down and row out if he had to. For now he would keep going.

The moist air smelled of wet stone. He was out of breath when he felt what must be a wooden door.

CHAPTER FORTY-ONE

K IPP RAN HIS HAND along the rough wood surface. It was a round door about six feet high. The metal handle squeaked as it turned, and the door swung open to a bright sunlit garden terraced into the side of the mountain. The tumbling waterfall to the right of the garden sent a thick white spray over the trees, bushes, and flower beds. There were two more terraces overhead, connected by stone stairs along the right side of each wall. Above that he glimpsed a temple or fortress built into the side of the mountain. He'd not seen it through the mist from his small boat, nor from below when the sun had broken through the gray veil just before he reached the river cave.

Approaching the wall at the edge of a sheer drop, Kipp wrapped his arm around a sapling and peered down. The waterfall filled a rippling pool far below, which narrowed and deepened before it disappeared into the dark cave. This was the source of the river he'd come in on.

The sound of a child's laughter made him turn abruptly.

"Aum," said Kipp. He gave a quick smile, hoping his sudden appearance had not alarmed the little girl. "I found your garden. I hope this is all right."

"My garden?" she said with a laugh.

"Your master's garden, then," he guessed, "or your mistress's?"

The girl ran in a circle around him. She was barefoot and dressed in a long white gown that complemented her smooth bronze skin. Her thick belt was shot with golden threads; her dark braided hair was adorned with flowers. He saw the wealth in her clothing, though it was simple in design. He might have been wrong to say "master" or "mistress"; perhaps the word *parent* would have been better. She was likely the child of the one who dwelled in the great fortress or temple above.

"I am looking for someone. Do you know Mistress Omaja?"

"Did the titauns bring you?" asked the girl. She was swinging now on a frail orange tree branch, her weight bending it like a bow.

"Yes, that is how I came here." He saw no reason to lie to the child.

The branch broke with a sudden loud snap. The girl fell and landed on her feet.

"Now you've broken it," Kipp said.

"I did not break it yet."

Jumping up, branch in hand, she swiftly attached it to the orange tree. Kipp stepped up and ran his hand along the wood. There was no seam. It was as if it had never broken. "How did you do that?"

The girl grabbed her dusty copper-colored sandals from beneath a flowering bush and ran up the stone stairs to the next garden terrace. Kwaja tugged Kipp toward the stairway. He reached the top in time to glimpse the hem of the child's white gown blowing conspicuously behind an apple tree. He had not come here to play. The little girl was becoming annoying.

"Does Mistress Omaja live up in that temple?" he asked as he stepped around the tree. He was met by a young woman of startling beauty. He had caught her in the act of slipping on her sandal. She wore the same style of dress and belt as the little girl. Bright flowers shone in her coiled braids. Kipp's mouth went dry. His heart pounded. He had never spoken to such a woman. Her face was the mature flowering of the child's. *She must be the little girl's older sister.*

"Please forgive me, Sa, for stepping so abruptly into your garden," Kipp said awkwardly. "I came here looking for someone."

"It is the only reason for one such as yourself to come here," she said matter-of-factly. He wondered what she meant by "one such as yourself." He glanced down at his torn, dusty clothes and realized how disreputable he must look to one so clean and finely dressed.

"I am not as I appear to be," he said quickly. "I am no one's servant. I am my own man."

"So you own yourself?" she said with a wry smile.

"I . . ." He could think of no clever response. "I came a long way to see Mistress Omaja. I don't have time for games."

"Who has time?" she asked. Another trick question. She turned about and walked gracefully up the last flight of stairs. His heart thudded as he followed. Though the smallest, the highest terrace garden was the most magnificent of the three. The ground, bushes, and trees were riotous with flowers. His eyes were drawn to a marble fountain richly carved with flying dragons in the center of the courtyard at the base of the temple stairs.

A middle-aged woman sat on the fountain edge, beckoning Kipp closer. He looked about for the young woman who had just come up the steps. Was she somewhere behind the trees, or had she gone through the double doors into the temple? He could see from here that the richly patterned doors were wide open.

Kipp circled the fountain. The twelve-foot-high marble dragons spouted water from their mouths. Below them, lions, antelopes, and wildebeests were carved on the round rim surrounding the pool. Horses and dogs were also hewn into the stone. Kipp thought of ChChka and Epopo encamped near the singing towers. Was it night there still? How much time had passed?

The woman sitting upright on the marble edge looked remarkably like the two girls. *This must be their mother*, he thought as he gave a quick bow. A woman this age deserved respect.

"Do you like the titauns?" she asked, lifting her hand to the marble dragons. The fountain spray made a small rainbow over her head.

Kipp gazed at the open jaws spewing clear jets of water. The white marble carvings were masterful. "They are handsome, Mistress."

"Only that?" She looked surprised.

"They are not like the living titauns," he admitted. "No art can come close to them."

She stood abruptly, walked up the steps and between the marble pillars, her white gown fluttering in the mountain breeze as she passed through the large double doors. Had she dismissed him? Kipp bit the inside of his cheek. Detch. He should have said the fountain was beautiful instead of being so brutally honest. He did not understand what was expected of him here. The woman had questioned him without introducing herself or asking his name. All three of the females he'd met so far had talked with him or teased him casually as if they had already been introduced. They had not ordered him to go nor asked him to stay.

Kipp wiped his boots on the grass, ascended the steps, and passed through the temple doors. The large oval pool inside the great room sent reflected light along the walls as the river had done in the passage, only these walls were smooth green marble. More light beamed down from a crystal dome high in the ceiling. Kipp glanced up in wonder and instantly felt the heat against his upturned face. He'd never seen or heard of a glass or crystal dome. Who had made it?

You do not know where you are, he reminded himself. *This might be the One World where Ahyuu's First Beings dwell.*

Beyond the inner pool, an empty throne was draped in colorful silks with a harp to its left, a loom and long table to its right. The woman he'd spoken to outside was seated before the large loom, working the shuttle, but it was the table along the wall to her right that drew Kipp's eye. It was full of bright bouquets, and platters mounded high with tantalizing food.

Fruits, nuts, breads, jams, cheeses—Kipp's nose twitched and his mouth watered. If he were a man with no manners, he would run over and stuff himself. His stomach growled audibly but he stayed where he was.

"You are unclean," the weaving woman said.

"Mistress?"

"Go," she said, pointing down a hallway on the other side of the pool. "Change," she insisted.

He headed for the hall to do as he was instructed, though he did not know what she meant by "change" until he saw the fifth room down the long passage. Through the open door he heard the sound of falling water. Along one marble wall, a thin, clear waterfall tumbled from ceiling to floor, disappearing through a grate at the base. There were small washcloths, bronze ewers, wooden buckets, a round soap ball on a thick white string, and larger cloths for drying off. And in the farthest corner, a set of new clothes hung from hooks.

Kipp stripped off his coat, boots, and soiled garments. Naked but for Kwaja tied to his right leg, he stepped under the chilly falls, working the soap ball against his skin. As the dirt washed off in layers, gray soapy water streamed down the drain. He shivered as he scrubbed his hair.

When he was clean, he dried off and tried to dry Kwaja, too, before slipping on the new breeches. The clothes were finely made. He especially liked the shirt, which seemed to be woven out of the same white cloth the girl and the two women wore. It was longer than his old work shirt, falling halfway to his knees, but the length helped hide the damp spot on the pants where the sack had soaked through. Drawing in the shirt with his old belt, he took the knife from his cracked boots and slid the sheathed point under the leather belt.

He had not been asked to greet them with upturned hands, to remove his boots or turn over his weapons. He would openly wear his hunting knife. The only other thing he took from the mound of filthy clothes was Sor Joay's tinderbox. The left-hand pocket of his new trousers was just large enough to slip the box inside, though it bulged a little. He'd grown used to carrying it.

Last, Kipp draped the finely woven gray cloak about his shoulders, slipped on the sandals, and wiggled his free toes. This was the strangest and least familiar part of his new garb. He bent down and rubbed the last smudge of dirt from the top of his foot and caught a glimpse of himself in the mirror when he stood again: a tall, lean figure, taller than most grown men he'd met. He braided his clean hair, pulled out the tinderbox, and found the stone the titaun had dropped in the bottom of the vessel.

Flushing with pride or arrogance or both, he quickly strung the moss agate on the leather strap and wove it into his braid before he could change his mind. He sang a line of Jilly's favorite song under his breath.

"Neither a master nor servant you'll be,
For you are a child of the high country.
Sing high for the highlands,
Sing low for the low.
You will have plenty wherever you go.

"Sway low, sweet morning grasses,
Whispering softly where the wind passes.
In the bright summer
And deep winter snow,
You will have plenty wherever you go."

He was pleased with his reflection now. What other man could claim a dragon's braid-bead? It was an honor beyond measure. Back in the great room, the woman still worked her loom. A turquoise cloth was forming under her hands, the color of the sunlit sea. She did not look up from the loom but gestured to a bench at the long table where a plate was waiting for him.

"Taka, Mistress." Kipp gave a formal bow. It seemed to fit the room, his new clothes, his mood. He felt sure he'd find the Daughter of Time somewhere in this new land of temples, gardens, and pools. Omaja might even be here in this very temple, the empty throne to his right, her throne. If this were so, he'd be well dressed and well fed when he met her. He was surprised, if a little worried, that they still had not exchanged names, but customs must be different here.

Alone on the hard stone bench, Kipp ate his fill of bread, fruit, and cheese; drank the water; and sipped the wine in the elegant silver chalice. The wine was sweeter and richer than the mebe juice he'd tasted in the village. He fought the urge to gulp it down. His mother had taught him to be civil and would have expected him to display good manners here. He ate as if she were watching him, and stopped when his throat began to tighten. Since the night of the fire, he couldn't picture her round face, light red hair, and kind blue eyes for more than a moment without a strong choking pressure coming to his throat.

The woman, who did not in the least look like his mother, left her loom when he'd finished his meal. A strand had loosened from her coiled crown of braids. She appeared older now. Tiny wrinkles gathered around her eyes. Maybe it was just a deception of the light from the windows and the inner pool. Still she was the same woman who had met him outside at the fountain, who had ordered him down the hall to change.

He thanked her again. Stood and bowed again. "I am Kipp Corwin," he said as politely as he could. "May I ask your name?"

She crossed to the harp and plucked a few cords. "You know it," she said with her back to him.

"Mistress?" He skirted the long table and went to her. Had her coiled hair been streaked with gray when he'd first seen her? Had her torso been this thick? How could he have missed that?

He stepped closer and halted. She swiveled slowly on the harp stool.

"You," he said. "What are you doing here?"

"I live here," said the Sanuu Witch.

Kipp backed away. "You've tricked me, witch!"

He spied the lightest braid tucked deep into her crown of hair. Blond. His hair.

"What have you done with the Daughter of Time? Where is she?"

"Where is she?" she asked, standing. "She is here."

319

"Where?" He rubbed the scar on his neck where she'd cut him with her blade in the mountain hut. "Did you imprison Omaja somewhere in this temple?"

"Stop," she said.

One word, but it made him stop and turn back from all the halls he was racing down in his mind. He paused a moment longer, then said what he suddenly knew—and still only half-believed: "You are Omaja."

She did not deny it. He said the next unbelievable thing his heart had known before his mind. "You were the little girl in the garden, the young woman behind the tree, the weaver, the Sanuu Witch back in my world."

The floor swayed under him. He was speaking to a First Being, a timeless one.

"Kipp," she answered, calling him by name. "And you are the master of the sack I wove."

A shaft of light lit her loom. "I don't want to be its master." The words came out in a strangled cry that shamed him, but he could not help himself. "Take it back, Mistress Omaja. You made it. You can destroy it."

The drawstrings were around his waist, the damp sack roped to his leg. "I have it here," he said. "I only need to cut it free."

She lifted her hand to stop him.

"But you have to destroy it," he said again. His blood raced. His temples were throbbing. He'd come a long way to bring her the sack. He wanted it destroyed now.

"I am telling you to wait." Her words were forceful. She was young and strong again behind them. Her beautiful bronze face shone with perfection. Her youthful looks and curved figure awakened passions he had only felt for Zalika before this. *She is old*, he reminded himself. *She is the Sanuu Witch.*

"I'll do a task for you," he blurted out. "Whatever you ask, I swear I will, as long as you take it, Mistress."

"You must meet someone and speak with him. Then if you wish me to destroy Kwaja, I will."

Kipp's heart leaped. "I'll meet this person. Tell me who. Tell me where to go. I'll leave now."

"He is outside."

Giving a quick bow, he raced around the inner pool, his lank body running in a flat reflection along the surface. Outside he saw roses, chrysanthemums, purple and golden iris, and on the edge of the high garden terrace, a cloaked figure leaned over the low wall. Was this another First Being like Omaja? What would speaking with him have to do with destroying the sack?

The day was sunny, but Kipp felt the damp chill from the misty air roiling around the waterfall as he turned onto the path and walked between the trees. The man's cloak was light gray like his own. Kipp wondered if he, too, had been sent off to bathe and change. His steps slowed to a sudden halt at the foot of the cherry tree. He knew those shoulders, that long lean back. It was a detching trick! Why did he have to talk with him? *Speak. That was all she told me to do. Say something. Now.*

"Did the titauns bring you here?" Kipp asked hoarsely.

"They did," said the Gwali. He had not yet turned around.

"They did not bring your hounds." Kipp did not try to hide the relief in his voice.

"Nor yours."

"Mistress Omaja said I only have to speak with you and she will destroy the soul sack. You cannot stop her from destroying what she made." Kipp tried to sound assured, though he was afraid. "She is more powerful than you. She is a First Being and she is older than anyone."

"And younger," said the Gwali.

Was the Death Catcher joking? Did he actually crack a joke?

The Gwali turned, his long cowl overshadowing his head.

He was but twelve paces away. "You have hidden your face from me," Kipp said.

"You will understand too much if I show it to you."

"Why do you pretend to be who you are not? Why speak with an Escuyan accent when you are not a nomad?"

Kipp liked the way the Farland people spoke Zolyan, spicing the pronunciation and deepening the words as if the land were speaking through them. The Gwali's imitation offended him.

"How should I speak, Kipp?"

Kipp winced, hearing the Gwali say his name. "I've done what Mistress Omaja asked me to do." He turned to go, looked down at his sandals where a garden snail was passing through the moss. He had almost crushed it.

"Before I leave, I will see your face." He was staring at the little snail, still trembling. "I am not afraid to look."

CHAPTER FORTY-TWO

A
RE YOU SURE you want this?"

"I told you I am ready." Kipp hadn't promised to look at the Gwali, only to speak with him. But he was driven now to see the one who had chased him so many months, followed him beyond the end of the world, flown with dragons to find him here.

"Before I remove the cowl, I tell you it is not a trick. It is who I am."

"Do it."

Old hands gripped the sides of the gray hood. "Open your eyes. Tell me what you see." He flipped it back. From deep in shadow a face appeared.

Kipp grasped a low cherry tree branch to steady himself. "You . . . you said this is not a . . . a trick," he sputtered.

Sor Joay's dark eyes were flecked with gold, two night pools set in a hardened desert face.

"They told me you were dead." Kipp could barely breathe. Here was a monster, an evil demon of death—his sworn enemy. Here was the man he'd known since he was four, the one who took him to the Farlands and taught him to hunt and fish, the man he had loved and admired all his life. Sor Joay. The Gwali.

Kipp felt sick, dizzy. A man with a dragon's braid-bead did not faint like a young girl. Still he had to sit on the ground or fall. He chose to sit and lean against the tree. Legs bent, he rested his elbows on his knees as waves of heat crossed his face.

"I did not want to know this."

"I tried to keep my face from you," Sor Joay said.

"I thought you were one thing," Kipp said bitterly. "You turned out to be someone else."

Sor Joay drew closer to the stone wall. "I disappointed you."

"You are my enemy!" Kipp stood again, anger straightening his spine. "You took my mother and father. You took Royan. He was only nine years old! How could you . . . do that?" His voice cracked with emotion.

"Kipp. I did not take them. They died in a fire."

"The fire? Oh, the fire was to blame?" Kipp tore Sor Joay's tinderbox from his pocket and hurled it into the waterfall, where it disappeared in the wet mist. The soundless fall didn't satisfy Kipp's rage. He should have smashed the hand-carved lid first, broken it to pieces in front of Sor Joay. He wiped his wet eyes, breathing hard. Smashing the lid would not have been enough. He wanted to strangle the old man.

"You came to our house with your hounds," he said between clenched teeth. "You let Kwaja take their souls." His words tasted like venom in his mouth. His lips felt numb.

"I opened Kwaja. I helped them on their way."

"Don't make what you did sound kind. It was evil! You know it was! I trusted you. I—" His throat tightened. "How could you let yourself turn into the Gwali?"

"The same way you did, Kipp."

Kipp's heart leaped. "Liar! I stole Kwaja to stop you. To stop death."

"I also went after death for taking my wife away from me."

Kipp pressed his palms against the wet wall, watching the water pummel the pool below. It did not wash away what he'd been hearing.

After a time he said, "I do not want to hear your story."

"You do."

"You will lie to me again."

"I never lied to you, Kipp."

They were both looking down at the water now.

"Tell me after I bring Kwaja inside to be destroyed."

"If you destroy Kwaja, Safra will be lost to me. I will never see my wife again."

Kipp leaned his forehead on his palms. Everything he'd eaten in Omaja's temple threatened to come up again. For a moment he could not move.

Sor Joay said, "Let me tell you my story now. Will you do this for the one who first told you about dragons? For the one who took you hunting when you were a boy?"

For the man I once knew, thought Kipp. His heart was aching. He managed to say, "I will stay a few minutes longer."

"That is a long time in this timeless place," Sor Joay said.

Mist came around the two men like hands as Sor Joay began in a familiar place, the time he took Kipp to see the Sanuu Witch. "Safra had been gone less than a year then. I wanted a potion to bring her back. I thought the witch had power to help."

"Did you know who she was back then?"

"How could I know such a thing? I thought she was a witch with powerful potions. That was all."

He shook his head. "That powder did not work for long. I only felt Safra's presence for a moment, and she was gone. By the time I left your father's farm, Safra had been dead for eight years. Soon after I returned to my village, I went on my last Lostwalk in search of death. I was already an old man. I did not see a reason to live any longer." They watched a leaf twirl down beside the waterfall. "I was not afraid to go. I'd had a vision of where Safra had gone: a beautiful place. The witch's potion had given me that much, a seeing of the place where her spirit was. I wanted to go there. Do you understand?"

Kipp didn't speak, waiting to hear more.

"I caught up with the Gwali on my Lostwalk, but he would not take me. Kwaja opened only long enough for me to see a glimpse, then Kwaja closed again."

"Why?"

"I had tried to hurry my death. An Escuyan man does not take his own life. I had not gone so far as that, but I had stopped eating, stopped drinking. After a time that is the same thing. I was an old man, but it was unacceptable because it was not yet my hour to die."

Kipp thought of the bone thrower, who had asked him to open the sack for him, of Sor Twam, who was even now on his last Lostwalk.

"You are young," said Sor Joay. "You do not understand the feeling of being ready to go. It comes to some men and women, not to all."

Kipp noted the new wrinkle lines around Sor Joay's eyes and mouth. "Aren't you afraid?"

"I had nearly died from hunger on my Lostwalk three years ago, when the Gwali came to me with Kwaja. I went inside a little while before I came out again. What I saw made me want to see more. But I was not allowed to."

"What did you see?"

"You know Kwaja is not really a sack. I think you have discovered this."

"What do you mean, Sor?"

"In the time you have had Kwaja with you, did you ever reach inside?"

"I did. There was no bottom there."

"Just so."

"What is Kwaja then?"

"Kwaja is a passage."

Kipp leaned against the wall to support himself. The mist softened the old man's face; drops gathered in his long gray braid like dew on a spider's web.

"What did you see when you went inside, Sor?"

"I cannot speak of it."

"I want to know." Kipp ran his finger along a crack in the wall. "Show me."

"It is not in my power to do that. You will have to speak to Omaja."

CHAPTER FORTY-THREE

IN OMAJA'S TEMPLE, Kipp stood with Sor Joay beside the pool. A wind gusted through the open doors, sending ripples across the water. The smell of the sea was on it.

Omaja perched before her loom in her young woman's form. Her arms moved in rhythm as she fed the shuttle through the warp and threads. Kipp cleared his throat. He did not know how to start. On the long table to the right of the loom, the flowers in the vases bloomed and died, bloomed and died in rapid succession. They had not changed like this earlier. Brown and crumpled, bright and fragrant, the flowers flashed old and young the way Omaja had, though she had changed more slowly.

"Approach," she said, leaving the loom to sit on her throne. She was regal in her white gown, though she wore no jewels and no crown other than flowers. Stepping closer, he bowed.

"Mistress Omaja, I spoke to this man as you asked me to do." Sor Joay had come to stand beside him.

"I can see that," she said.

"I have a request to make before you destroy Kwaja."

She adjusted her gown, waiting.

He forged ahead. "I have kept Kwaja with me close to four months now. This . . . thing has been tied to my body. I fought its destiny with death many times." He paused, unsure. "I am only human. It took great strength to tame it." *Tame* wasn't the right word, but what was? "I ask to see inside Kwaja, Mistress, before it is destroyed."

"Do you wish to die?" she teased.

"Not to die, Mistress. Just to see." He had looked inside before and found only empty dark. He wanted more than that. "I wish to walk inside Kwaja, the way Sor Joay did." His heart pounded in his ears as he waited for an answer.

The Daughter of Time turned to the old man. "You told him this?"

"He looks at me and sees the Gwali, Mistress. What else could I do?"

"You could let him see what he wishes to see. This is something he must work out for himself."

"The boy wants to understand, Mistress."

To Kipp she said, "Is that what you want?"

Kipp nodded.

She paused a long while, then said, "There will be a cost."

The words rang in his mind. The Sanuu Witch said just the same when he'd asked her for a potion. His hand went unconsciously to his new braid with the mysterious dragon's braid-bead.

"Not your braid this time," she said. "That is a small thing for what you are asking."

Kipp let his hand drop.

"There are few mortal beings who pass into Kwaja and come back to this world again. Those who do are changed." She looked into his eyes. "If you do this, you will not be the same when you come back. Your life will change forever. It will move in ways you cannot yet understand."

"She is right," said Sor Joay. "I was an old man when I stepped through Kwaja. I could not ever return to my former life after that, do you see?"

Kipp swayed a little on his feet. "My life has already changed forever, Sor. It did the night you took . . ." He shook his head. "The night I left my little brother with . . ."

Kipp felt the choking in his throat. It was here again, the feeling that something was about to burst. Kipp looked from Sor Joay to Mistress Omaja. "I have to think," he blurted out, and raced outside.

The moist sea wind had strengthened, but it did not cool his skin. A fire was building inside him. He knew what it meant to have your life change forever, to lose your old life and never be able to return. How could he face this again when he'd lost so much the first time?

He felt Techee burning as he ran. The nightmare had returned, only this time he was awake. He could not run away from the flames, the smoke. He was in the inferno again, standing with his arms spread out wide against the Death Catcher. The hounds gathered before his eyes.

Even as he raced down the garden steps, he was there again, screaming, *Get back!* Standing sentry before the burning doorway. He felt the heat wash up his backside. The house had already fallen. There was no house and no door, only a pile of blazing timbers; still, Kipp had not let the Gwali past.

He had been the wall. He had been the door against the Death Catcher, and he had been locked. But the door of this memory could not burn behind him forever. He turned toward it, felt the heat stinging his face.

Kipp raced down the stone steps to the lower garden terrace and sped past the apple trees. It had not been the Gwali bringing death that night.

Death had already come. He had left Royan with the tinderbox. His family had burned because of what he'd done. Kipp had known at the time he should not ask Royan to light the fire. Mother's stove was old, needed repair, was dangerous to light. He had not cared. He'd wanted to run away after his own dream and capture Lightning. To rescue the family from financial ruin, to be the hero.

All the hatred he'd felt these past few months for the

Gwali was turning back on himself as he flew across the lowest terrace and kicked open the round door.

He half-ran, half-fell down the cold spiral stairs . . .

. . . into thick darkness

. . . into his own chest, where his heart broke.

CHAPTER FORTY-FOUR

H E FELT EMPTY WHEN the tears left him. In the clammy stairway the sound of his jagged sobs echoed, doubling and redoubling his cries until they were more than his own, until they belonged to him and Mother and Father and Royan, until he heard his family crying with him.

He did not know how long he'd been here in the dark. The stairwell was silent now, except for his gulps and hiccups and the small knocking sounds of the boat tied below. But he was less alone. For the first time since the fire, he felt close to his family again.

He could see his mother's freckled face, round though she'd grown as thin as the rest of them from their years of hunger. He saw his father's eyes, dark green as kora leaves, his determined jaw and slightly crooked nose. And Royan, his happy, annoying, excitable little brother. It hurt to remember them so clearly, but not as much as he'd feared it would.

It was night when he left the deep stairwell, but the outside world was not as dark as the tunnel below. The moon was out. Stars crowned the mountain. The wind had softened to a low sea breeze when he climbed to the highest terrace and approached the stone temple, gleaming pale white against the side of the mountain. The double doors were still open. He entered, his sandals lightly slapping the marble floor.

At the long side table, Mistress Omaja and Sor Joay sat eating a meal.

"Come join us," said Sor Joay. He filled a plate for Kipp with fruits, breads, and cheeses, and poured wine into his chalice.

Kipp's nose was stuffy and his eyes were swollen from crying. He was too spent to care. In the glow of the oil lamps, he noted the Daughter of Time had let herself age while he was gone. Kipp felt relieved.

He did not speak about where he'd gone and why. They did not ask; they simply let him eat. He was less ravenous than he'd been earlier, so he was able to taste the food this time and appreciate the tart cheeses, the flavorful fruits. There was no meat, but he did not miss it.

Sor Joay spoke quietly across the table as he sipped his wine. Kipp did not try to follow much of what he was saying. His ears still rang. His head felt puffy. He'd never wept so hard for so long. He realized with some surprise that he did not feel less of a man because of it. His body felt hollow, yet stronger somehow. He had turned toward the burning door, gone inside, and faced his shame.

"I have decided," he said around a mouthful of bread. Sor Joay stopped mid-sentence to listen.

"I want to enter Kwaja. My parents and my brother went that way because of me. I want to see where they have gone."

"Because of you?"

"I loaned Royan the tinderbox, Sor. He was too young to tend the stove, and he started the fire. I should not have left it with him."

Omaja cut a slice of yellow cheese and laid it on her plate. "You will only be able to go in a little way, Kipp," she said. "Not as far as they have gone, if you are to live."

"I know that, Mistress."

Omaja dropped a handful of dried cranberries on the cheese. "You prevented others from passing through Kwaja all the time you had it with you. You let only one soul inside. Is that not so?"

Kipp tried to swallow his last mouthful but couldn't. How did she know about Sag Eye? "I saw one man go in, Mistress."

"Because you could not stop it?" asked Sor Joay. A braid-bead clinked against his chalice as he leaned forward.

Kipp took a gulp of wine, caught his warped reflection in the silver cup, and abruptly put it down.

"It's a long story, Sor." *Strip off your shirt. Show them the worm lines across your back where Sag Eye whipped you. The scars are still there.* Kipp sighed. "Sor Saggorn was a cruel man. He was very sick when he captured me. He died before he could bring me in."

Kipp used the napkin to wipe the damp sweat from his palms. "I wasn't fast enough to stop Kwaja that time." His eye passed from Sor Joay to his empty plate. "I didn't try as hard as I had with all the others."

There. It was out. Mistress Omaja cleaned her knife and got up from her chair, her blade glinting yellow in the light of the oil lamp. Kipp blinked at the sharp edge, remembering the cut she'd made across his neck in the witch's hut. She'd warned there would be a cost, but he didn't want to feel that blade against his neck again.

Omaja turned the handle to pass the knife to him. "Slit the rope you have used to bind Kwaja."

"I will use my own knife, Mistress." Kipp excused himself and left the room for a more private place to lower his trousers and cut the rope. In a shadowy alcove down the hall, he slit the bonds. They were dirty and had a foul smell, though the sack did not.

Sheathing his knife and tucking it back into his belt, he returned with Kwaja draped over his palms. The black sack was slightly damp from his bath earlier. It hung limp over his upturned hands. He hesitated a moment before handing it to Mistress Omaja.

Sor Joay took the oil lamps from the long table and placed them around the edges of the inner pool. Kipp had seen sunlight shimmering across it earlier in the day. He was startled when Mistress Omaja passed Kwaja to Sor Joay, pointed to the water, and said, "Get in."

"What? Now?"

She kept her finger out.

Don't do this. You don't have to do this. Kipp removed his cloak and sandals, took off his belt, shirt, and pants, and laid them on the floor beside his knife. Looking down at the pile, he thought better of it, stooped, and carefully folded the new garments, placing his belt and knife neatly on the top. He no longer had the tinderbox to add to the tidy stack. He could have turned now to show them his scars, but he did not.

"Is this what I must do to see inside the sack?" he asked, confused.

She gave no answer, continuing to point. Beside her, Sor Joay gripped the neck of the sack, the drawstrings dangling over the back of his hand. Kipp faced the water. The lamps sent a golden glow along the surface, but the center was completely dark. *I have come this far. I will go a little farther.* On the edge, he lowered himself in and let out an involuntary gasp. It was incredibly cold. Shivering, he moved his arms and legs to stay afloat. His feet did not touch the bottom.

"Now swim out into the middle." He saw Sor Joay fingering Kwaja's mouth as he swam out.

"Float on your back," Omaja ordered. "Lie completely still."

"I will sink," Kipp said through chattering teeth.

"Lie still."

The skylight overhead was full of stars. The smallest slice of moon peeked out of the low right corner. Kipp floated, hands and feet stretched out. He tried to relax.

"The water is too cold," he complained.

His words were answered by a searing wind racing through the open door. The oil lamps blinked and quickly sputtered out. Kipp shivered uncontrollably. A strange crackling sound filled his ears. He turned his head and gasped. Ice was swiftly forming across the inner pool. Before he could scream or swim away, ice crystals surrounded him and froze him in place. He couldn't move his arms or legs; he saw with horror thick ice forming across his torso, crackling white to clear.

Kwaja floated over the pool. Its mouth opened slowly. Kipp let out a strangled cry, sucked in another shivering breath, heard the sound of horses running, hoofbeats slowing, fading, his heartbeat thudding sluggishly. A last vaporous ghost breath rose from his mouth.

Wind blew out the stars and it was dark.

He was floating up from the black pool, looking down at the frozen boy in the ice. The boy looked terrified in death. So cold down there. Dark above and warm. He drifted toward the warmth, passing into Kwaja's mouth or through the sky dome; he could not tell which, for the way seemed very wide. How rich the darkness was and how thick, but he was not afraid. Farther in he saw small specks of light appear. Stars flaming, shimmering. The specks grew larger. They touched now and became a single brilliant beam. The bright, warm beam held him in its glow and ran like honey through him. The sweetness of it, like Zalika's kiss, awakened him.

He felt the worries the frozen boy had carried all his life slowly drop away. The beam was more than light. *Primordial light,* he thought, *like Ahyuu's light in the One World.* He swallowed it, was cradled in it. No hunger here. There was plenty. He spotted an outline far away. A mountain, a valley. He flew toward it, heard a sound like wind or water flowing though him.

I am like a leaf twirling down a swift river.
Lighter than the leaf.
Brighter than the water.
Glory to Ahyuu.
Glory. Glory. Gl—

CHAPTER FORTY-FIVE

FREEZING. SHIVERING. DARK. *The Gwali walking over the ice, pulling me out. The hood falls back. Sor Joay helping me across the frozen pool. Teeth chattering. Body numb. How is it I am even walking?*

Too cold. I want to go back into the warm light. Let me go back. I want to go back.

I am weeping. I can hear myself weeping. I cannot feel my face.

Omaja's says, "Bring him to the fire."

In a sleeping chamber down the hall, Sor Joay draped Kipp's dry cloak about him, added a thick blanket over that, and helped him sit before a blazing fire.

There was a jug and two cups on the small table between the stuffed chairs. Sor Joay filled the cups with kora. "Try to drink this."

Kipp's hand shook violently. Half the warm kora dribbled

down his chin, staining his new gray cloak. As the numbness left him, sharp pains entered his hands and feet.

He turned to Sor Joay. "I f-froze to death?"

"It is one way to die." The old man poked the fire. "Omaja promised you would come back. It was not your rightful hour. I had to trust her; still, it was hard for me to watch you go."

"How l-long was I dead?" he managed to say through chattering teeth.

"A matter of minutes. No more."

"You sh-should have let me stay. I saw a land ahead. I was almost there." His words were broken ice, crackling with emotion.

"You couldn't go in too far. I warned you about that."

"But you didn't tell me that I'd want to s-stay," Kipp blurted.

"Drink. You will feel better soon."

Kipp obeyed out of habit. Soy Joay had been his teacher since he was a young boy. The stinging pains intensified as the fire brought his sensations back. He knew the pain was the price for leaving his body, for going where he was warned not to go before he was wrenched away so suddenly from the forgiving light.

"What will you do now?" Sor Joay asked at last.

Kipp thought. His hands on the armrest looked white and bloodless. "I don't want her to destroy the sack."

"I thought you would not." Sor Joay looked into Kipp's

eyes. Both had gone into the passage, both had felt the light beyond the darkness. They shared it now, a smile breaking first on the old man's face, an answering smile on Kipp's.

"If I'd known what Kwaja was, I would never have stolen it from you, Sor."

"I'm glad you don't think me evil anymore."

Kipp shook his head. "You are the guardian of the passage."

Sor Joay nodded. "It's been an honor to open the passage to those who are ready to go through."

Kipp was still shivering. There were more blankets on the nearby bed, thick ones shot with gold and crimson threads. Sor Joay caught his glance and brought yet another covering. He knelt and wrapped it about Kipp's legs and feet.

Kipp spoke again. "Back in our world, you are the Gwali. Why don't you tell people you aren't evil, that you are the guardian who brings passage to those who die?"

Sor Joay stood again and poured himself a second cup of kora. "Death is a mystery. I am not allowed to speak of what I do."

"But why?"

"The Gwali can only reveal his true self to the souls ready to enter Kwaja."

"But I saw you, the butcher in town saw you when you came after me, and the elder in the village by the river saw you—he told me so."

"The Gwali can be seen if he wishes it, but that is not

why they saw me. I did not have Kwaja with me then, Kipp. It's Kwaja's power that gives us flight, makes us appear and disappear."

Kipp nodded. "Still you revealed yourself to me the night the farm burned."

Sor Joay blew the steam away from his kora cup. "I was not surprised to see you had Naqui powers. I sensed that power growing in you when you were young. It's one of the reasons I stayed working with your father for so long. It is the only reason I went against Escuyan custom and let you take me into the dragon cave."

"I thought I found the cave, Sor," Kipp said.

"You did. Still there are many caves hidden in the Pinnacles. I could have let you steer me into another one, but I waited to see if you would find the titauns yourself."

"So you knew where we were when we first entered?"

"I knew, and when you found it, I knew also that you had Naqui powers. No man can find the cave without this power unless he is shown there by another."

Sor Joay turned the white bead on his long braid, the sign that he had been a married man. He had not removed the marriage bead when his wife died.

"Your powers helped you see me and the hounds the night of the fire, Kipp, even though Kwaja made me and my dogs invisible to the others there. But your vision was not complete. You saw only the darkness. The Death Catcher with his black sack. Not the light beyond it. That is how it is with the living. That is how it would still be with you if you had not gone in."

"I had to go inside and see the passage myself once you told me what you saw."

"You did not have to go in."

"I wanted to."

Sor Joay laughed suddenly and leaned back in his chair. "You are so much like your father."

Kipp smiled. "We are both stubborn men."

"Like wild horses," Sor Joay added.

"My girl is that way, too."

"Zalika." The old man said her name before taking a sip.

"Zalika." Kipp wiggled his toes under the blanket, then opened and closed his hands. There was less pain now in his extremities. He still felt stiff and sluggish. "I used Kwaja's power to free her from OnnZurr. ChChka and I flew her over the wall."

"I know."

The answer surprised him. "How do you know, Sor? I didn't think you were close enough to see me then."

"I wasn't. You flew far with Kwaja. I had to follow on the ground. I am only human, you know," he added with a wry smile. Sor Joay crossed his extended legs at the ankles. "When I came to Omaja's temple, she showed me all the places you took Kwaja when I was too far behind to find you."

Kipp fixed his eyes on the red embers. Sor Joay had seen what happened at the fair, and after with Sag Eye. He'd seen him going after Jilly and Zalika, seen him traveling later with Sor Twam. Why had he asked about Sag Eye then?

"Sor, you didn't seem to know about Sag Eye's death."

"Omaja showed it all to me. I saw Epopo free you after the man whipped you." He made a fist as if he'd knock Sag Eye down himself if he could. The gesture made Kipp's eyes prick with tears. He would have fought for him.

Sor Joay cleared his throat. "Your hands were free, but you did not move from the tree. I could not tell whether you tried to reach Kwaja and close the mouth before Saggorn died."

"How did she show you where I'd been?"

"She made a seeing for me across the surface of the inner pool."

"But"—Kipp frowned—"how could you see all of it? The places I went and the things I did with Kwaja are all in the past now."

Sor Joay refilled Kipp's cup. "What is the past to the Daughter of Time?"

Kipp rubbed his hands together. The color was returning to his fingers. The old familiarity he used to feel with Sor Joay was also coming back.

"You fought me all those months, Sor, and you loosed your hounds against me to steal the sack. Why didn't you just show yourself and tell me who you were?"

"You were angry and saw only what you wanted to see. I could tell you were not ready to look."

Kipp shot a glance over at his old teacher and took in his long face with the strong wide jaw, a face he'd known since he was small.

Sor Joay kept his eyes on the fire. "I also thought I might spare you," he said. "You are very young."

"Spare me? What do you mean?"

The old man stood and drained his mug. He seemed suddenly annoyed. "We will talk another time."

"I want to talk now."

"You are not ready."

"I am, Sor."

"Then I will say that I am not." Sor Joay set his cup firmly on the table. "You died and came back. That is enough for one night. I am old and need my rest."

He went to the door. "Try to get some sleep." He closed it behind him with a click.

Kipp swallowed the rest of his kora and poured more from the thick pitcher on the table. He drank it down in great gulps, remembering the warm light that filled him in the passage. Delicious light. He wanted to feel it flow through him again, to get lost inside it. But kora is only a drink. It tasted bittersweet, and the last two gulps were gritty. Kipp licked away the grounds till his teeth were smooth again and dragged himself to bed.

CHAPTER FORTY-SIX

K IPP AWOKE IN the temple room. The fire had gone down to red coals. Dropping his feet on the cold bare floor, he quickly slipped into his sandals. Sor Joay had hung his wet clothes by the fire and they were dry now. Kipp dressed, belted his shirt, and walked silently down the marble hall, through the great room, and out the door.

The moon had set and the stars hid beyond the pale blue predawn light. Across the fountain, Kipp spotted a gray hood. Sor Joay sat on one of the scalloped marble seats, resting his back against the fountain lip. Kwaja was draped across his lap. "I could not sleep," he said, looking out at the sea.

"I slept." Kipp sat next to him and told him his dream. It was the same nightmare he'd had since the farm burned, only this time the dream had ended with Mother, Father, and Royan entering Kwaja.

"Royan was just a boy," said Kipp. "Why did he have to die so young?"

Sor Joay sighed. "I do not know the answer to that."

"I thought the Gwali might."

Looking down, Sor Joay opened his hands resting on the black sack. "The one who guards Kwaja must know what the passage is. Otherwise it would break his heart."

The sky was lightening, and the sea beyond was sheeted in violet. "So everyone who has ever guarded Kwaja has gone inside?"

"Yes. But not everyone who has stepped inside becomes the guardian."

Kipp thought about this a moment. Suddenly restless, he stood and paced a little. The first night he stole the sack it seemed as if Zalika had died and her soul had already drifted into Kwaja. He thought he'd seen it enter her again before he rode off. He remembered what she'd said later on the hill above the village, something about a strange dream she had the night she'd hit her head: *I was soaring through the night sky all the way to the golden edge of day.* He'd heard the awe in her voice when she spoke of it, and the long sigh after. He looked down at Sor Joay. "Zalika entered Kwaja."

"After she fell, she stepped inside as you did—only briefly."

"You would not have taken her that night?"

"I would not. Her injury released her into Kwaja for a moment," Sor Joay said. "But she was not meant to stay that time. It was not her hour to go."

"So I stole the sack for nothing."

Sor Joay did not agree or disagree. The fountain hissed overhead, the marble dragons frozen in flight, spitting water, not fire.

Kipp turned and crossed his arms. From here he could see the dome of the sun coming up beyond the sea.

Sor Joay spoke. "The titauns will be here soon."

"How do you know, Sor?"

"Omaja told me." He took a folded paper from beneath his cloak and handed it to Kipp. "I have some land near the Twilgar Mountains. A man and his wife train a few horses for me there."

"You still train wild horses, Sor?"

"I am Escuyan," he answered. "It is a good way to make a living if it is done well." He placed his hand on the sack and spread his fingers wide. "You will see where I marked the map. There is more than one hut on the land. It would be a safe place to bring Zalika and Jilly."

"Sor, how is it you own this place?"

"The last Gwali passed it on to me before he died."

Kipp's hands shook as he unfolded the map. "Taka, Sor. They cannot stay with Sa Minn in the village forever, and they have nowhere else to go." He scanned the stained paper and found the place Sor Joay had marked nestled in the foothills. It looked to be a good hundred miles north of his father's old farm and closer to the coast, but it was in the highlands, a place Kipp loved.

He circled the tiny dot with his thumb, wanting to express his gratitude. He might train horses there the way Sor Joay had taught him to. This sanctuary would be an enormous gift for the three of them.

Kipp looked into the old man's eyes. "You are coming with me on the titauns, Sor. You can show me this place yourself." He folded the map along the creases, and held it out.

Sor Joay did not take it. Kipp kept it out between them. His chest began to tighten.

"Sor?"

His teacher's dark skin, proud nose, and fine wrinkles caught the morning light. "I do not want to break your heart," he said.

"Don't, then."

"My hour is here," Sor Joay said. "I am ready to see Safra."

Kipp sat again. He wanted to put his arm around Sor Joay's shoulder, hold him to the earth. "Wait a little longer, Sor."

"A man cannot change his hour."

"Omaja can. I will go for her."

Before Kipp could leap up, Sor Joay put his hand out. "Not even she can do that."

Kipp's heart pressed against his chest. It was hard to breathe. Beside him, Sor Joay looped Kwaja's drawstring around his first finger. "Would you want me to go against my hour after what you saw last night?"

Kipp stood, dropped the map. He was suddenly cold, very cold. "Don't ask me to do this, Sor."

"You cannot stop my death by wishing for another day."

Sor Joay held out the sack. Their eyes met. Kipp had flown into the passage, seen where his beloved friend was about to go. Last night when Sor Joay had walked him to the fire, he'd wept like a child, begged the old man to let him go back into the passage, though it was wrong to ask for that when it was not his hour. Even now he would go inside again if he could. He had flown beyond worry and regret, into Ahyuu's primordial light.

"You remember," said Sor Joay.

"I remember."

Sor Joay kissed Kipp's hands, first one, then the other.

A drawstring is a simple thing to pull, a sack an easy thing to open. Even so, it broke Kipp's heart to see his friend take his last breath and slip into death. Sor Joay's head hung over, his braid touching his knees. Kipp laid him gently at the base of the fountain and opened the passage for him.

This time, though it was dark inside, Kipp glimpsed flecks of light like captured stars deep within Kwaja's passage. In only a moment, his friend was gone, the passage empty again.

The wind changed. Looking up, Kipp saw the titauns wheeling over the island.

The one who guards Kwaja must know what the passage is. Otherwise it would break his heart.

353

The dragons' wings took on the sunlit morning, and their scales flashed blue-green over the sea. This dawn was not like the light Kipp had seen in the passage, not as rich as the place where Sor Joay had gone, but it would do for now.

Kipp slid the map into his pocket and tied Kwaja around his waist.

You remember, Sor Joay had said.

His last words, the only ones that gave Kipp the courage to step up and take what was passed to him, what was meant for him all along.

ACKNOWLEDGMENTS

M Y WARMEST THANKS TO Regina Griffin and Ruth Katcher for their unwavering guidance and keen-eyed edits; to my agent, Irene Kraas, who is tireless and true; to Mary Frances Albi for her support, Tristan Elwell for the magical jacket art, Anne Diebel for the exquisite book design, and Heather Saunders for the detailed Zolyan map to help readers find their way.

I'm ever grateful to my critique group Diviners: Peggy King Anderson, Judy Bodmer, Katherine Grace Bond, Justina Chen, Holly Cupala, and Molly Blaisdell, who critique my raw chapters week after week. And to Jaime Temairik, for her beautiful illustrations and games on my Web site.

Mary Harris and Rebecca Willow at Parkplace Books in Kirkland, Washington, can always be relied on to suss out terrific research books. These brave booksellers invited revelers to sing, dance, dine, and otherwise frolic at my book-launch party. (Party photos at Heidi Pettit's site: www.litartphotography.net.)

And finally, I must thank PlayPumps International (www.PlayPumps.org) for creating inspiring and innovative solutions to the problem of clean drinking water in sub-Saharan Africa. After researching drought-ridden lands to create an authentic Zolyan landscape, I knew I had to do something to help people who struggle with severe drought. I was fortunate to find PlayPumps International, whose mission is to install four thousand PlayPump® water systems in ten countries in sub-Saharan Africa by 2010, and bring clean water to up to ten million people.

It's an honor to sponsor a PlayPump on behalf of the book. Interested readers can find the *Stealing Death* Water for Life challenge page at www.janetleecarey.com/PlayPumps.

side of time? Kipp moved his torch to the left and to the right, listening to the wavering fire speak in sudden ripples, like a flag beating in the wind.

The longer he looked, the more he liked the new idea. This is what the circle said, dragons flying in and out of time, and the place the last titaun seemed to fade into the sky was directly over Titaun Koy.

Kipp drew back. "How can the edge of the world be there at Titaun Koy when there is land beyond?" he asked.

Sor Twam smiled. "How does a circle have a beginning and an end?"

Kipp thought a moment. "It does only if it is broken." He turned back to the painting. "Sor, do you really think the dragons will fly me to meet the Daughter of Time?"

"Omaja lives beyond time. The titauns are the only ones who can take us there." He traced a dragon's wing with his index finger. "We can only go, Kipp. We can only ask."

They stood beneath the painted dragons flying beyond this world. They would go to the singing towers; Sor Twam to see titauns on his last Lostwalk, Kipp to ask them a great favor.

"Grandfathers," Sor Twam said, "we are coming to see you. We are walking to the edge of the world."

CHAPTER THIRTY-NINE

TWO MILES FROM Titaun Koy, they passed the charred orchard and the black woodpile that was once Kipp's house. Kipp didn't speak a word. He would not stop here to stand on the ruins of his old life.

"What was it like to grow up here?" asked Sor Twam.

"We were always hungry." He kept walking, leading ChChka across the dirt road and through the burnt stubbles of grass. What did it mean to grow up here? It meant looking through his bedroom window to watch the moon rising over the dragon's jaw or to catch the distant smoke of the Sanuu Witch. It meant beauty, hard work, and hunger.

The highlands just below the Twilgar mountain ranges were not a place to try to tame the land. Kipp had always known that they were too high up, too close to the opalescent sky. Their farm was a testament of his father's desire to be an independent man, a conqueror of the last place anyone dare plant and reap. The thin air here in these foothills was rich with the scent of untamed land. Even the sparse trees leaned out as if looking for a way to flee.

Wild horses, goats, lions, and birds were all at home here where the four winds ruled. It was not meant for man.

Kipp felt the raw spot on his leg where Kwaja's cords rubbed against his skin. Sor Twam swayed in the dust-covered saddle, the setting sun washing him in gold. Their moving shadows tilted out at an angle as they traveled west toward the base of the Twilgar Mountains.

"It was good to live here. We were a family." Tears pricked his eyes. The word *family* was dangerous. "We were also alone. Pickers came and went at first. Later we could not afford to pay them. So we worked by ourselves. My father was the only kora farmer up at this elevation. People said you could not grow kora up here. That was why he came. To prove everybody wrong."

Sor Twam gave a low laugh. "You and your father are the same."

Night came slow across the highlands. The sky grew darker and was glassed with stars like a great shattered window by the time they reached the stony terrace of Titaun Koy.

TeySaaNey. The singing towers marked the place where the dragon's teeth stood. The teeth were the towers, the towers the teeth. That was what the cave map said. Trees grew where the high, rocky shelf met the greater mountain slope. Kipp tied ChChka to a low branch. Sor Twam rubbed his hands excitedly, but Kipp felt uneasy. He still wasn't sure they were in the right place.

Near the edge of the dragon's jaw, he found his friend scratching Epopo behind the ear and gazing up at the granite teeth.

Sor Twam tipped his head. "Do you hear the towers singing?"

Kipp listened to the wind blowing around the stone towers. It slid up and down from a high-pitched whistle to a low moan. He had climbed Titaun Koy many times when he was young with Sor Joay, returned three months ago alone to pursue the wild horse across the wide, rocky shelf. Later that same night he'd chased the Gwali up this mountainside. Each time he'd come up here, he'd heard the wind blowing through the dragon's teeth. He had not thought of it as a song.

"I think it is the wind, Sor."

The old man kept staring up. Kipp remembered what Sor Twam had said about TeySaaNey. *Songs swirl inside and come out again. One tower is Past, one is Present, one is Future. Beyond these towers and their song of time, the dragons fly.*

He wanted to believe it was true. He did not have Sor Twam's believing heart. There were many stars out now, and the full moon looked down. Kipp could see the face in it— the dark sorrowful eyes above the bright cheeks.

Titaun Koy was milk-white where the crags did not make shadows. Kipp listened to the night breeze. The wind was